THE GAME

By the Author

Live and Love Again

Best Laid Plans

New Life

The Game

The Game

by

Jan Gayle

2022

THE GAME

ISBN 13: 978-1-63679-126-5

This Trade Paperback Original Is Published By
Bold Strokes Books, Inc.
P.O. Box 249
Valley Falls, NY 12185

First Edition: March 2022

Credits
Editor: Shelley Thrasher
Production Design: Susan Ramundo
Cover Design By Tammy Seidick

Acknowledgments

Bold Strokes Books for giving me a chance to write novels.

Shelley Thrasher, my editor, for not only editing but helping me become a better writer.

My family and friends for continued support and encouragement.

Dedication

To my beautiful wife, Jules

Chapter One

Ryan's tires crunched on the icy gravel as she drove her Toyota Tundra into the empty parking lot of the Los Alamos County Golf Course at seven a.m. No one would be there for at least another hour and no golfers for another three hours for the first tee time at ten a.m. Even then there'd only be a few diehards, but Ryan was an early riser. Besides, she could do some paperwork while she waited for the sun to come up. It was the kind of paperwork she hated—inventory sheets, repair requests and bills—but it had to be done. If she was the pro at a bigger course or still on tour, she wouldn't have to do all this course management, but it wasn't too bad. It was even kind of fun knowing she was basically in charge of the entire golf course. Over the past year and a half since she'd started, she'd been able to figure out most of her administrative responsibilities. Thankfully, the staff was willing to help her, and many of them did most of it.

As the cold February wind blew across the mesa, Ryan pulled her quilted, Callaway golf sweatshirt tight around her neck—it wasn't enough for the early morning cold. Even her long underwear wouldn't stop the cutting New Mexico winter wind. It would be cold on the course all day today—too cold for golf—but it had already been twenty-two days since she'd been able to play because of the snow cover. No way would she let it be twenty-three.

She looked over at the Pajarito Mountains just before she tucked inside the club bar and restaurant, Cottonwood on the Greens. The mountain was still covered in snow and would be through April, at least. Snow levels had exceeded the average annual snowfall this year, causing the local ski resort to have a bountiful season. Despite its small size, it offered about two dozen runs and six lifts, some carrying skiers to nearly twelve thousand feet in elevation. Ryan had taken advantage of the little resort several times this winter. No one could golf when the greens were covered in snow, and she could swing into a net for only so long before she feared the net would consume her. Skiing was the next best alternative, aside from having a drink, and she wasn't much of a drinker. Thankfully, she could take part in Tuesday-night karaoke at the local pub with her friends—most of whom she'd known her whole life.

She shivered as she let the door slam closed behind her. Each night Rebecca insisted the heat be turned down to a ridiculously low temperature. She told Ryan that it only needed to be warm enough to keep the pipes from freezing, so it was cold in the bar, but getting out of the wind made it almost feel warm. She trotted over to the thermostat and pushed the needle way too far to the right. It wouldn't heat the place any faster, but it was satisfying to push it up to eighty. Besides, Rebecca would set it where she wanted it when she came in. With the heater running, Ryan went to the kitchen to grind some coffee beans. Rebecca was always happy to have hot coffee when she arrived.

Rebecca Sanchez-Whitney, the bar manager, part-time chef and waitress, and all-around great friend, would be there in the next hour. Even if Ryan swore she didn't want anything for breakfast, Rebecca would insist she eat some eggs before going out to play. She'd probably even try to talk her out of playing in the cold today. The wind would make it almost impossible to control the ball, but just feeling and hearing the smack of her titanium driver against hard plastic would be worth it, even if the wind turned her ball right back into her face.

"How long have you been here? It already feels warm," Rebecca called across the dining room to where Ryan sat at her favorite table. She had papers stacked in several neat piles in front of her. Ryan's table sat next to a window with a view of the driving range, three greens, and two tee boxes.

"No, not yet. It just feels warm compared to outside." Ryan walked over and met Rebecca at the kitchen door. "I've only been here twenty minutes or so, but the coffee should be ready."

"Oh, bless you. It's nasty out there. Tell me you're not going to play." Rebecca's slight Spanish accent was noticeable in only a few words. She pushed wisps of her long, black hair out of her face and followed Ryan to the kitchen.

"You know I'm going to. I told you yesterday I couldn't wait another day."

"Yeah, but it wasn't blowing forty miles an hour when you said that." Rebecca cut each word short and snapped at her as she pulled off an ugly striped knit cap that looked like she'd used only small pieces of leftover yarn to make it. She probably had. Her dear friend was the most generous person she knew but pinched every penny when it came to things for herself. Rebecca tugged each arm out of her puffy pink winter jacket and hung it in her locker next to the back door. She was ten years older than Ryan, but six inches shorter and about twice as big around.

Ryan couldn't remember a time when she didn't know Rebecca. Every day during the summer and after school, Ryan had followed her mother around at the golf course, and Rebecca was usually there. Ryan's mother, Janet Gibbs, had been hired as the full-time course pro golfer at Los Alamos just weeks after Ryan's father, a nuclear physicist, moved them to "the Atomic City" to take a job at the Los Alamos National Laboratory. Ryan hadn't even started school yet when they arrived, and two years after they got there, her workaholic father, whom she barely knew, had died instantly of a heart attack, leaving her and Janet on their own, in the middle of nowhere, with no family. But soon they made the town their home. Because of their ubiquitous presence at the golf course, everyone there knew them and became their family.

Rebecca was one of the many locals who took in Janet and Ryan. Or, more accurately, Janet took Rebecca in. The second oldest of thirteen kids, when Rebecca turned sixteen, her mother sent her to make money for the rest of the kids. She started working as a waitress in the club bar when she was still too young to serve alcohol. With little support from her own mother, she soon became like a second daughter to Janet and an older sister to Ryan. She worked her way up to manager and happily stayed in the town where she was born and raised.

Rebecca had remained single until a couple of years ago, when she and Eddie finally married after dating for nearly eight years. Because she'd spent so much time caring for Janet, she hadn't had time for a relationship, not even with Eddie, who didn't need much of anything to keep him happy. Rebecca was Ryan's stabilizing factor, especially when she felt like she was spinning in one of those carnival rides where the bottom drops out. For the past two years, she'd experienced that sensation a lot. Seeing Rebecca angry at her was odd. Of course she teased her and mothered her, but rarely was she so visibly mad.

"Oh, well. I've played in worse weather." Ryan poured two cups of coffee and handed one to Rebecca.

"How do you drink that with nothing in it?" Rebecca snapped again. She went right to the coffee bar back in the dining room and started pouring sugar and creamer into her cup.

"I'm a coffee purist," Ryan said and took a sip. She followed Rebecca, hoping for an explanation. "I wonder how you drink it with all that junk in it."

"Well, if I can't talk you out of going out there in this crap, I'm going to make you eat some eggs—bacon too." Rebecca headed back to the kitchen. "Perhaps if I can keep you in here a little longer, the sun will warm things up a bit."

"Bec?" Ryan tentatively called her name, fearing more anger. She slowly walked back to the kitchen.

"What?"

"Is something wrong?" She tilted her head around the kitchen door to see Rebecca lighting the stove.

"Oh…" Rebecca turned and leaned on the stove with a hard swallow as she tried to hold back tears, but they began to stream down her face as soon as Ryan moved to take her in a hug.

"Oh, Bec. What is it?"

"I started my period." She sobbed into Ryan's ear. Nothing ever slowed Rebecca, certainly not menstruation, but Ryan knew she was upset today because she and Eddie had been trying to get pregnant.

"I'm so sorry." Ryan squeezed tighter and tried to think of something to say. "You haven't been trying that long. It'll happen. Just give it time."

Rebecca pushed back from the hug and wiped her tears on her sleeve. "Ry, I haven't used birth control since we got married over a year ago. Eddie's almost forty-five. We wanted to get started right away so we could have more than one. I just don't understand. My mother got pregnant when she even looked at any old bum, and I can't get pregnant with the most wonderful man in the world."

"Have you gone to a doctor?"

She sighed and dropped three pieces of bacon into the skillet she'd put on the flame. The sizzle was almost deafening, but Rebecca continued. "Eddie thinks it's him 'cause he's older, but I don't know. I don't want to find out it's me. We both want kids so badly." She wiped her face again.

"Well, maybe you should find out. Maybe it's something simple they could do to help you." Ryan had no idea what she was talking about.

"I know we should go, but it's never simple, and I'm scared of finding out that we can't have kids at all."

"Oh, Bec, I…" Ryan tried to give Rebecca another hug, but she pushed her away.

"I'm done crying. I have work to do, and apparently you need to go freeze your tiny little ass off, so go. Get out of my way." Rebecca hugged Ryan with one arm while turning the bacon with her other hand and then pushed her out of the kitchen.

Ryan knew Rebecca was done and there was no need to press her more. "Where's Eddie working today? I'll play nine on whatever side he's working on. You can make him a thermos, and I'll take it out to him." Ryan yelled back into the kitchen to be heard as she watched Eddie walk back and forth from the work truck to the maintenance shed carrying large boxes.

"Eddie is smarter than you. He's not going out there today. He's working on those carts you put on his list last week." Rebecca's tone had already changed, and she even sounded cheery. "I guess all the parts came in yesterday. He was stopping at the depot on the way in to pick them up, and he's got the boys tuning up the mowers. He'll probably end up working on them himself."

Edward Thomas Whitney III, Rebecca's husband, had been working at Los Alamos for nearly thirty years and as the head greens' keeper since Janet promoted him. Eddie and Rebecca had met when she started working in the bar. Los Alamos was small, and the locals all knew each other, but since Eddie was twelve years older than Rebecca, they hadn't exactly run in the same crowd. It took them several years to finally realize the age difference wasn't a good-enough reason not to be together.

Rebecca set a full plate in front of Ryan.

"You're not eating?" Ryan asked.

"Already ate. I have to get the menu done for lunch, and John's not coming in till noon today, so I have to cook and serve too, if we get folks for breakfast. Some of them crazy retired old men will be here pretty soon too, debating about whether they can make it for nine holes in this weather."

"Mmm-hmm." Ryan started eating her eggs and bacon as Rebecca returned to the kitchen. "Thank you," she called back between bites. She wanted to console her friend, but Rebecca had moved on. If she wanted to talk more, she'd give Ryan a sign, even if it required some interpretation, just like she did this morning.

By nine a.m., a handful of folks was at the bar, mostly men, but a couple of women had joined them for Rebecca's breakfasts. The wind hadn't slowed at all, so most of them wouldn't be going out. They were there for the social experience more than the golf, even when the weather was good. The ones who played would come in for their coffee right before they teed off.

"Hey, Bec. I'm going out to check on the guys. I'll be in the starter booth at ten. After I send out the first group, if anyone shows up, tell Patty to let them start with about ten minutes between them." Patty worked in the pro shop and was the cashier and starter during the slow months. Ryan brought in part-time summer help when things got busy—mostly high school kids or college students home for the summer.

"Okay. You come in if you get too cold out there. Hear me?"

"No such thing," Ryan yelled as the wind yanked the door out of her hand, and a gush of cold air blew through the dining room.

"Ryan, close that door. You trying to freeze us out?" Charlie Parker raised from his reclined position when the wind blew paper napkins off the big group's table.

"Hush up, Charlie. Come out here and play with me."

"You're crazy, Ryan. I ain't going out in that." He nodded in the direction of the big windows.

She walked on out. She could've gone back and forth teasing Charlie all morning long. Like many of the older golfers, he'd known Ryan most of her life. Charlie was actually one of the few guys Janet had let help Ryan with her swing when she first started learning at about five years old. He'd been the course pro before Janet and had hired Janet on the spot after he watched her play when she first arrived in town. She'd gotten her LPGA teaching-pro card the previous season when they were still in Washington state.

Ryan kicked some rocks off the cart path as she walked to the maintenance shed. Two cars pulled up as she crossed the lot. One belonged to Donnie Jones, who was thirty-something—just a bit older than Ryan—and likely hadn't worked a day in his life. His family was richer than Donald Trump said he was and was skilled at getting out of work, but he was a great guy—generous and a lot of fun. Ryan knew he was there to try to play golf, because he played any time he could. She didn't recognize the other car, but it was a fancy white Escalade, rivaling Donnie's silver BMW, so they were likely together.

"Hey, Ryan. You going out today?" Donnie called from the back of his car, where he was unpacking thousands of dollars' worth of golf equipment.

"Yeah. After I get the first group out. In this weather, it might be just you guys out there."

"Yeah. It's probably about six weeks from any real play." He walked over to her with his friend at his heels. "You want to play with us, Ryan? This here's Mark Staton. He might just beat you."

"You golf?" Mark asked. He eyed her up and down as if he doubted she could even identify a golf ball. He was tall, with thick dark hair, and she assumed most women would find him attractive except for his too-big gut. He was probably no older than Donnie, but he had the beer belly of a fifty-year-old.

"Are you kid…" Donnie started but stopped when he saw Ryan shaking her head at him. He tilted his head a little like the RCA dog but seemed to understand she didn't want him to say any more.

"Mark, you say?" Ryan quickly started talking.

The man looked down at her and nodded.

"I'm just a humble, local, golf-course manager. You look like you can strike the ball," she said and smiled at Donnie, who clued in quickly.

"Yeah. Ryan's from right here in Los Alamos. She and I went to school together. Right, Ryan?"

"Yep. When you bothered to show up." They all laughed. "I'd love to play with you guys, if you don't mind draggin' me along."

"Of course. Why don't we make things a little more interesting and play five-dollar skins?" Donnie asked.

"Oh, I think twenty would be much more interesting," Mark said as he threw his big, expensive bag over his shoulder and walked to the driving range.

Ryan shrugged and looked over at Donnie, who just smiled and picked up his clubs. "He's got plenty of money." He winked and started following his friend. "See you at the number-one tee in ten–fifteen minutes?"

"Sounds good. I'll check on the guys and meet you out there." As she walked away, Ryan overheard Mark say, "Damn, she's hot." And Donnie quickly responded. "Dude, trust me. You *are* not her type. Just play golf."

Ryan shook her head and proceeded to the maintenance shed. She was never surprised at the size of some men's egos. Donnie was probably right about him. He wouldn't miss a penny even if she took every hole, but she'd definitely feel it if she lost.

She went into the large Morton shed to check on Eddie's maintenance crew. Like every day since she'd returned home, Eddie was happy to see her. Even after more than a year, he still asked her almost daily how she was doing. Sometimes she dreaded going out to say hi to him because of the sad look he gave her. But she loved him so much, and she knew eventually they'd both move on. Eddie had become a surrogate father after Ryan's dad passed away. Eddie and Ryan's mom treated each other like siblings, often to the point of spatting with each other about how the course should be run or what type of training Ryan should have to improve her game.

Ryan always told him she was fine, even when she hurt from head to toe from missing her mother. Sometimes the pressure she felt in her chest from her mother's absence was so heavy, breathing was difficult. She knew he missed her almost as much as she did, so she smiled and told him everything was good.

Today, Eddie's four full-time crew members were obviously glad to be inside. Snow removal put them out in the frigid conditions most of the winter. They were all buried under some piece of equipment or other, with Led Zeppelin echoing loudly in the big metal building.

"You going out there today, Ryan?" Michael, the newest member of the team, called out. He played every chance he got and was fascinated by Ryan's experience on the LPGA tour. He had big dreams, and she wasn't about to crush them, so she gave him a free lesson whenever their schedules matched up. The winter had been tough, and neither of them had played much since before the first snowfall.

"Yeah. I'm going out with Donnie Jones and a friend of his. Think you could hook me up with a couple of carts on the first tee while I get my clubs?"

"Course. I'll get them ready right now. You want the ones with heaters, right?" He laughed.

"You take it easy on those guys, Ryan. You know those fragile egos are easier to crush than eggs." Eddie patted her shoulder. "And don't get too cold out there. I don't think it's even reached forty yet." He turned to look at the digital thermometer hanging above the door of the shop. "Forty-two. Dang. That's too cold for golf, especially when you factor in the wind. You know your mom had a fifty-degree rule."

That's what her mom had said, but Ryan also knew she'd never turn down a chance to play, especially against someone as overconfident as Donnie's friend. "She lied, you know?" Ryan winked and grabbed her clubs from the corner of Eddie's office.

"I know. Good luck. Drinks on you tonight at karaoke if you win?" Eddie gave her a quick squeeze.

"Sounds like a deal."

❖

Ryan was swinging her 7-iron when her two competitors strolled over from the driving range.

"How'd ya hit 'em?" she asked as they approached.

"Man, the wind is carrying the ball ten to twenty yards to the west with each hundred yards down range. How do you play in this crap? You guys need to move to California."

"Nah. We love it here. Don't we, Donnie?"

"Yes, we do." Donnie was still smiling, clearly happy with the trick he was about to play on his buddy.

"You want to give up on the skins and just have a little fun hitting the ball," Ryan offered.

"No, no. Skins will make things even more fun." Mark secured his clubs to the back of the cart.

"Ryan, we haven't paid yet. I'll get you after we finish up."

"No worries, Donnie. I know where you live. You guys ready?"

"Yeah. Where's the women's tees?" Mark asked as he glanced down the fairway.

"Why? You wanna play from 'em?" Donnie asked and laughed.

"Our course is pretty short, and a lot of the red tees line up with the whites. On this short par four, all levels of play start from the same tee box," Ryan said as she tapped the side of the red, golf-ball-shaped tee marker sitting right next to the white and blue ones. She hated for people to call the red tees the women's tee since it was intended to be for beginning or limited-skilled players. More than a few men should use the red tees but wouldn't because they didn't want to be teased.

"You want me to play the reds?" This time Ryan had a hard time keeping a straight face, and Donnie actually had to turn away to keep his friend from seeing him bust out laughing. She hadn't played from the red tees since she was about ten years old.

"Well, I want to be fair," Mark said in all seriousness as he pulled his driver out of his bag.

"Perhaps my familiarity with the course will even out the game," she said. "Should I throw the tee to see who tees off first?"

"Sure." Donnie jumped in and moved up next to her, so they formed a small circle.

She tossed her tee in the air and let it land on the ground. It pointed at Mark, just as she'd hoped it would. "Your honor, Mark." She tossed it again, and it pointed at herself.

"You're number two," Donnie said and backed off the tee with Ryan. Then they watched as Mark placed his expensive Titleist ball on the tee he'd just forced into the hard ground. They exchanged a glance and a smile. They both knew what was about to happen. Ryan tucked her hands in her pockets, where she had stashed some hand warmers, and waited for the show.

Mark made a couple of practice swings with his driver. Ryan noted that the swing wasn't too bad, but in this weather even a perfect swing wouldn't help. Finally, he set himself up to the ball and took a massive swing that launched the ball off the tee like it had rocket propellent stored inside it. Just before it reached its apex, the ball took a nearly ninety-degree turn with the wind and started toward the trees on the far-right side of the fairway. The grounds crew had taken care of most of the pockets of snow on the fairways and greens, but the rough still had a lot of the white stuff. Finding that ball was going to be like…well…searching for a white golf ball in the snow.

"Shit." Mark yelled as the ball landed in the snow and brush. It was still in bounds, but it would be a tricky shot to get it out of the trees.

"Yeah. That wind's a bitch," Donnie said, fighting to keep from laughing.

Ryan grabbed her 3-iron and set up her ball. On a clear day with such hard fairways, she could nearly hit the green with her driver on this three-hundred-and-forty-five-yard par four, but in this wind, she was going to keep the ball low and hope the hard ground would give her a good roll. Ryan blew on her hands, steadied herself in the wind, and took one practice swing before moving up to the ball. With a slightly shortened backswing, she made solid contact and watched the ball travel with a slight draw down the fairway just over two hundred yards. The line drive she hit kept the ball out of the worst of the wind, and she was in good shape for a birdie.

"What club was that?" Mark asked.

"It was a long iron, Mark, ol' boy. You better leave that driver in the bag today." Donnie placed his ball and swung away with no hesitation or practice swing. His ball bounced up just a few feet behind Ryan's. Donnie had been playing this course his whole life and knew every bump and divot almost as well as Ryan did.

Donnie and Ryan both parred the first hole and waited patiently as Mark double-bogeyed. Ryan was actually impressed that he'd been able to get out of the mess with only two strokes over par. They moved to number two, with Mark owing both Donnie and Ryan twenty dollars.

Number two was a short par three, with a sand trap on each side of the green.

"Donnie, you first." Ryan nodded, giving her old friend the honor.

"What're you going to hit, Ryan?" Donnie asked.

"I ain't tellin' you. You want a penalty for asking for advice? Hit the ball." She teased Donnie as she waved her 5-iron in his face so he could see the number.

Donnie smiled and grabbed his 5-iron. In his typical style, he put his ball down and swung away. It carried to the fairway through the gust of wind and was safe on the back right side of the green.

"Damn, dude. Don't you ever use a practice swing?" Mark asked.

"Nope. I might waste my best shot."

Ryan laughed as she approached the box. "Yeah, Mark. He has only so many good shots in his bag."

Mark laughed, and Donnie lightly shoved Ryan's shoulder as they passed on the tee box.

Ryan choked down on her 5-iron and, like Donnie, swung as soon as she placed her ball. Again, the ball traveled down the fairway only a few feet above the ground and landed ten yards in front of the green.

"Oh. That's too bad. You choked up too much," Mark commented as he walked up to the tee.

"No, she didn't, dude. Look." Donnie pointed to the green, and they all watched as Ryan's ball did just as she'd intended. It rolled across the hard ground and slowly crawled up on the edge of the green about five feet from the hole cut in the front center of the green.

"Damn. The ground must be as hard as concrete." Donnie held out his gloved hand, and Ryan fist-bumped it.

Ryan was sure after the first hole that Mark would've figured out the wind and bad-weather conditions, but instead of trying to keep the ball out of it, he chose a short iron and swung with the same power he'd used on the first tee. Again, his ball soared off the tee and went straight up in the air. And again, the wind pushed it to the west, which was right back toward him. It landed about twenty yards in front of the green. She was starting to feel a bit bad for him, because on a good day that ball would've probably hit the center of the green.

"How can the wind move that little ball so much?" He looked at his club face as if he could find the answer there.

"Welcome to New Mexico," Donnie said.

"Okay. I get it. Keep it low."

Donnie and Ryan laughed, and she patted Mark on the shoulder. "Yep. You got it."

After Mark finally caught on along the way and quit hitting the ball high in the air, he managed to be a bit more competitive but couldn't quite master the line-drive shot. They were all freezing and exhausted from fighting the wind when they were ready for the turn after the ninth hole, so Ryan convinced them they should call it quits and go in for a burger. She'd gotten her fix. In a few weeks the weather would be better.

"All right, all right. I give." Mark followed Donnie and Ryan off the ninth green after yet another bogey. "I guess I owe you both a bundle of money, and I've been properly schooled on playing in high winds in this freakin' desert, so I better pay for the round, Donnie." Ryan could tell this man never considered money.

"Rightly so, and I think you should pick up lunch as well," Donnie said as he climbed in the cart.

"Fine!" Mark said.

"Ryan, we'll meet you in the clubhouse after we take our clubs to the car," Donnie said.

"Right on. Want me to have Rebecca get some burgers started for you?"

"Yeah. Thanks. Extra green chiles for my friend." Donnie smiled that mischievous grin again.

"Seriously?" Ryan asked. New Mexico's green chiles were amazing and unlike any other pepper in the world, but they were an acquired taste, and some seasons they were extra spicy. This fall's harvest was one of the hottest Ryan could ever remember—just the way she liked them. But she wasn't sure Donnie's California buddy could handle the heat. "No. I won't do that to him. I'll have Rebecca put them on the side."

The guys met her in the clubhouse, where they enjoyed the warmth and Rebecca's amazing burgers and fries. Mark handed Ryan a wad of cash as soon as he sat down, and she pushed it back at him.

"I can't take that," Ryan said. "I had a blast playing with you guys today. Let's call it even since your boy and I played a little trick on you."

"Yeah. He told me you won like a bunch of LPGA tournaments, but a cocky ass like me needs to be put in his place, and you earned every penny. That was some serious course management out there. I can strike a good ball, but you handled the course."

"Well, thank you, Mark. But not only have I played a few LPGA tournaments, it was pretty unfair of us, since Donnie and I have been walking this course our whole lives."

Donnie chimed in between big bites of gooey cheese and green chiles spilling off his burger. "What? Unfair? No way. He thought he was going to kick our asses. It was just a pleasure to be a part of watching you beat him."

When Ryan finished her burger, she said good-bye to Mark and Donnie and headed back to the pro shop to send Patty home. Only one other group came out after Ryan's group teed off, and they turned around after the third hole. It was brutal, and if she hadn't been having so much fun playing, she'd have turned in early herself. It was nearly one o'clock, and given the slow day, she could handle anything else that might come up. She tried to give the staff a break whenever she could, because as soon as the weather warmed up, there'd be no breaks and lots of long hours.

CHAPTER TWO

It was nearly six p.m. before Ryan left the golf course. Besides the afternoon restaurant crew, she was the last one to leave. Adrienne and Nathan, a husband-and-wife team who did everything by themselves during the winter months, took over for Rebecca and her crew at two p.m. every day. During the summer months, when the restaurant was as crowded as the course, Ryan again relied on students to backfill her regulars.

With the overcast sky and the sun long behind the mountain, only the sparse streetlights lit Ryan's drive to the little adobe house her mother had left her. After her mom died, Ryan was sure she would sell the house, but she'd finally gotten used to the memories and found being there comforting. She could always sell, but for now she'd stay right where she was.

As much as she wanted to grab a book and curl up next to her wood stove with a glass of wine, it was Tuesday, and if she didn't go to the Pajarito Brewpub for karaoke at eight p.m., someone would come over and drag her out. But first she wanted to go home and take a warm shower. She'd been cold since she came in from her nine-hole game with the boys.

Before she jumped in the shower, she poured some vegetable soup into a bowl to heat up. Rebecca had sent it home with her after their dinner Sunday night. As much as she loved Pajarito's pub food, she'd eaten badly all day, so a cup of veggie soup sounded amazing—not to mention warm. If she hurried, she might even get through a couple of chapters in her latest novel before she had to leave the house. The book, a debut novel by K.T. Rivers, was amazing. She'd had to make herself stop reading last night so she could finally get to sleep.

❖

The parking lot was pretty empty when Ryan swung her big truck into the spot nearest the door, but she was early, as usual, and most of the regulars wouldn't arrive until right at eight. She'd secure the group's normal table next to the stage, even though the owner always put a reserved placard on the coveted high-top.

"What can I get you, Ryan? Your usual and a menu?" Tiffany, their regular waitress, asked. Even in the dead of winter she wore a tank top and short shorts with cowboy boots. It wasn't very warm in the pub, but if you ran around the room serving drinks all night like Tiff did, it probably got pretty hot, even in March.

"Just the beer, no menu, and put everyone's drinks on me. I won some money today."

"Right on. Should I set them up now or wait?" Tiffany was great. She knew everyone's drink orders and kept their glasses full all night.

"Nah. Let's wait. It'll be a minute before Adrienne and Nate close the restaurant, and Rebecca always makes her and Eddie late."

"'Kay. Be right back."

Ryan looked around and saw, like usual, that more than half of the clientele were locals whom she knew. She nodded a greeting around the room and walked over to Ms. Ilene's table. Her salt-and-pepper hair was done in a perfect football-helmet-shaped roll and style, the same one she'd worn for fifty years, and her cotton blouse and new blue jeans were pressed with tight creases. She came to karaoke almost every week, and even though Ryan's group invited her to sit with them, she always refused. She kept a seat available on the off chance her son would come join her. Ms. Ilene had been the local elementary school's third-grade teacher for nearly forty years. She'd finally retired two years ago, and now she volunteered full-time at the library. Everyone in town knew her, and anyone under the age of forty-five had probably had her as a teacher. She loved every one of her students, even the difficult ones.

"Evening, Ms. Ilene."

"Hi, there, Ryan. You beat your gang here again."

"I normally do. Are you going to sing tonight?" Ryan asked as she leaned on the back of one of the chairs at Ilene's table.

"It depends on how many folks sing. They don't need me if the young people want to." Ilene looked around the room, assessing the talent. It was a rare night when she didn't perform at least one Loretta Lynn or Patsy Cline song. When she did, Ryan would make Adrienne or Rebecca two-step with her. Ryan was a better lead than most of the men, so they never refused her.

"Well, you know we love to hear you sing. Is Buddy coming tonight? You know you can always sit with us."

"Oh, thank you, honey, but he might just show up." It was true that he did come by once in a while, but it was rare, and he was usually pretty drunk when he arrived. Ilene would have to take him home early—small-town drama.

"All right, ma'am, but you know you're always welcome. Buddy too." As Ryan walked back to her table, all her friends entered the bar at the same time.

After Tiffany delivered the drinks, they raised their glasses to Mark, the rich Californian who had no idea how to play golf in the cold New Mexico wind. His money lasted through the whole night, and none of her friends paid for a single drink or snack. Neither did Ilene, who ended up singing two songs. Rebecca even got Ryan up to sing "Girls Just Wanna Have Fun." Most nights Ryan could fight her off, but after Ryan's third beer, she had no fight left and followed Rebecca up to the stage as if she were on a leash. They had a blast—they always did.

Ryan was so grateful for her extended family. They truly cared for her, but at ten thirty, she started saying her good-byes.

"Oh, come on, Ryan. One more," Rebecca begged. It was Eddie's turn to drive, so she was feeling no pain. After Rebecca's disappointing morning she was taking full advantage of her designated driver.

"Tomorrow's going to hurt as it is. I gotta get some sleep," Ryan insisted.

Thankfully, Eddie agreed and piped up. "Yeah, Bec. We should go too."

"Oh, you guys are no fun." Rebecca pouted but fell right in line behind Eddie when he started toward the door.

"Good night. I'll see you tomorrow." Ryan gave Nate and Adrienne a quick hug. They didn't have to be in early, so they were staying until the last amateur sang.

"Thanks for the drinks. We'll see you tomorrow." Nate stood to give her a hug. "Rebecca's in for a tough morning." He nodded toward the door as Rebecca staggered away on Eddie's arm.

Ryan caught up with Eddie and Rebecca and sent her friends off with a hug. "I'll see you in the morning, Bec. You're okay, right?"

She nodded and climbed into Eddie's Ford pickup.

"Yeah. You'll see her, but you might not want to expect her normal happy self." Eddie gave Ryan a big hug. "You okay to make it home? I can drop you off and pick you up in the morning."

"I'm good," Ryan said.

Eddie nodded and started his truck.

She watched them drive off and stood for a minute staring across the mesa before she headed for her own truck. The clouds had cleared out, and she could see the moon—almost full—and a sky covered with stars. The only constellations she could identify were the Big and Little Dippers. They seemed so close, she felt like she could almost reach out and grab their handles.

As she headed toward her house, her truck seemed to take over, and the next thing she knew, she was sitting at the gates in front of the city cemetery. She zipped her Carhartt up tight and put on her sock hat. After the sun went down, it had dropped below freezing again. She searched through the center console until she found her little Mag light. This stop was not an unusual occurrence for her, so it was right on top. When she got out and walked robotically through the headstones, she didn't bother turning on the light. Her familiarity with the path and the bright moon made the light unnecessary.

Her mother's headstone was a modest piece of granite sitting alone in a small plot in a new area of the cemetery. Ryan had struggled desperately with the decision about where to bury her. Her father's family, whom she barely knew, had insisted that she be buried back in Washington with her husband, and her mother's family was originally from Montana, but no one was left, so it was just her. After giving it way too much thought, she finally decided her mom would want to be here. Janet had fallen in love with New Mexico the minute they arrived, and she loved her Los Alamos family—her only family. So Ryan spent almost all of what remained of her savings and promotional money for the service, cremation, and burial plot. Everything else had already gone for medical costs. Ryan was lucky to still have the house left in her name, but what else did she need? She had a job that she loved, great friends, and a home full of memories.

Just before she reached her mother's marker, Ryan tripped and fell flat on her face on a pile of remaining snow right in front of the stone. She missed cracking her cranium on the edge of the stone by only a couple of inches.

"Shit, Mom. I guess that third beer was one too many. It's always the last one, right?" She laughed, and the sound bounced around eerily off the canyon walls. Finally, she sat down next to the stone and leaned against the side of it.

"I miss you so much, Mom." Tears began to stream down her face. "I can't cry, or my tears will freeze to my face." She wiped both cheeks with her gloved hands and sniffed.

She turned and faced the back of the stone, pulled off her right glove, and ran her finger along the outline engraved there. It was a female golfer completing her follow-through with a driver. The finishing form was perfect—just like her mother's. Below the image in fancy looping script it said, "Fairways and Greens." The phrase wasn't original, but whenever Ryan saw it there, she could hear her mother calling it out to her before one of her matches. She traced the letters too, then shoved her hand back into the glove.

"Mom, I'm sorry. I wish I'd made it home sooner. I wish I'd made them try everything. I was stupid and selfish, and I'm so sorry." She sobbed as she laid her head on the hard, cold marble. "It's my fault you're not still smashing the little white ball and telling me to keep my head down."

She mumbled her mother's mantra, "You're good, Ryan, but you're no Annika Sörenstam. Keep your head down!" While the golfing community referred to her as the next Nancy Lopez, and that was for sure an honor and high praise, her true hero was Annika. Her mother was referring to how quickly Annika always raised her head during her swing. For Annika it worked, but when Ryan did it, her ball hooked sharply, and she spent a lot of time in the weeds looking for it. She even heard her mother's words in her head during the fourth hole of the tiebreaker at the British LPGA Open Championship, hours before she saw her for the last time. If she'd only listened, she'd have won the tournament, but Ryan shouldn't have been there in the first place.

Finally, she got up on her knees—the snow and wet ground seeping through her jeans making her legs cold. "I miss you so much. Some days it's impossible to walk in your shoes. I think I mess up more often than I get it right, but I'll keep trying." She lightly stroked the side of the stone. "I wish you were here." Janet Gibbs had died of ovarian cancer two days after her forty-eighth birthday and soon after Ryan arrived home from her second-place performance at the British Open.

CHAPTER THREE

"I started the coffee," Ryan said when she heard the restaurant door slam. She didn't look away from the window she was staring through. "Did you see the tall blonde on the driving range? Beautiful woman, ugly swing. She needs to relax. She's strangling that club." Ryan continued to focus on the view out the window overlooking the nearly twenty acres of lush grass that made up the driving range and practice greens. Just a few weeks of New Mexico sun had turned everything green, and the only snow was what remained at the top of the mountain. It was so early, the sun was just beginning to rise and brighten the Pajarito Plateau.

"It's pretty amazing. Her ball actually goes straight most of the time." Ryan couldn't help evaluating the women's swing, even though all she wanted to look at were her sexy long legs and her well-defined shoulders displayed so nicely in her tight-fitting, black Body Armor. It was difficult to see what her face looked like, but Ryan didn't have any problem fantasizing about how beautiful she must be.

"Yeah. I saw the girl. I brought her here, and thanks for making me coffee," Maggie Hart replied from across the large dining room.

Ryan spun around at the shock of not hearing Rebecca's voice, as she had expected. Instead, the one she heard was familiar but totally unexpected. "Mags, what the hell are you doing in the middle of...what do you call it here...the middle of fucking nuclear nowhere?" Ryan rushed over to give her old friend and coach a hug. Maggie looked exactly the same—short bob groomed to perfection, even so early in the morning; tall, lanky body with copper-tanned legs that didn't stop; and a cocky smile that always stopped Ryan in her tracks.

"You look amazing." Maggie enveloped her in a hug. "I love the highlights in your hair." Maggie ruffled Ryan's hair as if she were a child. "The extra neutrons around here must be good for you." Maggie had made fun of the history of Los Alamos and its infamous reputation as the birthplace of the US nuclear weapons' program from the minute she met Ryan and found out where she was from. Oddly, Maggie seemed to know more about the Manhattan Project than anyone Ryan had ever met, outside of the science geeks who worked at the Department of Energy National Laboratory on the edge of town.

As they held each other in an extra-long hug, Ryan knew exactly when she'd hugged Maggie last. It had been over nineteen months since she got off the plane in Denver, returning from her last professional golf tournament, and got on the last flight to Albuquerque. During the entire flight across the Atlantic and on to Denver, Maggie had been trying to convince her to stay on the tour. There was no question; she was at the top of her game. In just two years, she'd won eight tournaments and barely lost the British Open in a tie on the fourth tiebreaker hole during playoffs. Even though Ryan wanted nothing more than to win a major championship, Maggie couldn't convince her to change her mind. Ryan knew she'd waited too long already. She had to get home.

Finally, Maggie backed away slowly and pulled Ryan into a kiss that was too passionate and lasted too long, especially since they'd agreed to only be friends. Ryan tried to back away at first but soon relaxed into the familiar arms wrapped around her and the calming effect of human contact. She'd cared very much for Maggie and knew the feeling was mutual, but Maggie would never settle down. Ryan never made the mistake of falling too deeply in love with her, but she did enjoy her company. Maggie gently forced Ryan's lips apart—something Ryan didn't fight—and flicked her tongue across Ryan's lower lip. While she was sure Maggie would've followed her to the back of the building to her office to finish what she'd started, Ryan finally ended the kiss instead.

"You look good too, Mags, and you feel good. I've missed you." Ryan stepped back and looked her up and down before she lightly ran her index finger across Maggie's cheek. "Your new girl must be taking good care of you."

"No. It's not like that," Maggie said.

"Yeah, right."

"No. I mean it."

"She's not gay?"

"Well...she is, but..."

"But she doesn't want to date her coach." Ryan watched Maggie's face. "She's smarter than me." Maggie had likely tried. She couldn't turn down a challenge, especially a tall, blond one.

"No, just different. We didn't click like you and I did."

Ryan took Maggie's arm and guided her to her table next to the window. "So...that's Katherine Reese. I should've recognized her. You want to tell me why she's hitting balls on my driving range? And how in the world does that woman win tournaments with that swing?" She hadn't recognized the professional golfer who'd drawn a lot of attention during the first part of her rookie season but had slowly fallen in rank after the middle of her second season and was nowhere to be seen this season. Ryan had never met her. She had qualified for the tour the year before Ryan left, but she'd seen her play only a couple of times. She'd been impressed until Katherine just dropped off the leaderboard like a has-been musician disappears off the Billboard charts. Ryan hadn't watched many professional tournaments since she buried her mother, but someone around the clubhouse was always giving her the tour stats.

"Well, that's why she's here. She learned that swing when she was a kid, and she's scared to death to change it. I need your help to convince her it's worth it. You know better than anyone what a new swing can do." Maggie had convinced Ryan to make a few small adjustments to hers when she first started on tour, and it took her from being a great golfer to a tour champion. She lost a little distance at first, which was discouraging, but after she realized how much better her control was, she was happy to give up a few yards and eventually gained them back with time and practice. Ryan hadn't been too willing to give up on her swing at first either because her mother taught it to her, but after Maggie showed Janet what she wanted Ryan to work on, Janet agreed, and Ryan had no choice.

Maggie sat in the chair next to Ryan, and they both watched as Katherine hit ball after ball with the exact same motion. It was as repeatable as if she were a robot but as unpredictable as New Mexico's weather. Ryan admired the fact that any of the balls went where she aimed, let alone most of them, but that swing would fail when she needed it the most. It was why she'd once spent so much time at the top of the leaderboard but hadn't won in over a year.

"I'm not in the business of teaching professionals. That's your job," Ryan finally said.

"Ryan, I think she'll listen to you. She talks about your career all the time. She knows how hard you worked to become so good, and she always wants me to tell her about you."

"What do you tell her about me, exactly?" Ryan asked, elevating her voice and frowning.

"Chill out. I don't say anything."

She glared at Maggie.

"Really…nothing, but she respects you. She might listen to you, but enough about that for now. I haven't told her why we're here yet. She thinks it's some weird get-away for a break from the tour. But…let's talk about you. How are you? Are you seeing anyone?"

"Hmm. I suppose you have nothing to lose since she's not winning, but I don't think she'll listen to anyone. Besides, from what people say, her temper is unattractive on the course. I'm not sure I'd want to work with her, even if she wants to change. On the off chance she agrees, she needs to drop out for a month and stay here and work on it every day. Are you willing to stay here and leave your other clients?"

"You didn't answer my question. How are you?" Maggie repeated her question.

"I'm fine, Mags. How are you? Since I haven't even received a call from you in nearly a year, I can't imagine that you care that much about how I'm doing." She stared out the window, refusing to look at Maggie and pretending to care about the players filling up the range. They were mostly old guys with too much time on their hands since they'd retired from the labs.

Right after she left, Ryan had tried several times to talk to Maggie, but her calls always went to voice mail, and she never received a return call.

"I'm sorry. I suck at sickness and death. I…I…"

"You're not unique. Everyone sucks at it. But shit…I don't even care. You had stuff to do, right?" Ryan looked back at her.

"When are you coming back?" Maggie ignored Ryan's sarcasm, probably because she knew Ryan was right.

"I told you when you asked the last time we talked. I'm not coming back. This is what I do now." She held out her arms. "This is my club." She pointed at the range. "I teach every day in this beautiful spot just like my mom did, and that's what I want."

"Come on, Ryan. You can't stay here. You're a professional golfer." Maggie put her hand on top of Ryan's and squeezed. "You can't stay in hiding and hope that will make you feel better."

Ryan pulled her hand away. "I'm not going to talk about this. If you want me to talk to your girl, I will, but I refuse to fight with you about something I've already decided and you can't let go of." Ryan tried to walk away, but Maggie grabbed her hand and held her to the table.

"Okay. No more talk about the tour, but won't you have a cup of coffee with me first? She needs to get worn out before she'll maybe listen." Maggie released her hand and gave Ryan a pouty look.

Ryan nodded her head. "Okay, coffee."

As she headed for the kitchen, Rebecca burst through the door. "I'm late. I'm so late. The alarm didn't go off and then… Oh, who are you?" She stared at Maggie.

Maggie rushed over and held out her hand. "I'm Maggie Hart. I was Ryan's coach before she left the tour."

Rebecca had heard Ryan tell many stories about Maggie Hart. Ryan had told her the good, the bad, and the ugly about Maggie—about how she missed her and how she hated her for not staying in touch. Given the way Rebecca was scowling, Ryan was a little worried she might give Maggie a piece of her mind.

"You're Maggie. Not what I imagined." Rebecca looked over at Ryan, shrugged, and walked right to the kitchen.

"Well…I guess she knows who I am." Maggie watched as Rebecca left. "I'm not sure if I should be flattered. I'm thinking not. Who's that?"

"My dearest friend in the world, and she's not fond of people who make me sad."

"Look, Ryan, I…I'm sorry. I suck at being a girlfriend."

"I just needed a friend." Ryan poured the coffee into two cups. "But let's move on. That's my new philosophy on life, 'cause you sure as hell can't change the past." If only she actually followed that philosophy.

❖

Ryan and Maggie managed to quickly make it past the hard feelings and started telling stories about their short time on the LPGA tour together. Maggie caught Ryan up on the status of all her old friends—women still traveling every week to a new venue for a professional golf tournament. Ryan wouldn't admit it to anyone, but she missed it. She even loved all the travel—seeing new places and meeting new people. But most of all, she missed the fans. LPGA crowds were small compared to the men's tour, and because of that fact, the player's relationship with the audience was so much more intimate. She had earned herself quite a following in just two seasons. It was fun to hear them cheer and encourage her along the course. Some women hated the crowds, but she loved them. She often talked with the people throughout the game. During one game in Texas her first season, two girls followed her through the whole tournament and asked her to dinner with them on Sunday night after she won. She agreed, and they had a great time, but Maggie got so jealous she threatened to quit. It was funny now, and even Maggie laughed when Ryan reminded her, but it sure wasn't funny then.

"Well, should we go meet your girl?" Ryan watched through the window as Katherine poured out the last few balls from her fourth large bucket. She had to be getting tired after over an hour and nearly two hundred balls, but she still looked amazing.

"Yeah. I guess we'd better. She's going to wonder where I've been. She's probably glad I wasn't out there trying to get her to adjust her swing." Maggie took the last sip of her coffee, which had long ago gone cold. "Um…just so you know, she's going to be a little grumpy. She hasn't been hitting them too well, as you may have noticed."

Ryan had watched Katherine's practice balls slice over and over again. They were landing farther and farther to the right with each swing. She'd switched to her short irons, and even then, her ball took a dramatic turn at the end—at least most of the time. Additionally, Ryan had watched her temper flare, and her clubs were taking the brunt of her anger. She'd repeatedly smacked her long irons against the ground when the ball went astray.

"Have you talked to her about her temper?" Ryan asked as they strolled across the putting green out to the range.

"Yeah, but she's young."

"Hmm. We're all young when we start, but if she doesn't get that under control, she'll lose her fan base and, even worse, her sponsors."

"She's about to lose most of her sponsors if we can't help her. She'll have to start from scratch, but her family can afford to keep her on tour as long as she can maintain her tour status," Maggie said.

The LPGA tour was not a good way to get rich. Most players barely made enough to live on, let alone pay the cost of travel and earn any real money. It was all about the sponsors. Professional women golfers just didn't get the publicity that male athletes did, so even the sponsors weren't as generous as the golfers needed them to be. For most players, losing a sponsor could badly affect a career; losing all sponsors was a death sentence unless you had your own money.

"Maybe golf isn't her game. Does she play Ping-Pong?" Ryan spoke quietly as they approached Katherine on the range.

"Give her a chance." Maggie punched Ryan's arm.

"Ow." Ryan punched back. "Fine."

"Hey, Ryan. Are we going to see you on the course today?" one of her students called from the end of the range. "Tom and I are going out as a twosome in about twenty minutes. Wanna come with us?"

"Hey. Thanks, but I'll be going out later. Maybe I'll see you in the bar after we're done." As the weather warmed up and the course got more crowded, Ryan wouldn't be able to get out and play as much as in the off-season, but she could usually walk on with a group that didn't have a foursome now and then. The locals all knew her and liked for her to join them for a round, but they were smart enough not to bet against her.

"Where have you been? I've been out here smashing balls for like two hours." Katherine exaggerated as she snapped at Maggie. "Wait. You're Ryan Gibbs." She had turned her attention toward Ryan.

"Yes, and you're Katherine Reese." Ryan held out her hand. "Welcome to Los Alamos."

"What are you doing here?" Katherine quickly shook Ryan's hand without making eye contact and turned away. She placed another ball on a tee before addressing it with a wide stance. Ryan didn't say anything while she was preparing to swing, but she couldn't help but notice that the angry blonde wasn't quite as tall as she'd thought when watching her on TV and earlier this morning through the window. She was probably about five feet nine inches—a little shorter than Ryan—but her legs were every bit as long as they looked from afar, and tan and firm as well.

Katherine gave the ball a little more power than she had when she didn't know anyone was watching, and despite her efforts to strike the perfect shot, it made a sharp right turn about a hundred yards down range and missed the one-hundred-and-fifty-yard marker by about ten yards. If she'd been on the course she could've recovered, but the shot was messy and not at all one a professional golfer should make. She didn't smack her club on the ground this time; she simply stared down range. Ryan wondered if she was trying to find something to blame it on, but the wind was moving only a few knots across the range in the opposite direction. If anything, it actually kept it from going farther off course.

Just before things were about to get more awkward than Ryan could handle, Katherine turned and spoke to Maggie. "Why are we here?"

"I want Ryan to look at your swing. She changed hers at the beginning of her career, and I think she could help you."

After that shot she couldn't possibly defend her swing, so she just stood there leaning on her 6-iron.

The silence was painful again, so Ryan took up the conversation. "I know it can be scary to change after you've had success with it, but I think we could make a few adjustments, and you wouldn't have to deal with that unpredictable slice." It would require a complete makeover, but Ryan believed she'd have better results if she fibbed a bit.

Katherine turned and spoke quickly. "First of all, what do you know about coaching golf? You were at the top of a game many would die to be able to participate in, and you quit. And second, if I wanted to change my swing, I wouldn't have had to fly all the way out to this godforsaken place to do it." Katherine slammed her club into her bag.

Maggie put her hand on Katherine's bag so she couldn't walk away. "Listen. If you want me to be your coach, you're going to have to spend some time here and work with Ryan. She's one of the best coaches I've ever seen, and that is extremely rare for a professional golfer."

Ryan knew Maggie wasn't taking much of a chance with her threat if Katherine was serious about golf. Maggie was a highly sought-after coach. Ryan was a little confused as to why she'd taken Katherine on as a client in the first place, but when she first hit the tour, she'd been pretty impressive. And she was beautiful—one of Maggie's criteria for who she coached.

"Mags, look. If she doesn't want to do it, then—"

"No. She may not want to, but she needs to, and this is a bye week anyway. She's never going to win again consistently if she doesn't make some changes. Her course management and short game are also suffering. You know as well as I do, confidence is the true winner of this game, and she's losing it."

"Do I need to be here for this?" Katherine tried to pick up her bag.

"Yes, you do." Maggie forced the bag back to the ground.

For a few minutes they all stood in the middle of the driving range, while players on both sides of them stood and stared. To break the tension, Ryan finally suggested, "Why don't you come out tomorrow morning at sunrise, and we'll play a game. We'll just enjoy the course and get to know each other." She couldn't forget the insults Katherine had thrown at her, but she wanted to try to help her, and spending time with a sexy, hot chick was never a bad thing, if only she could calm down a bit.

"If I beat you, then I go home." Katherine responded to Ryan but stared at Maggie.

"Excellent idea," Maggie said and smiled at Ryan. "You know you can't beat her, especially here on this course. You've never played it."

"I'm not good enough to beat the great Ryan Gibbs. Is that what you're saying?"

"No. She's not saying that." Ryan gave Maggie a stern look.

"Give me two strokes a side—because you have the home-field advantage," Katherine said.

"Ah…well…"

"Scared?" Katherine asked.

She appeared to be enjoying herself. She'd pushed her sunglasses up on top of her head, and Ryan couldn't help but stare at her emerald eyes, so bright and clear they didn't quite look real. And then she finally smiled. She was truly beautiful when she let go of her stress and anger.

"No. She's not scared. I'll have you here at seven, and we'll see what happens." Maggie finally took her hand off Katherine's bag so she could carry it away.

"See you in the morning, Ryan." Katherine said, and then she grabbed her bag and took long strides toward the parking lot.

"I thought you said she liked me?" Ryan took Maggie's arm and started escorting her toward the rental car.

"I thought she did. I didn't expect that reaction."

"I'm not sure how constructive this is going to be, but I guess we'll have a little round of golf in the morning. Did you bring your clubs?"

"No. I'm not playing. This is between you two. Maybe after eighteen holes she'll be ready to listen, especially after you kick her ass."

"I've never found that to be a successful way of getting what you want."

"It worked on me," Maggie said and picked up her pace. Katherine was already sitting in the white Camry rental when they reached the car.

"What makes you think I'll beat her?" Ryan asked.

"You will." Maggie raised up for a kiss, and Ryan obliged.

CHAPTER FOUR

At the sound of her phone alarm beeping, Katherine turned over and switched it off. It didn't wake her though. She'd been awake for over an hour. The large-blade ceiling fan had managed to transfix her. The mesmerizing effect of the slow, steady movement had kept her from getting up when she first woke up just after three in the morning. That and the thought of playing golf with Ryan Gibbs.

Now it was five and she finally sat up. She had a routine. Every morning for the past three years she got up at least an hour before she had to so she could write. She was about halfway through her second full-length novel, and it was better than anything else she'd ever written. The first one she wrote, while still in college, was on the bookshelves of booksellers all over the country—clearly it wasn't bad either. She'd used a pseudonym, K.T. Rivers, and been picked up by a small publisher. Katherine didn't believe much would come of it, but after Julia Roberts gave her novel an enthusiastic review, she'd sold thousands of copies. Even her family didn't know of her success, but writing was her passion, and one day she would write full-time.

Katherine loved golf, but not as much as her sister, Marie, did. They'd played nearly every Sunday since she was about eleven years old, with her dad and her uncle at their private club. They'd teed off at seven every Sunday morning until Marie enrolled at Stanford. Uncle Harold and her dad had been members forever. Her Grandpa Johnny had been a member of the exclusive club since he made partner in one of LA's most prestigious law firms in the early sixties. According to her father, her grandpa had waited nearly twenty years for one of the other members to die so he could get that Sunday tee time. It was handed down to Uncle Harold when Grandpa Johnny passed away, the same year Katherine turned eleven and Marie was thirteen.

They'd both been taking lessons since they were old enough to hold the clubs. Uncle Harold didn't have any kids, so he agreed to let them play on Sundays, even though almost any member would have paid to be a part of their foursome. Marie was always better than Katherine, probably because she liked the game more. Katherine enjoyed being with Uncle Harold and her father more than the golf, because it was one of the few moments she got to spend with her dad. But Marie wouldn't have minded if the rest of the family stayed at home as long as she got to play. Katherine was a natural athlete, though, and the game came pretty easy for her. With a few lessons and some tips from her dad, she was playing under par by the time she was sixteen.

It was a little harder for Marie, but she became determined to make it on the LPGA tour after she watched Annika Sörenstam win the Kraft Nabisco Championship live at Mission Hills Country Club. She spent every spare moment hitting balls on the driving range, tapping in putts on the practice greens, or working on her short game. By the time she was in high school, she was a highly competitive golfer, and when it came time for college, Stanford was waiting to put her on their golf team. It took only one year on the university team and a third-place showing in the US Amateur Open before Marie was ready to try the LPGA qualifying school.

Katherine continued to play every Sunday, with an occasional round with a friend during the week while she was in school, but she never felt the desire to compete like Marie did. As good as she was at any game she played, she much preferred a quiet place and a long classic novel. She was only ten years old the first time she read *Pride and Prejudice*, and from that moment she wanted to be Jane Austen. She entered her first story in an adult writing competition when she was twelve and won third place and two hundred dollars. The money meant nothing to her, but placing in a competition for adults was all the recognition she needed to be inspired to become a writer. And maybe someday she could still do that, but for now she had only early mornings and late nights. She dedicated her days to living Marie's dream. She had to win at least one major tournament.

The first year it looked like it would be an easy goal, but on her current path, it would never happen. Her faithful swing had abandoned her. She hadn't placed in her last ten rounds and had even missed the cut in the last two. She needed to do something if she was going to succeed, but the last person she wanted help from was Ryan Gibbs, even if she was as sexy in person as she looked on TV—sexier. Katherine didn't want to think about that now. She had only an hour. It was time to write. She'd been running paragraphs through her head since she woke up—even if most of them included images of a tall, beautiful, tanned golfer.

With a cup of black coffee in her hand, she strolled over to the writing desk where she'd set up her computer last night. After walking around the beautiful foothill property surrounding the bed-and-breakfast Maggie had rented for them and then having a late dinner with her, she'd had only a couple of hours to write last night before she was too exhausted to focus on the screen.

In addition to the large plot of land surrounding the property, the Southwestern-style decor was incredible. She'd lived her whole life in California and traveled all over the world with her wealthy family, but she'd never experienced the quaint Spanish-influenced style that filled her room. The big chunky pine desk she sat at had large, solid tree branches for legs. They matched the bedposts and headboard, creating a warm, natural wood feel in a room with knotty-pine tongue-and-groove boards from the floor to the chair rail. She took it all in as she reclined in the out-of-place, modern, leather office chair in front of the desk. This could be a wonderful setting for a future story. She made a note in her journal before she started typing.

She set her cup down, and by the time she stopped to take a sip, the coffee was cold, and it was after six a.m. The story wasn't flowing as well as she'd hoped, despite her efforts to make it come. For some reason—one she wasn't quite sure she'd ever understand—she'd agreed to play golf with the last person she ever wanted to meet, let alone spend four hours walking a golf course with. Katherine had seen pictures of Ryan and even watched her play on television, and she'd always thought she was cute, but in real life, standing only a few feet away, she was truly stunning.

Her dark-brown hair was cut in a Tomboy style, pulled forward and messy, with blond highlights. Katherine wanted to run her fingers through those thick locks. Despite the boy haircut, no one would ever mistake Ryan for a man; her full red lips and flawless copper complexion confirmed her femininity. Just looking at her lips, especially when she smiled, made it hard not to want to kiss them. She had a beautiful heart-shaped face, with subtle little dimples on each cheek, but best of all were her eyes. Maybe it had been the sun yesterday, but Katherine wasn't sure what color they were—blue or green or blue/green. Whatever the color, they were translucent, and Katherine was almost convinced the woman could see inside her. Watching her walk the golf course might have a detrimental effect on her game—not that it could get much worse at this point. But she needed to beat her so she could get back to the tournaments, figure out what to do with her swing, and win a major. Then she could go on with her life. When she'd started this project, she had no idea how much she would regret it, but she had to finish. She never left anything incomplete.

Katherine had been so distracted with thoughts of Ryan, she hadn't written much this morning. Why had she wasted her precious writing time thinking about a woman she just wanted to hate? Ryan Gibbs had broken her family and ruined her life, but she seemed different, didn't she? She was probably humbled because she was working at a tiny course in the middle of nowhere instead of strutting down the fairways of famous courses with dozens of fans cheering for her. Katherine shook her head, trying to get thoughts of Ryan out of her mind. Then she punched the save button before she got up and threw the rest of her cold coffee into the sink. She'd be out of the shower just in time for Maggie to knock.

❖

"Hold on," Katherine yelled as she padded across the floor barefoot to open the big wooden door.

"You're not ready?" Maggie held two cups of coffee from the downstairs dining room. "I had a great breakfast—eggs, bacon, the works. I kept thinking you'd come down and join me."

Katherine took the coffee and rushed back over to the bench in front of the bed to put on her shoes. "You know I don't eat much breakfast." She grabbed a yogurt as she passed the small refrigerator next to the door.

Maggie backed into the hallway as Katherine closed the door behind her. "Yeah, but this was super good, and it is part of the deal. It's a bed-and-*breakfast*."

"Yeah, well, I still don't like a big breakfast." She locked the door and followed Maggie down the stairs.

CHAPTER FIVE

Katherine saw Ryan swinging her driver on the range as soon as Maggie pulled into the parking lot. Damn. Why did she have to look so good—like amazing, actually. Katherine had known Ryan was good-looking in that tall, slim, super-sporty kind of way—just the way Katherine liked them—but she didn't know how good-looking she was until she walked up on her out of nowhere yesterday morning.

Katherine knew when Ryan dropped out of the tour nearly two years ago, right before she made it through Q-School, but she had no idea where Ryan had landed or why she left the tour. And when Maggie insisted they take a break to New Mexico, as odd as it sounded when she suggested it, Katherine didn't question the choice and certainly didn't expect they'd be going to see Ryan Gibbs. She knew Maggie had been Ryan's coach. That was part of the reason she wanted her on her team now, but meeting Ryan face-to-face was not in her plan.

Katherine observed as Ryan struck the ball effortlessly. Katherine was used to being the tallest woman in most groups, but Ryan was taller than she was. Ryan's sun-streaked brown hair was lighter than she'd fantasized about this morning. She stayed in her seat, watching each perfect swing and the beautiful form with every follow-through. Even though Ryan had been off the tour for nearly two years, she was probably still as competitive as the best in the world.

"You should hit a few balls to loosen up," Maggie said as she tapped on the passenger-side window of their rental, standing outside the car waiting for her.

"Okay." She got out and continued to stare while Maggie got her clubs out of the trunk.

"Like what you see?" Maggie asked, but Katherine didn't answer when Ryan approached.

"I have a few balls left from my bucket, if you want to hit some before we tee off." Ryan strolled toward them with her 5-iron over her shoulder.

"More of those old, chewed-up range balls?" Katherine called back as she grabbed her clubs from Maggie.

When Ryan reached the car, she gave Maggie a quick hug. "Good morning."

"Good morning to you." Maggie held on to the hug.

Those two had had something between them, but Katherine wasn't surprised. Maggie had quite the reputation. She'd even tried to get her to go out with her, but she had too many things to focus on to get involved with someone, especially her coach. Oddly, though, she was a bit jealous as she watched them embrace.

"I'm sorry. Our little town club can't afford Titlists, but I did try to pick out the best balls we have." Ryan turned to Katherine with that perfect smile, as if everything was going to be okay.

"It's fine." Katherine walked ahead to the range.

"We need to tee off a few minutes early to get ahead of the first tee time, or we'll be waiting until late this afternoon," Ryan called out from behind her.

"Fine." Katherine snapped again.

She could hear Ryan and Maggie talking as she walked down the slope to the range. They were discussing the owners of the bed-and-breakfast. Ryan laughed, and as much as Katherine didn't want to like her, that loud, honest laugh was endearing. Hearing it made her feel good—almost happy—despite having to play golf with a woman she should hate.

❖

"Did the MacIntyres not take good care of you?" Ryan asked and nodded ahead of her toward Katherine.

"Nah. They were great. How'd you know where we stayed?"

"I know everything that happens here," Ryan said. "Are you kidding me? As soon as you left yesterday, I got like a hundred phone calls asking me if I knew who the golfers were who were staying with Dick and Terry."

"Seriously. This town isn't that small."

"Oh, yes, it is," Ryan said as she approached her bag and waited for Katherine to finish her swing. "I'll meet you over at number one in about fifteen minutes."

"I need to feel the greens," Katherine grumbled.

"Okay. We can push it to twenty and should still be able to get off number one before the first tee time." Ryan looked over at Maggie for an explanation.

Maggie shrugged, and they both walked over to the tee box, where Ryan had two carts waiting for their round.

"Is she always so intense? That might be part of the trouble with her game." Ryan fastened the strap around her club bag on the back of the cart.

"I guess she's just a little upset that I sprung you on her. I thought she'd be excited to meet you. She's always talking about you. She even tells stories about your final round at Q-School."

"Not my finest moment. How would she know about that?" Ryan pointed to the clubhouse. "Coffee?" She hated the memory of Q-School. She'd been so cocky and sure of herself, she'd nearly failed to qualify. Somehow after a good scolding from her mom before the final round, she pulled it out only one stroke below the final cut. It was pretty embarrassing now.

"Who knows?" Maggie answered and turned toward the clubhouse. "Nah. No coffee for me. I'm going to head out and leave you two to the game. I thought I might drive up to Santa Fe. I've always wanted to check it out."

"Don't miss the Plaza and the Georgia O'Keeffe Museum, but this could be interesting, and you'll miss it."

"I'm sure it will be, but she needs a break from me." Maggie moved in for another hug and raised her head for a kiss.

Ryan turned so Maggie caught her on the cheek instead of the lips. "Hey, Mags. We're not a thing anymore."

"I know. I…ahh…well, okay. A girl can dream, can't she? It's good to see you." Maggie turned to walk away, then called back. "See you in a few hours."

Ryan walked down to the fairway sand trap while she waited for Katherine to join her. She'd asked Eddie to put some more sand in it yesterday, and she wanted to see how it looked. He'd added just enough and smoothed it all out, like she'd known he would. As she walked back to the tee box, she watched the beautiful blonde on the practice green. The sun, which had just popped up over the mesa, was shining on her hair, making it look silver from the long distance. The chill in the air hadn't deterred her from wearing shorts, and Ryan couldn't help but admire her golden, tanned, long legs. If she would only lighten up a bit, Ryan was sure she would enjoy getting to know her, but for some reason Katherine seemed to despise her. Plus, it wouldn't be good to get involved with someone on tour. That was drama, and Ryan would never see her—not as long as she stayed in Los Alamos.

❖

Katherine tapped in three putts, one right after the other, before she collected her practice balls and headed toward the first tee box. She admired Ryan's fit body as she walked up the fairway scanning the course. Katherine couldn't help but hope she had on shorts under her warm-up pants.

"How ya hittin' 'em?" Ryan asked before they met at the carts and Ryan took off her warm-up pants, revealing a pair of black short shorts.

"Fine." Katherine turned away so Ryan wouldn't see her smile.

"That's good. I got two carts so we could speed up play a bit. We should be okay after the first hole, but I want to get out of the way soon. I know the first foursome, and we don't want to be anywhere near their tee shots," Ryan said. "They're good guys. Just not good golfers." She laughed a little.

"Mmm-hmm." Katherine barely acknowledged Ryan and pulled out her driver. "Me or you?"

"Ahhh…well…ahhh…do you want me to tell you about the hole?" Ryan asked.

"No. I'm fine. I saw the course guide. Apparently, your biggest hazard here is the wind, and it appears to be pretty calm today. Besides, I thought you were in a hurry."

"Yeah…but not that big of a hurry, but…Okay. You go ahead." Ryan shook her head and went to get her driver.

Katherine placed her ball on the left side of the tee box to give her a mostly straight shot around the slight dogleg on the first hole. She used her normal swing, and it worked. The ball landed in the exact center of the fairway about two hundred and seventy yards down range, leaving her a chip and a putt for birdie. "Dang," she said as she watched the ball roll down the fairway, and she slightly smiled. As much as she didn't want to admit it, she was nervous—even the television cameras didn't make her nervous, but Ryan Gibbs did—and that shot surprised her. It was exactly what she was hoping for but had no idea if her swing would actually work, and the long roll she got was an extra bonus.

"Nicely done," Ryan said and placed her tee and ball in the center of the tee box, then picked a spot in the distance and set up to her ball. Ryan's club impacted the ball, causing a metallic *tink* that all golfers associate with a titanium driver head contacting the hard, plastic coating of a golf ball. Ryan's ball lifted off with a slight draw at the apex, but Katherine wasn't following the ball. With a stroke like that, it was definitely going to hit in the center of the fairway. Instead, she stared at Ryan's follow-through. She held it like a designer model posing for a photo shoot until her ball stopped rolling down the fairway. When Katherine finally looked, she saw it had landed about two feet to the left of her own.

"Did you try to hit my ball?" she asked and climbed into her cart and drove toward the balls before Ryan could answer.

Katherine was waiting when Ryan caught up to her. Ryan's ball was about six inches behind hers, making her farthest from the hole, so she was supposed to play first.

"I didn't try to hit yours. It's the best spot for the second shot. See the bunkers around the green—too far to the left or right of here and you put those suckers in play." Ryan pulled out her 9-iron and started for her ball. "Did I unknowingly do something to piss you off?" Ryan turned and stared at her.

She shook her head and looked down at Ryan's ball, waiting.

"Okay. It might be a long day." Ryan backed away from her ball and took a couple of practice swings before setting up to it and sending it to the green, where it landed about three feet from the flag stick. Katherine admired how quickly Ryan went from anger to serious-golfer-with-no-emotions in a matter of seconds. It was a skill she needed to master.

Without a word Katherine repeated the action, and her ball also landed only a few feet from the hole. She relaxed a bit as she walked to her cart. She might not even need those two strokes per side if she kept striking them like that, and maybe her swing was okay. And maybe she didn't need to be so mean to this woman. She was trying to be nice, but how could she respect her after she quit the tour—an opportunity she stole from her sister.

This time Ryan was the one to drive off. Katherine looked back at the tee box to see if anyone was waiting on them, but no one was there. She saw a lot of activity around the clubhouse as the morning golfers got ready for their game—carts moving back and forth, golfers hitting balls on the driving range and around the practice green—but they didn't need to rush. Maybe she should chill out a bit and try to enjoy the game. She was playing with one of the best golfers in the world, even if she was a quitter.

Katherine drove up next to the green, grabbed her putter, and walked up to her ball. This time she was the one slightly farther away, so Ryan was the one waiting. She'd already removed the flag stick and was lining up her putt. Her focus was intense, as if she were the only person on the course.

"You beat my sister in the final round of Q-School," Katherine said before she hit her ball without even lining it up.

"What?" Ryan rose from her squatting position as the ball hit the edge of the hole and lipped out.

"Damn!" Katherine reached across the hole to avoid walking in the path of Ryan's line to the hole and tapped her ball in for a par.

"What did you say?" Ryan asked.

"Can't you play and talk at the same time?" Katherine walked over to pick up the flag to have it ready to replace as soon as Ryan hit her ball.

"Ahh…okay." Ryan tapped her ball, and it rolled straight into the back of the cup. She reached down to pick it up before Katherine dropped the flag back in the hole. Ryan shrugged and walked to her cart.

"Nice birdie. You probably always birdie that hole, don't you?" Katherine caught up to her.

"Not always, but, yes, it's an easy one. You should have birdied it too." Ryan gave her a quick glance before she climbed in her cart. Katherine couldn't help but notice those green, no, blue eyes. Katherine was probably staring, but then Ryan pulled her sunglasses back down and covered her eyes. Katherine had only her own reflection to stare at now. She didn't have time to respond before Ryan took off. She couldn't decide if she was glad or sad that she'd managed to make Ryan mad and now she wasn't talking to her. But she still looked good even when she was angry—pretty hot actually. She parked her cart behind Ryan's and watched her set her ball up on the second tee.

"We don't have to hurry anymore, in case that's why you rushed that putt," Ryan said as she raised up and looked over at her.

"Okay." She climbed up on the tee box and stood behind Ryan, watching her practice swing. "Sorry if I've been a little grumpy."

"Ahh…okay. Why are you so grumpy?" Ryan backed away and stood behind her ball—listening but still looking down at the green.

"I…I…I guess I'm sick of being told to change my swing, and you're the last person I want to hear it from."

"Okay. I don't understand why, but I don't have to tell you anything about your swing. Do what you want. We don't even have to play if you don't want to." Ryan was clearly done with the attitude.

"No. I want to. Tell me about this hole." She looked down at the short par three. "Have you ever had a hole-in-one here?"

"Ahh…no. I've actually never had a hole-in-one."

"Never? You're kidding?"

"Nope. Very close many times, but it never drops." Ryan popped her ball off the short tee it sat on and bounced it on the face of her wedge. With one quick flick of the wrist, she caught the ball and set it back on her tee. "There's not much to say about this hole. It's pretty straightforward. It's a short one hundred sixty-five yards to the center. You can see the hole is cut to the left today. It's a good location for an aggressive approach. Don't hit too much club. It's deceivingly close, and," she tapped on the blue tee markers, "since these are so close today, it's more like a hundred and fifty yards. The greens are still a little damp, so you won't get much roll. I'm going right at the flag."

"Okay." Katherine backed up. "Go for it. Today might be your hole-in-one day."

Ryan laughed and approached her ball.

Katherine smiled as Ryan's ball flew nearly straight up in the air. They both watched as it came down hard on the green two feet from the hole and bounced to a position fractions of an inch from the pin.

"Oh my God. Can you believe that?" Katherine was yelling from the back of the tee box. "Go in. Go in!"

"Beat that." Ryan bowed low and backed off to let her play.

"Truly, that was amazing. It's like you're shooting darts. I thought for sure it was going in." She placed her ball in nearly the same spot as Ryan and stood back to zero in on the flag stick.

Her ball landed in the center of the green about six feet from the hole. When they got to the green, she let Ryan tap in her easy birdie before she missed her first putt by inches. She was now two strokes behind.

"Well, that's your two strokes on this side," Ryan pointed out.

"I guess I'd better birdie through the turn."

"Or we could quit this silly competition, and you could work with me."

"Seriously." Katherine raised her voice. "My swing has been serving me well so far today. It's my putting that's given you two strokes. Damn it. Just keep playing. You haven't won yet."

"Okay. You're right." Ryan headed over to the third hole.

They played the next six holes with little conversation. Ryan went on to birdie three more holes and even eagled the second par five. Katherine had held her own on the unfamiliar course, and with the exception of the first two holes, she'd matched Ryan's birdies and was only behind one stroke, considering the proffered two strokes. She was becoming confident that she could beat her on the back nine.

As they approached the last hole on the front side, Ryan caught up to her on the tee box. "Would you like something to eat?"

"It's not even nine o'clock yet."

"So, Rebecca will make whatever we want." Ryan shrugged and pulled her cell phone out of her bag.

"Wow. Is that like the first iPhone ever made?" She looked over at Ryan's cracked screen and dented frame.

"No. I've just had it for a while."

"A while? Like a decade? I'm surprised it still works."

"Do you want breakfast or not?"

"I'm good."

"Well, I didn't have anything, so I'm ordering a breakfast burrito. You go ahead and tee off." Ryan made a quick call while Katherine teed off on the four-hundred-and-fifteen-yard par four. She slammed her driver down hard on the ground as she watched her ball take a dramatic right turn. "Damn it."

Ryan walked up just in time to see the ball land in the high rough on the right side of the fairway. "You can get out of that. I've been there before."

"Right. Like you've ever missed the fairway." She stormed back to her cart and sat down while Ryan teed off, placing her ball in the center of the fairway yet again—almost like a robot programmed to birdie every hole.

Ryan waited in the fairway while Katherine headed to the rough to find her ball. She was so disgusted she got out of her cart and stomped into the high grass, kicking it around trying to stir up her ball. But instead of stirring up the ball, she discovered a huge nest of bees. Despite her intense bravado all morning, she squealed like a four-year-old and started running back to the cart. When she finally got there, she discovered the bees had followed her. She swatted and shrieked while flailing around the center of the fairway.

❖

Ryan was cleaning the dirt out of her 7-iron when she first heard and then saw Katherine screaming and racing across the fairway.

"Wait. Wait," Ryan yelled before she dropped her club and went into action. She reached for the rain poncho she carried in her golf bag and ran toward where Katherine was still flapping her arms. When she reached her, she threw the poncho over Katherine's head and shoulders. With Katherine covered, Ryan caught her and kept her still. As she held on, Ryan felt several stings on her arms and legs.

"What are you doing? Let me go." Katherine squirmed under the cape.

"Stay still. I'm going to get you to the cart, and we're going to outrun them," she said as she pushed Katherine toward the cart and settled her in the seat before pushing the gas pedal as she climbed in herself. The golf cart kicked forward, and she grabbed Katherine's arm to hold her in. She guided the little cart toward the clubhouse as fast as it would go.

"Can I take this off?" Katherine had calmed and sat motionless in the seat next to her.

"Oh. Ahhh…" She glanced behind her to see if the bees were following, and seeing nothing, she agreed. "Yeah. We're okay." She screeched to a stop, locking the cart's brakes and sliding several inches on the concrete patio.

"What are you doing?" Eddie said as he stepped out of the restaurant while she guided Katherine from the cart.

"She's been stung." She pushed past Eddie.

"Is she allergic?" Eddie bent to pick up Katherine. Ryan let go of her and grabbed the door to let Eddie in.

"Bec, get the eppie," Eddie yelled across the room.

"I'm not allergic." Katherine spoke but Eddie didn't hear.

"Rebecca, hurry." He yelled again as he sat her on the nearest chair. Only a handful of patrons were getting coffee and breakfast, but all of them stopped and watched the commotion.

"I'm not allergic." Katherine elevated her voice enough to be heard this time.

"Oh, thank God." Eddie exhaled.

"Here, here. I got it." Rebecca jogged across the room, her large bosom bouncing as she approached.

"It's okay. She's not allergic." Ryan leaned down and pushed the hair out of Katherine's face. Then she began to scan her arms and legs. "Where are you stung?" She continued searching and called back to Rebecca. "Get some hydrocortisone and some Motrin."

"Okay. I'll be right back." Rebecca scooted back toward the kitchen.

"I don't think I have any stings." Katherine examined herself, then looked up at Ryan. "But you! Look. She pointed out a sting on Ryan's neck and two on each arm. "Here. Sit down." She got up and pushed Ryan into the chair.

"Shit, Ry! Are *you* allergic?" Eddie asked.

"No. I'm fine." She tried to get up, but Katherine pushed her back down.

"Where's that lotion?" Katherine yelled in the direction of the kitchen while she gently touched the sting on Ryan's neck. "Oh my God, that must hurt." Katherine's face was only a few inches from Ryan's as she kneeled next to her.

Ryan could feel Katherine's breath on her face and finally relaxed into the light touch and pampering she was getting.

"Here." Rebecca approached. "I'll put it on."

"No. Here." Katherine took the lotion.

In the meantime, Eddie returned with a glass of ice water. "Take the Motrin." He prompted Rebecca to give her the pills. Ryan popped the pills while Katherine continued to examine her.

Ryan watched Katherine squirt a glob of Cortisone cream in her hand and start rubbing it over each sting she found. "How do we know if the stingers are still in there?" Katherine looked back to Eddie and Rebecca.

"Bumble bees don't leave their stinger unless you kill them when they're stinging. She should be okay," Rebecca said.

"I'm fine." Ryan tried to get up again. "We have a game to finish."

"No! We are not playing golf with you looking like this," Katherine declared.

"What? I look so bad you won't even play golf with me?" Ryan took hold of Katherine's shoulders. "Really. I'm fine."

Eddie laughed in the background.

"Are you the groundskeeper?" Katherine asked.

"Yeah. I'm Eddie." He held out his hand but pulled it back when he saw all the lotion on Katherine's hands. "Who are you?"

"I'm Katherine Reese. Her clubs and the cart are in the fairway in the middle of number nine, and some golfers were coming up behind us. Can you get it?"

"Katherine Reese. Well. I'll be damned. I thought Ryan was the only pro we had to deal with around here," Eddie said. "You aren't as tall as you look on TV."

"Ahh… Can you get the cart?" Katherine asked again.

"Better send one of the boys out to get it, Eddie. She's not going to let me finish this game." Ryan finally relaxed in the chair while Katherine continued to treat each red mark she found.

Katherine kept mumbling about another one and another one as she continued to softly apply ample amounts of lotion. It was a little ridiculous at this point, but Ryan was enjoying Katherine's touch and her kindness. And having her so close wasn't a bad thing either. She could smell the coconut of Katherine's sunscreen and the citrusy clean smell of her hair each time she leaned down to cover another spot.

"Twelve. You were stung twelve times. That can't be good. Are you sure we shouldn't get her to a doctor?" Katherine looked back up at Rebecca, who stood alone now, pointing out spots on Ryan over Katherine's shoulder.

"There. Thirteen and fourteen. And fifteen—there's one near her armpit there on her right arm." Rebecca pointed. "I don't know. Maybe we could take her over to the clinic." Katherine got up to follow Rebecca.

"Hey. I'm still here," Ryan said.

"Yeah. I'll get my car. You can tell her how to get there," Rebecca called over her shoulder with Katherine on her heels.

"No. I'm not going to the clinic. Just get me a glass of tea. I'm fine. And I'm starving. Did you get the burrito made?"

"No. I didn't make a burrito," Rebecca said and frowned at Ryan. "You came in yelling for help for this woman who ended up taking care of you. There was no time for a burrito. Hi. I'm Rebecca." She held out her hand to Katherine. "Nice to meet you, Ms. Reese. We've watched you play."

"Nice to meet you, Rebecca. It's Katherine, please. Can we get her some food and see how she is? Then I'll take her over to your clinic."

"Yeah. Putting food in her mouth is the only way to get her to shut up. What can I get you?" Rebecca stood in the middle of the room, holding the remaining lotion in one hand and a bottle of Motrin in the other.

"I'm good…"

"Bring the girl a breakfast burrito. You eat meat, right?" Ryan called from where she still sat.

"Yeah."

"Good. Two bacon-and-egg burritos coming up," Rebecca said and walked away. "Oh. Do you want red or green?" She looked at Katherine.

"Red or green what?"

"Give her a little bit of green."

"Maybe I want red. What is it?"

"Green chiles, a New Mexican pepper. They're spicy."

"Give me a lot of both. I like spicy food."

"You should put them on the side," Ryan added.

Rebecca nodded and disappeared into the kitchen.

"Thank you." Katherine sat in the chair next to Ryan. Her hair, long since fallen out of its neat little bun, brushed against Ryan's arm as she leaned in to examine one of Ryan's red bumps. "Do they hurt?"

She relished the feel of Katherine's fine hair across her forearm.

"I asked, do they hurt?" Katherine asked again.

"Ahhh. No. Not really. Some of them are a little uncomfortable and itchy, but I'm fine." She was face-to-face with those beautiful green eyes.

"You saved me from all those bees. I didn't get a single sting, and look at you. You have marks all over your arms and legs. Thank you." Katherine gave her a hug, and she wanted to hang on, but she held her only until she felt Katherine release her.

"You're welcome. I couldn't let you get stung on my golf course. What kind of host would I have been?"

"I'm sorry I was so grumpy this morning. If I'd been you, I probably would've let the bees eat me alive."

She laughed. "Hmm. It was tempting for a second." She lightly touched Katherine's arm. "Thank you for nursing my wounds. Now, when are we going to finish the game? We can probably get back out there after five, but I'm not sure we could finish before it gets dark tonight. Should we try?"

"No. We aren't going to do it today. You should go home and rest."

"I'm fine. I've been stung before—hundreds of times. I'll be okay. Tomorrow morning then?"

"Hmm. I'll finish the match with you tomorrow, if you let me take you home after you eat and be sure you get in a warm bath and some rest."

"What? No. I can't leave. I have work to do."

"You planned to play golf all morning. Whatever you have to do can wait until tomorrow. I don't finish the game if you don't go home."

"Man, you drive a hard bargain. Is everything a negotiation with you?"

Rebecca approached with two large plates overflowing with stuffed burritos covered in green chile sauce. "You have to be tough. Don't let her break you," Rebecca said to Katherine as she set the plates down.

"Oh my God. Am I supposed to eat all this in one sitting?"

"If you don't, she'll be insulted," Ryan said.

"No. I will not. You never eat a whole one." Rebecca pointed at Ryan. "Most days there's two or three leftover burritos in the fridge. Eat what you want, and I'll wrap up the rest."

"Thank you, Rebecca. It looks amazing." Katherine cut off a gooey, cheesy piece.

Ryan watched her take her first bite.

"Oh, wow. This *is* amazing. I love this…what is it…green chile?" She poured the side bowl of chile sauce over the burrito and took another big bite.

"See now, Ryan. You should never underestimate a person's green-chile tolerance. Let me know if you need anything else." Rebecca walked away.

She and Katherine started eating and didn't say a word until finally she pushed back from the table with more than half of the large burrito still on her plate. "I can never eat it all."

Katherine pushed back as well. "I want to. It's so good, but I can't take another bite."

"You girls stopped already?" Rebecca called from behind the bar.

"Yeah. I'm done. I'll get us some boxes." She started to stand, but Katherine stood and pushed her gently back down in her chair.

"I'll get it. Where are the boxes, Rebecca?"

"Sit. I'll get them," Rebecca said.

"I'm not sick, you know. It's only a couple of bee stings." She started pushing the food to the edge of her plate.

"I'm taking you to your house. Then I'm going to get you into your bed and stay and watch you to be sure you don't have some kind of reaction."

"No. You. Are. Not." She finally stood up. "I'll live, and what do you know about a bee-sting reaction? I have work to do."

"Okay, then no golf tomorrow."

She huffed. "Fine. I'll go home, but I'm not going to bed, and you're not staying to watch me. I'll have Terry come get you and take you back to your B and B."

Rebecca set two to-go boxes on the table. "Here you go."

"Rebecca, should someone keep an eye on her?" Katherine asked.

"Rebecca, nothing's wrong with me. Please tell her this is not the first time I've been stung at this course." It was the first time a beautiful woman she wanted to kiss had taken care of her though.

"Well, she always needs to be watched, but I don't think the bee stings will put her in any more danger than she normally puts herself in. She could use the rest though, and we can handle the place, so you should take her home. She'll probably be fine there." Rebecca knew she wouldn't agree to having someone babysit her all day.

"Okay. Where's your car?"

"Can you drive a truck?" she asked.

"Of course." Katherine stood and picked up the boxes. "Let's go."

After Eddie put Katherine's clubs in Ryan's truck, the two drove off to her house. Because she had called Terry before they left, she was waiting at Ryan's little house when they arrived. After a bit more fuss, Katherine finally went with Terry. Ryan washed her dishes and put a load of laundry in before she drove back to the course.

"You like her, don't you?" Rebecca asked almost as soon as Ryan walked in.

"Nah. She's a pain in the ass—terrible temper, grumpy, and arrogant."

"Hmm. That sounds like another pro golfer I know. They must make you all alike at Q-School." Rebecca's eyes gleamed. "But she's gorgeous."

"Well…she is very pretty."

"Pretty? Hmm." Rebecca put a tray in her hands and waved for her to follow her. As they walked around the room, Rebecca put the condiments and the salt and pepper on the tray to fill up before the dinner meal. "Does she make you miss the tour?"

"I don't know. We haven't talked at all about the tour." She stopped and stared out the window.

"Come on." Rebecca waved her arm in front of Ryan's face.

"Oh. Sorry." She caught up to Rebecca. "That's weird. Normally when I'm around other pros, that's all we talk about."

"Hmm. Well, she is a beautiful woman, and I think she likes you."

"Are you kidding? She hates me. I don't know why, but for some reason she's not a fan."

"Well, I don't know anything about her being a fan, but I watched that woman take care of you and worry over your bee stings. She likes you."

❖

Katherine took advantage of the extra writing time and sat in her room with all the windows open writing—between thoughts of Ryan. They had planned to meet again tomorrow morning to finish the game. Maggie would probably be upset that no progress had been made, but she had enjoyed getting to know Ryan. She was nothing like she thought, but she had seen her arrogance, and that person was probably still there somewhere. She'd join her again in the morning and then run away as fast as she could, if she could hold it together for ten more holes.

CHAPTER SIX

Wednesday morning started exactly like Tuesday, and Maggie was knocking on the door before Katherine was ready, yet again. After Maggie dropped her off and headed out to hike to some local hot springs, Ryan and Katherine headed for the ninth hole.

"Should we tee off again?" Ryan asked.

"No. I'll see if my ball is still there, or I'll drop. I'll trust you to place your ball as close to where it was as you can." Katherine smiled. "I hit the shot, so I need to play the consequences."

"Hey. I think I suffered your consequences." Ryan rubbed the small red marks on her arms and laughed.

"I guess you did. They look much better today. Do they hurt?"

"Nah. I'll give you a drop on the fairway, so you don't have to stir them up again." They walked to the edge of the rough. "No, wait. Are you playing a Titleist ProV1?"

"Yeah. It has a small check mark below the T." She walked up next to Ryan, and they brushed into each other as Ryan backed away. "Oh, sorry."

"It's okay." Ryan lightly touched her shoulder. "It has to be yours. I'm surprised it's still here. Any of my golfers would have snagged that if they'd seen it." Ryan backed away.

"Yeah. It's mine." She walked back to the cart for a long iron. If she could make good contact, maybe she could still hit the green and birdie out. Ryan was watching as she approached her ball.

"Hmm." Ryan sighed and walked back to the edge of the fairway.

"What?" She looked over at Ryan.

"I didn't say anything."

"No. You made a noise. What?"

"Nothing."

"You want to tell me how to hit this shot, don't you?" She stepped away from her ball and leaned on her 3-iron.

"No. I…I'm just glad I'm not there. Eddie has taken good care of the rough this spring. Looks like hell."

"Oh, thanks. Thanks a lot. You probably pay him extra for that." She took a couple of practice swings before she walked back to her ball and let it rip. The high grass caught her club face and turned it as it impacted the ball, sending it back into the rough on the right side of the green.

"Fuck." She slammed her club and carefully climbed out of the jungle around her.

"How do they not penalize you on the tour?" Ryan asked. "I don't understand why you get so angry. Don't you enjoy the game?"

"Seriously? You're asking me why I'm mad after I hit the ball back in the rough?" She forced her 3-iron back into her golf bag. "I'm sure you're not offended. I've heard worse come out of your mouth."

"What? Not on tour, you didn't." Ryan stopped and looked back as Katherine got in her cart.

"Never mind."

"Well, we all hit bad shots now and then. It's part of the game."

"You've never hit a bad shot in your life—not when you were paying attention."

Katherine drove away before Ryan even hit her ball. How could things have changed from the great time they'd shared yesterday to Katherine hating her again? Ryan was starting to think she needed to be injured for Katherine to be kind to her.

She walked over to her ball with a short iron, swung quickly, and set the ball gently on the green. She had no idea why this woman resented her so much. It might be easier if she let her win. Then she could let Maggie take her back to the tour, and Ryan could go on with her simple, quiet life. But those sexy long legs and the occasional glimpses of humor and kindness kept her from picking up her ball. When Katherine relaxed—just a bit—that beautiful white smile was enough for Ryan to allow her to yell at her all day.

They finished the last hole on the front and played the back nine with little conversation as Katherine's game became more and more unpredictable. Ryan was actually embarrassed for her. At the end of eighteen, she was down by six strokes, even with the four strokes she had been given.

"Well, you won." Katherine said as she unfastened her big touring bag from the cart.

"It seems so." Ryan got out of the cart and stood next to Katherine. Maggie hadn't returned yet, and Ryan didn't want to leave her standing in the parking lot alone. "Why don't you come in and have a glass of tea or a beer if you want, and Rebecca will fix us something to eat?" The parking lot was filling up, and golfers were beginning to mill around the practice green. It was going to be a busy day, but Ryan could take a few minutes to try to break through the ice that had formed around Katherine in the last two hours.

"No. I'm all right. Maggie knew we had only a couple of hours to play. She'll be back soon. Besides, you're probably ready to be rid of me if we're going to be seeing each other for swing practice every day."

"No. She won't be back in a minute. When has Maggie ever been on time? Please come and have a drink with me. Let's just talk. Listen, if you don't want swing lessons, that's fine. I wanted to help, but if you're good, I'll back off." Ryan held out her hand but let it drop when Katherine made no move to take it or head toward the restaurant.

"I'll come for lessons. I said if you won, I would, so I will." Katherine sat down on the hard concrete bench right in front of the parking lot. "Damn, this bench is hard."

"Yeah. Come on. Please. I haven't been turned down so harshly in a long time. You'll hurt my confidence."

"That's bullshit." Katherine looked up and glared at her from her position on the bench. "But I'll go in and have a glass of tea. No beer. It's not even nine o'clock yet. And you're right. Maggie won't be here for another hour."

"Great. I'll ask Eddie or one of the guys to put your clubs in the shed, and I'll meet you inside. Tell Rebecca two large iced teas." Ryan turned toward the shed but saw Michael coming toward her. "Hey, Michael. Will you take our clubs to Eddie's office?"

"Yeah. That's what he sent me out to do. How'd you hit 'em?" Michael slid into Ryan's cart.

"Good."

"Like always." Michael smiled.

"Nah. Just lucky," Ryan said and watched the young man drive the cart to the maintenance shed.

"Do you ever play badly?" Katherine walked up behind her.

"Shit! I thought you went inside."

"They love you." Katherine pushed her sunglasses up on her head.

"I love them back. Come on." She took Katherine by the arm and escorted her to the clubhouse. The ice was beginning to thaw.

"I'm sorry I was no fun today."

"Don't apologize. I'm sorry you didn't have a good time." She opened the door and waited for Katherine to pass through, and they walked together to the bar.

"Bec, got any tea made?" Ryan called into the kitchen.

"Yep. Pitcher's on the drink bar," Rebecca answered. "Want anything to eat?"

"You hungry?" Ryan turned to Katherine.

"I could eat half of a burrito, if you want to share." Katherine smiled.

There it was—that gorgeous smile that made her want to know what was behind the angry woman beside her.

"Okay. Excellent idea. Christmas?" Ryan asked as she headed for the kitchen. "It's what we call it when you get both red and green chiles."

"Then yes, Christmas."

In the kitchen, Ryan told Rebecca what they wanted.

"You're going to win her over with *my* cooking." Rebecca teased Ryan.

"Well, you know I couldn't win anything with *my* cooking."

"Right! I'll bring it out."

When she returned to the empty dining room, Katherine had drinks for both of them and silverware set up at Ryan's favorite table. "Thanks for getting the tea. Rebecca will have the burritos out in a minute. So listen. We don't have to work on your swing. You need to do what you want with your game."

"Wow. You know how to kill the mood. Do you ever talk about anything but golf?"

"Ahh…oh…I'm…"

"No. Listen. I said I'd work on my swing if you won. You won, so I'll work on my swing."

"What if it helps?"

"I'm sure it will." Katherine sat down and looked out at the large driving range and across to the mountains.

"If you think it will, then why were you so stubborn about it?"

"I…I…" Katherine looked back at her.

"What is it?"

"Change is hard."

"Hmm. Okay. I can't argue with that, but is that really what you were going to say?"

"It's quite beautiful here." Katherine spun her chair a quarter turn and looked across the street as two golfers teed off on number ten.

"It is. I love it." Ryan turned to see the same view. "Did you think I wouldn't notice you changed the subject?"

"Here you go, ladies." Rebecca carried two plates covered with chiles to the table.

"Oh my God. It looks like more than yesterday. I only wanted half." Katherine took one of the plates.

Rebecca laughed. "It's only half. I promise. It looks like more because of the chiles on top today."

"If you spend a week here, you'll soon find out Rebecca doesn't know the definition of just a little." Ryan took the other plate. "Thanks, Bec."

"I'll have to be careful, or I'll gain a bunch of weight."

"That's why you should go running with me before our practice tomorrow."

"What time do you run? If you're here at six a.m., I can't imagine what time you get up."

"It's not that bad. I get up at five. I could stop by and get you, and we could go up and down a short trail on that mountain." She pointed out the window, then ate a big fork full of burrito.

"Is that your teaching technique—kill your students, and then they can't prove whether you could help them or not," Katherine asked.

"I thought it'd be fun. You were admiring our mountains."

"Fun?" Katherine asked. "Fine." She too dug into her burrito. "Mmm."

CHAPTER SEVEN

Katherine had no time for writing this morning, since Ryan was right on time. She was putting on her running shoes when she heard a light tap on the door.

"One second," Katherine called and then bounded across the room. When she opened the door, she was staring at Ryan's smiling face—fresh and ready to go. "Seriously, do you always look like you're ready to take on the world?" Katherine closed the door behind her.

"I'm going to try to get you to change your swing, so I'd better be ready to take on the world," Ryan said and followed her down the stairs.

"Hey, Ryan." Terry stuck her head around the kitchen door.

"Morning, Terry."

"Are you going to miss your meal again this morning?" Terry addressed Katherine. "She won't even try my breakfast." Terry turned back to Ryan.

"Her loss."

"I'm sorry. I'm not a big breakfast eater." She stopped at the front door.

"But she'll eat Rebecca's burritos?" Terry said to Ryan and waved as she went back into the kitchen.

"How does she know I ate burritos?"

"She and Rebecca are best friends." Ryan held the door open for her to pass through.

"This town is tiny."

"Yep," Ryan said and started walking toward her truck.

"Okay, so don't do or say anything the rest of the time I'm here. Got it." She climbed in.

They drove the four miles to the trailhead with only a few comments along the way.

Ryan parked next to a bright-red Jeep Wrangler, the only other vehicle in the lot. Then she jumped out and threw the keys on top of the back tire.

"You're leaving your keys there?" Katherine commented as she stretched her legs on the back bumper.

"Yeah. No one will take it. That's Martha's Jeep. She'll be down when we get back and will probably wait for us."

"Oh…she's already on the trail?"

Ryan laughed. "Yeah. She probably started about the time your alarm went off. She's going on the outside loop. It's not as steep and only about a mile and half, but she's almost eighty, so it takes her a little while to finish."

"Did you say eighty?" she asked and looked at the bright-red Jeep again.

"Yep. The high desert is good for you." Ryan smiled and waved in the direction of the trailhead. "Last one up buys breakfast?" Ryan started jogging up the hill.

"Is everything a competition with you?" Katherine asked mockingly, then took off and passed her at a quick pace.

For twenty minutes Ryan ran behind her as she slowed with every few feet of elevation.

Finally, Ryan passed her as they were about to crest the short peak.

"You did that on purpose." She reached the top panting. "You walk this every day, don't you?"

"Most days in the summer. There's too much snow in the winter. Besides, I had a nice view on the way up," Ryan said.

"Ryan Gibbs, are you flirting with me?"

"Nah. It wouldn't work." Ryan moved to the edge. "Look." She pointed off to the west side and down on the small village with the golf course below them.

"Wow. It looks so peaceful from up here. You wouldn't know that dozens of people will be cursing their golf balls in a couple hours." She used her forearm to wipe the sweat from her face.

"It doesn't seem like you really like golf." Ryan stood inches from her. She could feel the heat from Ryan's arms.

"I…I like…I like golf. Why would you say that?" She turned away and sat on a boulder next to the edge.

"You talk about it like it's a chore or a job you don't like doing."

"I just have to win a major." She started back down the hill.

"What?" Ryan ran after her.

She reached the bottom ahead of Ryan and was already being interrogated by Martha Henderson, who had lived in Los Alamos her whole life. She had great stories, but she could also tear a stranger to shreds. She was relieved to see Ryan round the last corner.

"Good morning, Martha," Ryan called as she approached. "I see you've met my friend Katherine. She's a pro golfer."

"Oh, Ryan. I'd have to be dead to have not heard that already. Besides, I've seen her on the TV. I watch every time they show one of them ladies' tournaments. You know your mama used to come by and help me clean. She taught me all about it. I know the difference between a bogie and a birdie, and I learned about an eagle when you played in Illinois." Martha held up two fingers and shook them at Ryan, then turned back to Katherine. "This one here is having a bad season."

"Well, she's going to fix that," Ryan said and then turned to Katherine. "She doesn't pull punches."

"Right. I see that."

"Oh, I don't care about that," Martha said. "Everyone knows you're going to show her how to play golf. I want to know if she's your girlfriend. That's what no one seems to know." Martha gave Ryan a hug.

"Martha!" Ryan said. "No. Katherine and I are just friends."

"Hmm." Martha turned and headed for her Jeep. "I guess we'll see about that." She climbed up with both feet on the running board and hopped into the seat, stretching her short arms and legs to get in.

"Now don't you start any new rumors, Martha." Ryan leaned in the passenger side of Martha's Jeep and spoke through the open window.

Martha laughed loudly and looked past Ryan at Katherine. "What fun would I have if I didn't talk about you young people?" She put the Jeep in reverse and spun her tires as she pulled away.

"Oh my God. She's hilarious," Katherine said. "And you're going to teach me to play golf, are you?" She walked around the truck to get in.

Ryan just stood in the small parking lot looking bewildered.

"Well… Are you going to teach me or not?" Katherine yelled from the front seat.

Ryan jumped into the truck. "Listen. They like to talk and don't often have anything new to gossip about around here. I'm sorry she said that."

"She didn't lie. I am having a hard time."

"But I'm not going to teach you how to play golf. You're an excellent golfer." Ryan headed back to the golf course.

"Hmm. Not lately." Katherine sank into the seat.

They drove in silence until Dick and Terry's place was in sight.

"What did you mean about just winning a major?" Ryan asked as they pulled into the driveway.

"Nothing. Forget it. Maggie will be up now. She'll bring me by. What time do you want to start?" Katherine asked as she climbed out of the truck.

"Oh…mmm… It's a little after six now, so how about eight?" Ryan glanced up from her watch, and Katherine stared at her.

"Eight? Okay." She closed the door and walked to the front porch.

When she got there, she looked back at Ryan and noticed her confused expression.

CHAPTER EIGHT

Morning, Ryan. You're late." Michael passed her as he was moving carts from the maintenance building to the starters' shack.

"Only twenty minutes," Ryan called to his back.

"Ryan, it's about time," Eddie said as they met at the restaurant door. "Is everything okay? Bec's in there worryin'. She was sending me over to your place. Guess I don't need to go now." Eddie patted her on the shoulder as he walked past.

"Seriously, I'm only twenty minutes late."

"You're never late," Eddie said and kept walking.

Ryan grabbed the door and nearly fell to the ground as she pulled with all her weight, only to have the door open from the inside. "Where have you been?" Rebecca yelled.

"Holy shit. You almost knocked me off the step."

"I'll do more than that if you make me worry like that again." Rebecca grabbed her by the arm and guided her to a table.

"Can I have a cup of coffee and some eggs?" Ryan asked.

"Not until you tell me where you were and why you weren't answering your phone."

"Calm down. I went for a run with Katherine, and my battery died."

"A run?" Rebecca calmed down and actually started laughing. "That's your first date tactic. A shitty one, if you ask me, but you athletic types seem to like it." Rebecca stopped, looked back at her, and spoke quickly. "You asked her out."

"Well…no, not exactly. I mean I would've liked it to be like a date, but you were wrong. I don't think she likes me. She tolerates me, and now she's planning to go through the motions with the swing lessons. It's probably a waste of time."

"Hmm. I'm not usually wrong about these things." Rebecca got up and headed for the kitchen.

"That's it. You interrogate me, then walk away."

"I'm getting your eggs and coffee, your majesty." Rebecca turned and bowed. "And would you buy yourself a new phone? Your battery only lasts like five minutes."

She followed Rebecca. "You think she likes me? I think she's mad at the world."

Rebecca cracked two eggs into a skillet. "Well, that's why it's hard to tell if she likes you. She's mad about something, but it's in her head, not something you did. She can't let it go and keeps looking for someone to blame. Sometimes you're it."

"Do you get paid extra for psychotherapy?" She gave Rebecca a big hug from behind while she finished cooking the eggs.

Rebecca leaned back into her hug. "You know exactly how much I get paid, and I think I deserve a raise for all the worrying and counseling I do around here." She laughed.

"Coffee?" Ryan headed to the coffee bar. "You know I couldn't afford you."

❖

After Ryan finished her eggs, she and Eddie headed out to the back nine to annotate locations for the pins for this weekend's local tournament. The location of holes in the green could turn her moderately skilled course into a real challenge.

"So you and that cute little pro golfer, hmm?" Eddie said as they drove up near the back of the tenth green. "I guess it's probably not the first time you've dated a golfer." Eddie paused a minute, then looked over at her. "That was stupid. I mean. I…ahh. I'm bein' stupid, aren't I?"

"What do you want to ask me, Eddie?" She watched as two balls hit the green from the foursome coming up number ten. "Wait. Who hit that shot? I didn't know Dr. Dunn had that one in his bag." She spoke loud enough for the approaching group to hear.

"Oh, now, give me a break, Ryan. I was sneaking you drinks of Coke when you were little enough that your mama would have kicked me in the ass if she'd seen me." Sam Dunn, their retired family doctor, approached the green, rolling his clubs in a hand cart behind him.

"Oh yeah." Ryan laughed. "At least the Cokes didn't have rum in them."

"I wouldn't be too sure about that," Doc said and winked.

"Well, that was a nice shot, Doc." She met him at his ball with a quick hug. I haven't seen you out here in months. Are you doing okay?"

"Everything's great. Nancy had me out in Florida all winter." Sam pointed at his ball. "I got lots of practice."

"I see that. Are you playing in the tournament this weekend?" Eddie asked as he approached the green where the group was talking.

"Yes, I am. Are you figuring out where you're going to put the holes? You couldn't give an old man a hint, now could ya?" Sam winked at Ryan again.

"Make that putt and get off my green," Ryan said, teasing him.

"You let her talk like that to her ol' doc?" Sam said to Eddie before he set up to his ball and tapped it in the hole. "Birdie."

The other three local guys finished their putts and headed to the next hole. "See you guys later," Ryan called after them. "What do you think, Eddie? Front right?"

"Yep. Just what I had in mind. Tough but not impossible. It'll keep them moving around the turn." Eddie made a note on his pad and headed for the cart.

"Now, what were you saying to me, Eddie?" she asked as she climbed into the cart next to him.

"Oh, I…I guess I was, ah…wondering…I mean…you know… They say a lot of ladies on the tour are like you."

"Like me? Cute and sexy?" Ryan said with a laugh.

"Oh, now. Stop that. You know what I mean." Eddie grew red as he raced down the fairway in the cart he'd souped up to go a little faster than the players'. He wanted to get to the eleventh green before the group on the tee got to their second shot.

"Yeah. There are a few lesbians on tour. And yes, I've dated a couple of them. Does that bother you?"

"Oh, hell, no. I don't give a shit about any of that. I worry about you. I don't want you to be alone." Eddie's face brightened again. He jumped out of the cart at the same time he hit the brake and rushed over to the side of the green while the cart was still skidding to a stop.

"What? I'm not alone. I've got a whole family here. You and Bec and Nate and Adrienne. And the whole damn town. I'm not alone."

"You know what I mean. Me and Bec wasted too much time. I'm so lucky to have her. I wish I'd been brave enough to ask her out long before I did." He picked up some twigs that had fallen on the green from a nearby aspen.

"Well, you've got each other now, and who knows? She might have told you no if you'd asked sooner. She might've still been seeing what was out there," Ryan said and punched Eddie on the arm. "Listen. I know you worry about me, but I'm doing better every day. We both will always miss her, but you know she'd be pissed at us if she knew we were grieving so long. She'd tell us to play more golf."

"Yeah, she would, wouldn't she?" He stood in the center left of the green. "What about here?"

"Yeah. I like that location. I can eagle this one sometimes."

"Of course you can." Eddie punched her back. "You know I want you to be happy. I don't want you to regret not going back on the tour."

"What? Not you too." She led the way back to the cart. "Don't you like working for me?"

"Ryan, you know, 'cept for your mama, there ain't nobody I'd rather work for. It's just…you're good, kid, exceptional, and you know it. This little town ain't big enough for you, and there ain't many options for datin' either."

"Stop it. Don't worry about me. Get this thing moving. I gotta be back at the clubhouse by eight."

"You meetin' your friend, aren't you?" Eddie chuckled.

"I'm coaching her, Eddie. And she doesn't like me for some reason I haven't figured out yet." She reached over and put her foot on the gas pedal.

The cart lurched forward. "Whoo. Okay. I'm going." Eddie scooted to the next hole.

It was nearly eight a.m. when they arrived at seventeen. Before they got out of the cart, she looked at her watch. "Hey. I need to get back to the range. Put this one in the far back left."

"Really? You're gonna get a bunch of bogies with that." Eddie marked his pad.

"Yeah. I want to take some arrogance out of 'em before they hit eighteen. Put it in the front. Some guys will read it right and take advantage of the location, but some will fire it right by the flag and be below the hole." She tapped the location on his map.

"Okay. Dang, that's an interesting setup." Eddie circled the location and started back toward the driving range.

CHAPTER NINE

Katherine looked across the range and over at the putting green, and then she turned toward the maintenance shed. She didn't see Ryan anywhere. Every other time she'd arrived at the course, Ryan had been the first thing she saw. "She's not here," she said to Maggie, who was looking across the first tee and watching a group of young women tee off.

"She's here," Maggie said. "She practically lives here."

"I thought she was going to tell you good-bye," Katherine said and started pulling her clubs out of the back of the car.

"She's here. Chill out. Are you sure you don't mind if I return the rental?" Maggie asked again. "You could drive me down and bring the car back."

"I'm sure. I have nowhere to go until I can get out of here." She hefted her giant tour bag to the front of the car as Eddie drove up with Ryan. She looked amazing with the sun shining on her tan face and the wind blowing her hair.

"Hey, ladies. Sorry I'm late." Ryan jumped out of the cart. "Thanks, Eddie."

"Where've you been? I thought maybe you weren't going to say good-bye, and this one was hoping she was going to get out of a lesson. Either that or she was worried about you." Maggie leaned near for a kiss, and Ryan gave her one.

"Whatever," Katherine said and pretended to look for something in her bag.

"I was setting up for a tournament," Ryan said to Maggie. "Are you still dreading this?" She turned toward Katherine and gave her one of those heart-melting smiles.

She couldn't resist smiling back and couldn't blame Maggie for being so attracted to this woman. Ryan was kind of amazing. "No problem." Katherine would enjoy being here so much more if this beautiful woman was seducing her instead of trying to make her change her golf swing, and if she didn't have a memory she couldn't forget.

"So you're out of here, hmm? Don't like our little town?" Ryan asked.

"I actually love it here. Who knew?"

"I did," Ryan said and winked.

"My sister is begging me to spend some time with her and my niece since I have a week off—well…three more days. I go back to the tour next week." Maggie leaned in for a hug. "Thanks, Ry. I appreciate this, and we'll work out the compensation later. She needs to be ready for the US Open in six weeks." Maggie reminded Ryan of the upcoming major championship. "I'll see you again soon."

Ryan returned the hug. "Yeah. Let's not make it so long next time. Drive safe."

"Okay. I better hit the road." Maggie turned to Katherine. "I'll call, and we'll talk about a return date."

"Right, and I'll be a whole new golfer," she said.

"Well, at least try, please." Maggie hugged her too and then climbed into the rental and drove away.

"And then there were two. Ready to hit some balls?" Ryan asked.

"I guess we better, since that's what we're here for," she said, showing no emotion.

Ryan waved at Michael, who was standing at the door of the maintenance shed. "Bring me a cart, will ya?"

"Sure thing," Michael said and disappeared.

"Let's get this mammoth bag on a cart."

"Are you making fun of my bag? You had a tour bag too."

"No. I'm not making fun. I just prefer putting it on a cart to carrying it around, but you can carry it if you want." Ryan started walking to the range.

"No, wait. He's getting the cart. We should use it."

"My thoughts precisely." Ryan met Michael as he drove up.

"Anything else you need?"

"Nah. We're good. Thanks." Ryan patted the young man on the shoulder.

Michael leaned close and spoke softly. "Hey. I heard you were giving a pro a lesson. Can I watch?"

Ryan shook her head. "No! You have work to do."

"Right." Michael walked away.

"So I'm the local entertainment?" Katherine started for her bag, but Ryan picked it up for her.

"Not a lot happens around here. You're kind of a star."

"Me? They've got their own hometown star." She watched Ryan's biceps flex as she lifted the bag onto the back of the cart. It would be so much easier to continue to hate her if she wasn't so damned hot. "Shit."

"What's wrong?" Ryan looked back at her as she strapped on the bag.

"Nothing. Nothing at all. Let's get this over with."

"Right. Okay." Ryan got in and drove them to the end of the range where a reserved sign had been placed at the far edge of it.

Ryan climbed out and walked over to the open slot, but Katherine stayed in the cart.

"So what do you want me to do?" she asked while staring down at her phone.

Ryan walked back and stood in front of her. "Only one thing."

"What's that?" She didn't look up.

Ryan went around the cart and got back in and drove off the range toward the trees behind the first hole.

"What are you doing?" she asked.

Ryan kept driving without a word.

"Will you stop so we can get on with this lesson?"

Finally, Ryan stopped when she was hidden on a trail overlooking a small stream. Katherine could barely see it, but she could hear the water rushing down its path.

"Katherine Reese, what have I done to make you have such a strong distaste for me—dare I say hate?"

"What? Nothing." She looked at Ryan. She'd pushed her sunglasses up, and Katherine was staring into those amazing eyes. "Nothing. Just…"

"That! What is it?"

Katherine looked back at her phone.

"No cell service here, so talk." Ryan gently took her phone out of her hand and set it in the drink-cup holder.

She spoke softly without looking at Ryan. "You're the reason I'm trying to win a frickin' major tournament."

"What? Me?" Ryan looked right at her. "And that's a bad thing?"

She watched as Ryan crinkled her forehead.

"It is if you would prefer to be writing novels." She let the words spill out before she even knew what was happening. "Never mind. It's nothing."

"A novel? You write novels?" Ryan asked.

"What? Just because my swing sucks doesn't mean I can't do other things well." Heat rose up her neck. Why did this woman make her feel so inadequate?

"No. First of all, your swing doesn't need much, and second, I didn't know, and third, why are we working on your swing if you want to write books?"

"I have to win the major you couldn't win!" She spoke louder.

"I'm so confused." Ryan shook her head, and then, in a calm, soothing voice, she asked, "Why are you yelling at me?"

Katherine got out of the cart and paced back and forth with her arms crossed. Then finally she couldn't stand the silence any longer. "You took it all away from my sister, and then you quit."

CHAPTER TEN

Before Ryan could speak, Katherine started running down the hill.

"Katherine, wait." Ryan jumped out of the cart and chased her. "Wait. It's steep over there. Stop!" Just as she finished yelling her warning, she heard Katherine squeal, followed by the sound of leaves rustling and branches breaking. "Oh, shit, Katherine." She yelled again and started sprinting with both arms pumping toward the sound.

She arrived at the edge of the steep decline just in time to see Katherine skid to a muddy stop in front of the river. "Are you okay?" she yelled, then plopped down on her bum and began a somewhat controlled slide down the steep slope. She jumped to her feet seconds before running into Katherine, catching her balance only inches from the freezing river water.

"What the hell did you do that for?" Katherine said as she began to push herself out of the viscous clay-mud muck she'd landed in.

"Wait." Ryan ran over to her. "Stay there. What if you hurt your back or broke something?"

"Stop it." Katherine pushed at her. "I'm fine." She stood and started brushing uselessly at the mud that covered her designer golf clothes. "But now we're both at the bottom of this mud slick." Katherine shook her head and began to look around.

"Are you sure you're all right?" She started patting Katherine's arms and shoulders, but before she could check her legs, Katherine was backing away and pushing again.

"Would you stop that! My pride is the only thing hurt. But more importantly, how the hell are we going to get out of here?"

She finally backed away, accepting that Katherine wasn't injured. "Stop worrying. I know the way out." She started walking.

"Where are you going?" Katherine stayed put.

"It's a bit of a hike, so we should get going." She stopped and turned back to look at Katherine. She was possibly even more beautiful covered in mud, with barely a clean spot on her. Ryan laughed at the sight.

"What? Stop laughing. I had no idea that cliff was there." Katherine finally looked down at herself and laughed as well. "Well, at least I'm covered in mud by accident. You voluntarily ruined a clean pair of shorts." Katherine pointed at the mud caked on the back of Ryan's shorts.

She walked back to where Katherine stood. "Listen. Let's call it a day. No lesson, okay?"

Katherine nodded.

"Seems like we might need to talk a bit anyway, and this is a nice hike. If we go the long way, it'll take us right by my house, where we can clean up. I'm sure I have something that'll fit you. Then I'll drop you off at Terry's, and you can chill for today. We'll get started tomorrow."

"What about my clubs?" Katherine looked up the hill.

"We'll have cell service in a few minutes, and I'll call Michael to go get them and store them with mine in Eddie's office. They're safe where they are." She took Katherine's hand to lead her down the trail. "Oh, shit. Your hand—it's a mess. Let me see the other one." She held both of Katherine's scuffed and bleeding hands in hers. "Do they hurt?"

"Well…they do now." Katherine looked down at them. "Shit. How am I going to grip a club?"

“Come on. I have some stuff at the house. It looks like surface scratches. Oh…except this one.” Ryan lightly touched an inch-long cut on the side of Katherine’s right hand. It was clotted with blood and covered with mud. “That’s going to hurt.”

“Ow. Damn it! I can’t win.” Katherine slumped down on the boulder she stood next to.

“It’s not that bad. We’ll know more after we get the dirt cleaned off. Then if you need stitches, I can take you over to the clinic.” She put her arm under Katherine’s and started pulling her up.

“Stitches? Really?” Katherine stood. “The Open is about a month away. I wanted to make a run for it.”

“You still can. Even with stitches, it’ll be healed in a couple of weeks, but is that really what you want?” She started walking down the path next to the river with her arm linked to Katherine’s.

“It’s what I need.” Katherine pulled away but followed.

“Can we talk about why?” She looked over her shoulder to catch Katherine’s reaction.

“There’s nothing to talk about. My sister is gone, and my last words to her were ‘I told you so’ when she returned from Q-School,” Katherine said and sighed. “She missed the cut by one stroke.”

Ryan stopped and turned to find Katherine staring across the shallow river. “I’m so sorry about your sister.” She walked back to Katherine and hesitantly wrapped her arms around her. “You clearly loved her very much.” She wanted to provide some comfort but feared Katherine’s resistance. When Katherine finally relaxed into her hug, Ryan felt the fullness of her breasts and the warmth of her body. There was so much to this complicated woman—if she would only let go of that tight hold she had on her feelings.

Just as Ryan finished her thought, Katherine began to speak. “It was all she ever wanted. She wanted to play golf on tour. She loved it so much. I loved playing too, but I mostly just loved being with her and my dad and Uncle Harold. I never wanted to go on tour. It was a fun hobby for me, and I never took her seriously when she told stories of becoming a tour pro. I laughed at her.”

Katherine stood still, letting Ryan hold her, and she continued to talk as she began to sob in Ryan's ear. "She called me when she was still in it on the last day. She was so excited and sure her dream would come true. She talked me into driving there to see her qualify, and I was finally believing it might actually happen. Then you, this person no one had ever heard of, came out of nowhere with five birdies in a row. You were tied with her and so fucking sure of yourself." Katherine moved away.

"Marie Reese. Oh my God. Your sister was Marie." She backed away to see Katherine's face.

Katherine nodded.

"I got lucky. I'd been such an arrogant ass all week. I should've lost and had to do it all again, but I got lucky." She looked down at her feet.

"Yeah, you were an ass, but you didn't get lucky. You're that good." Katherine put a finger under her chin and gently tilted her face to look at her. "You deserved to be on the tour, but so did my sister. She would've made it the next year if I hadn't crushed her." Tears began to run down her face. "I've been trying to blame you, but I'm the reason she's gone."

Ryan slowly moved toward Katherine again. When Katherine didn't budge, she wrapped her in her arms again. They stood together without a word for several minutes. Finally, Ryan slowly backed away. "I'm so sorry. I wish I knew what to say." She wiped tears and a streak of mud from Katherine's face.

"You've put up with all my shit all week. I had to fall down a hill and get covered in mud to finally realize you had nothing to do with it." Katherine nestled back into her arms. "I'm sorry I treated you so badly."

"What? I didn't even notice," she said. Katherine leaned back to read her face, and they both laughed. "Do you know how absolutely gorgeous you are, especially when you laugh?" She spoke without thinking. "I'm sorry. I…"

Katherine shut her up with a kiss. She relaxed into the feel of Katherine's soft lips and warmed all over as Katherine pulled her closer.

"Don't be sorry," Katherine said as she eased away. "Did you say your house was near?"

"Ahh…" She swallowed hard. "Yeah. It's about a half a mile down the river. Ahh…I…I've been wanting to do that since I first laid eyes on you."

"Really?" Katherine took her hand and began moving in the direction she had started earlier. "Me too."

They walked in silence for several minutes until they reached a small gravel road, and suddenly Ryan was shaken from the fantasy she'd been running through her head. "I'll call Michael now. I can get two bars here." She held up her phone, and Katherine released her hand. She missed the warmth and comfort as soon as she let go.

She quickly conveyed the situation to Michael and tucked her phone back into her pocket. She hesitated for a second and then took Katherine's hand. "This way. It's not far." She pointed down the gravel road covered by a large canopy of aspens. "My house is a few more feet down here on the right."

"You know, it's actually quite beautiful here. And cool." Katherine shivered as a breeze came through the tunnel formed by all the trees.

"Oh, of course. You must be freezing. Your clothes are all wet. Come on." She led Katherine down the street more quickly, and in a few minutes, they stood in front of her small home.

"This is your house. Oh my gosh, it's so—"

"Tiny," she said.

"No. It's adorable."

"Is that what you call it?"

"You don't like it?" Katherine turned to look at her.

"No. I love it. It was my mom's house. It's just, I didn't figure someone…" She stopped.

"Someone?" Katherine asked. "You were going to say someone like me or something like that. Am I right?"

"I'm sorry. Maggie told me your family is wealthy."

"Wealthy? Hmm. Okay. Actually, my family is filthy rich." Katherine said it with a straight face.

"Oh. I…" She stammered while watching Katherine remain motionless and stone-faced.

Finally Katherine laughed. "Your face."

"What? I didn't want to insult. I…I…just…"

"Stop. It's fine. So we have a lot of money. It doesn't mean I can't appreciate a beautiful cottage. It's so cute."

"Cute?"

"Yes, cute, damn it. Show me the inside." Katherine pulled her toward the front door.

They walked into Ryan's warm cozy living area. Even though the days were warm now, and midday was even hot in the sun, the mornings were still chilly, and she often lit a small fire in her cast-iron woodstove before going on her jog. The coals from this morning's fire had kept the place toasty. "Here. Come sit by the stove. It's still warm." She dragged her desk chair over in front of it.

"It feels wonderful in here." Katherine started to sit. "I can't sit here. I almost forgot what a mess I am."

"It's okay. It'll wipe off. I'll get you some tea." Ryan started toward the kitchen.

"No. Wait," Katherine said and took her arm. "I should just get cleaned up." Katherine turned her so they were face-to-face. "I…well…I was hoping…" Before she could finish, Ryan leaned close and kissed her.

It started out soft and gentle, and slowly Ryan moved closer, and her mouth opened slightly to receive Ryan's tongue. As their tongues intertwined, Ryan's heartbeat increased, and a rush of pleasure washed through her. She almost couldn't believe she was kissing this beautiful woman who'd pushed her away all week. Kissing her in her own house with a shower and a bed twenty feet away. She quickly refocused on the pleasure she was experiencing, and with her hand behind Katherine's neck, she pulled her deeper into the glorious kiss. Katherine tightened against her, and she wanted to be closer and closer. She ran her hands down the side of Katherine's blouse and began to tug at the bottom. Katherine backed away from her enough to allow her access. As she began to pull Katherine's shirt up over her head, she felt the slimy mud through her fingers and jerked back.

"What?" Katherine looked at her.

She held up her dirty hands. "Let's get you in the shower."

Katherine nodded and followed her to the only bathroom in the house. "Here." She reached for Katherine's shirt again, and Katherine moved closer and stood still as she removed the dirty shirt. She paused and stared at the beautiful woman before her, then drew Katherine to her and took her mouth in hers, gently unfastening Katherine's bra as their tongues met again. She backed away, and Katherine's bra fell to the floor. She stared at Katherine's perfect, full breasts—perhaps a little too long.

"I can't tell if you like what you see or if you're disappointed," Katherine said.

"Oh my God. I'm not at all disappointed. I'm sorry. I... Well...actually it's been a while for me, and you're amazing." She slowly moved forward and cupped both breasts.

"Oh..." Katherine jerked away. "Your hands are freezing. Let's get in." She nodded to the shower.

"I'm sorry. I...Yes. You go ahead." She reached down to turn the water on.

"No. I'm not going without you." Katherine tugged at her shirt, blotched with mud from Katherine's clothes.

"I'd like that." She raised her arms so Katherine could take off her polo and stood there in her dirty shorts and sports bra.

Katherine began to kick off her shoes and push down her filthy shorts. "Take off your clothes." Katherine looked up shyly. She responded immediately and removed them, pushing down her jockeys before Katherine had finished.

When Katherine looked up again, she was holding the glass shower door open.

"Ryan, you're so sexy." Katherine spoke in a breathy voice and ran her finger down Ryan's side to her hip before she climbed in. "Oh, warmth," she said as she pulled Ryan in after her.

They met under the shower of warm water, and she pulled Katherine into another deep kiss, feeling her wet, slick body against her own. She caressed Katherine's shoulders and back as she plunged her tongue deeper, feeling Katherine respond. She moved her hands around to cup those beautiful breasts again and moved away from the kiss. "Warm now?"

Katherine nodded and returned to her lips. She caressed Katherine's breasts, feeling the weight of them and the smooth, silky skin in her hands. "Oh my God. I want you so badly," she said as she bent to take one of Katherine's breasts in her mouth. Katherine's nipple tightened and grew hard instantly as she dragged her tongue across it. Water ran over her head and face as she continued to take as much of Katherine's ample breast in her mouth as she could.

Katherine moaned and pushed into her, and she obliged by sucking and tugging lightly at the soft flesh while running one hand down Katherine's back and cupping her round ass—squeezing and massaging.

She raised up, flushed and breathing heavily. "You feel amazing." The passion building inside her was overwhelming; the muscles in her core ached with desire. She could see it reflected back at her in Katherine's eyes and pulled her into another kiss. As she did, she traced Katherine's curves down to her smooth, flat stomach, touching every part of her. Slowly she inched lower until she felt closely cropped hair guiding her to Katherine's vagina. Katherine pushed into her as she lightly touched Katherine's clit. It was swollen and hard, wetness building there. She ached to thrust deeply into her but hesitated.

Katherine backed away from the kiss. "Please, please, Ryan."

Her plea ended Ryan's resolve. Her own wetness built as she slowly moved her middle finger inside Katherine's vagina. They sighed heavily together. She pushed into Ryan's hand. "Oh, yeah."

"You feel amazing. I want to taste you."

"Wait. This first." Katherine rocked as Ryan added more pressure. "More." Katherine spoke so softly she barely heard her, with the stream of water running over them. She inserted a second finger and rocked with Katherine's rhythm while trailing kisses down Katherine's neck and shoulder.

"Oh my God, Ryan," Katherine gasped, the words barely audibly.

"Yes!" She moved with Katherine, matching her tempo exactly.

"Ryan… Oh. I'm going to come."

"Yes. Please." With one final, deep thrust, Katherine climaxed. As each muscle clamped down on her fingers, Ryan nearly came also.

Katherine collapsed into her arms. "Oh, Ryan. I didn't expect that. Oh…not to come so fast. I wanted to enjoy you so much more."

She laughed and tilted Katherine's head to look into her eyes. "We have all day. We can do this again and again." She kissed Katherine softly.

"You don't have to go back to work?"

"I'm the boss, and I haven't taken a day off since I started over a year ago, so I think I deserve one day." She nuzzled Katherine's nose and reached for the shampoo. "Besides, I've already told Michael I won't be in for the rest of the day. The worst part will be having to deal with Rebecca tomorrow when she teases me constantly." She began to gently massage the lather she'd created into Katherine's hair.

"Oh, so you thought you were going to get lucky." Katherine groaned and leaned into the spa treatment she was receiving.

"I was hoping."

"Well then, I suppose I should see if I can provide you the same enjoyment you gave me." Katherine kissed her deeply, and pure pleasure flooded through her.

She backed away. "Not until I get all this mud off you. Now rinse your hair."

Katherine moved under the running water and tucked her head back to rinse the shampoo from her hair. "Does everyone do what you tell them to?"

"Rarely, but I like it when they do." She ran her fingers through the long strands of blond hair to help get the soap out. Then she took a washcloth from the shelf above the shower and poured her honeysuckle gel soap onto it.

"Hmm. That's what you smell like." Katherine smiled as she inhaled deeply. "I'm getting the full treatment."

"I don't do things halfway. Now turn around." She scrubbed Katherine's back and shoulders and slowly slid the cloth across Katherine's tight, round bottom. "You have a gorgeous ass."

"Mmm. That feels so good. Keep it up, and I'll do whatever you tell me to."

She kneeled down and moved the washcloth slowly, gently washing the inside of both thighs and wiping the last bit of mud off the lower half of each long leg. "Turn around again, please."

Katherine did as she was told, and Ryan was now looking at her beautiful pussy. She leaned near and ran her tongue across Katherine's engorged clit, and Katherine jerked.

"Oh… Oh my…No. Wait." Katherine tugged at Ryan to bring her back face-to-face. "Let's get out. I want to touch *you* now."

❖

Ryan nodded and followed Katherine out of the shower and even began to gently guide her in the direction of her bedroom, trailing wet footsteps.

Katherine stopped her. "Towels?" she asked as she looked around the small bathroom.

Ryan hurried into the hallway and grabbed two large, fluffy bath towels and practically threw one at Katherine while guiding her toward her bed.

"Slow down. I thought you said we had all day." Katherine resisted and stood fast, drying herself until Ryan returned to her. She wrapped the other towel around Ryan's dripping body, then gave Ryan a deep, passionate kiss. She loved feeling Ryan's lips on hers, warm and soft but strong. Her desire rose as she felt it return. She slowly pulled the towel she'd wrapped Ryan in up to her head and backed away. She dried Ryan's hair, fluffing it in all directions and making the highlights stand out in deep contrast to her natural brunet, made darker by being wet. "I love your hair." She let the towel fall and ran her fingers through Ryan's hair, where it was shaved close to her head in the back and on the left side.

"I love the pampering treatment. I understand why you followed my every command. I feel helpless waiting for you to tell me what to do."

"Hmm. Good." She quickly ran the towel over her own wet hair, then leaned close to Ryan's ear and whispered, "Show me to your room."

"I thought you'd never ask." Ryan took her hand and led her the few steps to her bedroom. "I'm sorry it's so small."

"Ryan." She nudged Ryan gently toward the bed. "It's perfect." She didn't take her eyes off Ryan's. She kissed and nipped at Ryan's lips as she continued to move toward the bed. As they reached its edge, she reached around Ryan and pushed the comforter down before she lowered Ryan onto the deep-blue sheets. Then she began to kiss Ryan on the neck, her wet hair dripping onto Ryan's shoulder and chest. She spoke between each kiss. "You…worry…too…much…just…enjoy." She strung out the word enjoy while running her tongue along Ryan's clavicle until she reached the center of Ryan's chest, where she worked her way down slowly between Ryan's firm breasts. She cupped Ryan's boobs together, creating cleavage. "Very nice," she murmured, her lips against Ryan's smooth flesh.

Ryan moaned inaudible words, but they encouraged her to continue. She caressed Ryan's tit in one hand, gently rubbing her thumb over the hardening nipple. The other she took in her mouth. Then, satisfied that she had all of it in her mouth, she pulled back, sucking the nipple as she moved away.

Ryan pushed up toward her. "Oh, Katherine…"

"Yeah?"

"Yeah." Ryan tried to bring her back to her lips.

"Wrong way." Katherine held firm and moved slowly down to her stomach, licking and kissing as she went. She raised up briefly to catch Ryan's expression. She was encouraged by the passion in her eyes and continued to Ryan's closely cropped bush. She delicately ran her fingers through Ryan's slick folds but was forced to pull away when Ryan thrust forward. "Oh no. Not yet." She bent and consumed Ryan's clitoris with her mouth.

"Yes." Ryan called out and pushed hard against her tongue.

Encouraged, she began to lick and suck more intensely, feeling Ryan grow harder and wetter with every stroke.

Ryan groaned and began to rock, creating a rhythm beneath her touch. "Put your fingers inside me," Ryan said.

She raised up briefly from her focused efforts to speak. "Beg."

"Please, Katherine. Please."

"Mmm." She resumed flicking her tongue in sync with Ryan as she slowly inserted her finger into Ryan's silky, wet vagina.

"Oh… OH." Ryan increased the rhythm.

She responded with a second finger and increased pressure on Ryan's clit with her tongue.

"Oh my God," Ryan called out.

Ryan's thighs tightened around her as she climaxed. She raised up to look in Ryan's eyes as she felt her last shudder tingle through her fingers.

Chapter Eleven

Ryan lightly tugged at Katherine, who had laid her head on Ryan's stomach. "Lie next to me."

"Mmm-hmm." Katherine moved up, and together they righted themselves so they shared a pillow.

"That was amazing." Ryan kissed her before she put her arm under Katherine's head and pulled her close.

"It was, wasn't it?" Katherine tilted her head back and gazed at her.

She squeezed Katherine. "Are you cold? Your hair's still wet." She reached down to spread the comforter over them.

"I'm perfectly comfortable." Katherine put her left leg up across Ryan's. "I could stay like this all day."

"As nice as it feels, I wouldn't want you to get bored." She ran her hand along Katherine's side to the swell of her hip.

"Oh, well, then. I do like to be kept entertained." Katherine took her hand and began moving it to her center. "Besides, when you came, you did this to me." Katherine pushed Ryan's hand against her clit and forced Ryan's finger into her welcoming vagina.

She turned to get on top of Katherine and kissed her, starting at her lush red lips and moving down quickly. "I couldn't leave you wanting, now could I?" As she was about to reach Katherine's full breasts, her phone rang.

Katherine groaned. "Should you get that?"

Ryan raised up. "No. Leave it." She sucked Katherine's nipple since she hadn't given it enough attention the first time around. She didn't plan to make the same mistake again. But as she circled Katherine's hard nipple, the house phone next to the bed began to ring. Why hadn't she gotten rid of that damn thing? Her mother had insisted she needed the landline, and even though she resented the small bill each month, she'd never gotten around to having it removed.

She raised up again and sighed. "For real!" She stared at the old black phone her mom had put in her room when she was barely old enough to remember her own number.

"Ryan, it must be important." Katherine nudged her toward the phone.

"No. You don't know my friends. They're harassing me." Just as she was about to re-engage, the old voice recorder, which she'd forgotten was still connected, clicked on.

"Ryan! It's Eddie!" He yelled into the phone as if trying to get her attention without a connection. "Listen. I'm scared."

She heard the fear in Eddie's voice, jumped to the other side of the bed, and grabbed the old handset. "Eddie. What's wrong?"

"Oh, thank God, you're there." Eddie paused.

"What! What's wrong?" The last time Eddie said he was scared was the day before the British Open began. He'd told her to come home, and she was too stupid to do as he suggested. She refused to screw up again. "Eddie?"

"Ry, it's Becca. She—"

"What happened?" Ryan jumped out of bed and started for her dresser but cursed as she found herself tethered to the corner of the bedroom by the short phone cord.

"I'm following the ambulance to the hospital. She—"

"On my way." She slammed down the phone and ran to her dresser, grabbing socks and underclothes. "I have to go. She's my best friend in the world. I'm so sorry. I—"

"Of course you do." Katherine got up and sat on the edge of the bed. "If I can get some clothes, I'll come with you."

"Oh. Yeah. There. Get what you need." Ryan pulled on a bright-red University of New Mexico tee shirt and a pair of denim shorts." She hopped on one foot while jerking on one sock, then the other. "She's a private person. I should drop you off at Terry's."

Katherine put on shorts and a tee shirt more calmly but just as quickly. "I'll get my shoes." She headed to the bathroom, which was still steamy from their hot shower.

"I'm so sorry." She pulled on a pair of tennis shoes and grabbed a jacket as she headed toward the door. "Fuck!"

"What?" Katherine joined her at the front door.

"My truck is at the golf course." She was already punching buttons on her cell phone.

Because of the delay, Katherine slowed down and put on her dirty socks and shoes and wrapped her muddy clothes in a towel.

"Michael, I need you to bring my truck over to my house. Keys are in it. And have someone follow you so you can get back to work." Ryan spoke quickly while pacing from one end of her small living room to the other.

"Ryan… Did you hear about Rebecca?"

She held the phone away from her ear because Michael was yelling so loud.

As much as she wanted to shout at the kid to get his ass to her house this minute, she knew she had to bring things down or she'd get nowhere, so in a soft, calm voice she said, "Yes. Eddie called me. I don't have my truck. Drive it over here and have one of the guys follow you so you can get back to work. I'm going to take my truck to the hospital and meet Eddie there."

"Oh. Right. I'll be there in a second." Michael still sounded somewhat panicked. Then Ryan's phone went silent.

"Is he on his way?" Katherine asked.

"Yeah. I'm so sorry," she said again and took Katherine in her arms. Her heart was still beating too fast, and she was desperate for news of Rebecca, but she hated leaving this beautiful woman. "I just—"

Katherine hugged her. "Stop it. Don't be sorry. This is your friend. Of course you have to go." Katherine kissed her lips lightly. "I don't mind staying in the waiting room, if you'd like me to be with you."

"Thank you." She stepped away, holding both of Katherine's hands. "You should go and be comfortable at Terry's, and if it's okay, I'll come give you an update tonight."

"Of course. I'll want to know."

She heard the crunching of gravel in her driveway. "That's Michael."

Chapter Twelve

Even after Ryan's delay waiting on the truck, Eddie was still pacing the waiting room, anticipating the news when Ryan walked in.

"How is she?" She touched Eddie's arm, only to send him spiraling toward the ceiling.

"Holy sh…Ryan." Eddie grabbed her and squeezed so tight she almost had to ask him to let go before he finally did. Then he started talking as fast as he could. "They won't tell me. I can't get anyone to find the doctor. They keep running me off. Oh, Ry, she was so pale. She looked—"

"Eddie, slow down." She took hold of his big arms and slowly pressed him toward the row of chairs along the wall. "Tell me what happened."

He plopped into the chair and nodded. "After you called Michael, I told him I'd walk down and get your cart and clubs. I was hoping you were going to spend some time with that cute girl…" He stopped and looked around. "Where is she? Weren't you with her?"

"Please focus," she said. "What happened to Rebecca?"

"Oh… When I got there I saw where you had slid down the hill, and I thought it was pretty funny. I couldn't wait to tell Rebecca. I drove the cart back up to the restaurant to talk to her, but you know how it is. Six or eight folks stopped me to talk.

I finally got inside, and she was standing over the grill hanging onto the countertop. Before I could get to her, she crumpled to the ground like every muscle gave out at the same time. I yelled for help, and someone called 9-1-1, thank God, and, well, here we are. I'm scared—"

"Eddie, Ryan," Doctor Murphy called as he walked into the waiting room. He was a regular on the course, and they knew him well.

"How is she?" Ryan met him in the center of the room with Eddie at her heels. "Can we see her?"

"She's going to be fine. She was dehydrated and overheated. You're working her too hard." Doctor Murphy touched her arm. "She's going to be okay, but Eddie, she has something to tell you. Ryan, why don't you wait out here and let Eddie go talk to his wife?" The doctor winked at her and motioned Eddie toward Rebecca's exam room.

"Thanks, Murph." Eddie exhaled and walked toward it.

"Why can't I go in, Doc?" She looked over at him. "You know we're like sisters."

"Of course I know that, but some things you need to tell your spouse first." He winked again, this time with exaggerated movements for effect.

She finally got it. "She's pregnant!"

He started to shush her, but before he could make a sound, she was jumping in his arms, and Eddie was yelling for her. "Ryan!"

Two nurses pushed Eddie back into the room to keep him quiet, and Ryan nearly knocked one of them to the floor as she shoved her way through the door. Eddie caught her in a big hug before she could reach Rebecca. "Congratulations, old man. Now let me go hug my friend." Eddie released her, and she ran to Rebecca's bed, stopping short of pouncing on her. She still didn't have her color back, which took Ryan by surprise, but her smile was infectious. "Oh, my God. You're going to have a baby." Tears were running down her face.

"I know. You're going to be an aunt!" Rebecca squeezed her hand, her tears flowing too. They held each other for a minute before Eddie joined them in a group hug.

Eddie finally broke the silence. "We're going to have to find someone for the morning shift now, Ry."

"No, we are not!" Rebecca interjected before Ryan could process.

"We can talk about this later." She leaned back and looked at her friend. "You guys just weren't trying hard enough before."

❖

Ryan stayed at the hospital until Rebecca was checked out. After a full bottle of saline, Doc Murphy was satisfied that she'd be fine with some rest. Ryan helped Eddie get her into the truck, and they finally convinced her to take the rest of the week off and allow Marsha to help until Rebecca was too pregnant to work. Marsha was another local, who had grown up with Rebecca. She'd filled in at the golf-course restaurant since she was in high school and knew the operations well. Though she was a stay-at-home mom, her kids were all in school now, and her mother didn't mind watching them during the summer months if Marsha was needed at the course.

Ryan knew they'd have to do without Rebecca for several months, and maybe forever if she decided not to come back to work, but they'd figure that all out later. As much as Ryan could tell, Rebecca didn't like the plan. Only Doc Murphy's speech about the possibility of losing the baby had finally convinced her.

With assurance from Eddie that he'd keep Rebecca in bed and take care of her the rest of the day, Ryan headed back to the golf course. Even though it had been quite an eventful day, it was only two p.m., so a lot was probably going on at the course. She'd confirmed from the hospital that Adrienne and Nathan came in early to take over the restaurant, and Eddie's crew was managing just fine. Even Patty said things were running smoothly on the course, so Ryan called Katherine.

"I'm so glad to hear she's okay. And pregnant. That's exciting," Katherine said, but she didn't sound excited.

"Can I take you to dinner tonight?" Ryan asked. "There's this little dive bar in this village on the other side of the mountain. It's a beautiful drive and a cool place, if not a little scary."

"Ahh…Do you mind if I take a rain check? I've been writing, and I'd like to keep it going."

"Oh. Yeah. Of course. I'm glad you had time to write. That's great." She had to work to keep the disappointment out of her voice, but she was glad Katherine had been doing what she loved and tried not to take it personally.

"Okay. Thanks, and I'll see you in the morning. Maybe we can actually get a lesson in tomorrow."

She could tell that Katherine was trying to end the call, probably to return to her writing, but again, she had to push down her disappointment.

"Right. Although if you slid down a muddy hill again, I'd be forced to clean you up." She tried teasing to get a response, but Katherine was clearly preoccupied.

"Right. Okay. I'll see you in the morning." The phone went dead before Ryan could respond. She stared at it for a second and then saw Patty run to the starter booth from the pro-shop. Things were likely not as calm as Patty had claimed. Back to reality. She had a course to manage.

CHAPTER THIRTEEN

Katherine set her phone on the desk next to her computer, where the cursor had been blinking at her for nearly an hour. She hadn't exactly lied to Ryan. She'd been writing, but the words hadn't been flowing. Every single one was a struggle, and she was sure she'd have to rewrite most of what she'd managed to eke out.

All she could think about was Ryan's touch. She couldn't remember ever feeling so good with anyone before, but Ryan Gibbs? She'd spent the last three years hating this woman—blaming her. And wasn't she right to? Didn't she bulldoze her way onto the tour, only to quit when things got tough and she lost a big match?

She was so torn. The woman she'd had sex with this morning wasn't so shallow that she'd throw her whole career away because she'd lost, was she? She struggled to push any thoughts of Ryan away, but when she tried to return to her last chapter break and get her characters in her head again, she had to read the same paragraph over and over. Finally, she jumped out of the chair and trotted down the stairs. Maybe a walk would help.

"No golf today?" Terry popped around the kitchen door as Katherine reached the bottom floor.

"Oh, hi. I didn't know anyone was down here." She walked back toward the kitchen.

"Same. I thought the place was empty." Terry took her hand and guided her toward the table. "Are you hungry? I made some chicken salad, and Dick went to Santa Fe to get some parts. I hate to eat alone."

"Well…actually, I haven't had anything since my yogurt this morning." She sat at the table Terry had led her to. "Chicken salad sounds good."

"Oh, it is. I make it with apples. It's crisp and refreshing." Terry smiled, seeming truly pleased with her recipe. "Would you like something to drink? I have some sun tea on the porch. If you want to bring it in, I'll cool it with some ice."

"Sure. Back here?" Katherine stood and motioned to the back door.

"Yep."

"White, wheat, or rye?" Terry asked when she returned with the tea. "Set that on the counter." Terry obviously noticed her makeshift bandage of Kleenex and sports' tape on her injured hand. "Now what did you do?" The older woman's motherly tone sounded scolding.

"Oh, it's nothing. I cut it this morning when I fell, but it didn't seem that deep." She was rather amazed that she'd been distracted enough to forget about it, since when she finally got back to the B and B, it was hurting pretty badly and beginning to bleed again. She'd used some tissues from the room and a bit of tape she wrapped her ankle with on occasion. Her first-aid kit was in her golf bag, still at Ryan's golf course. The wound didn't look too bad when she'd put the Kleenex over it, but it had been oozing a bit and looked disgusting now.

"We can do better than that." Terry put the chicken salad back in the fridge and took a rather large first-aid kit from the pantry. "Sandwiches can wait. I want to be sure you don't need stitches. At the very least we need to clean that up."

Katherine sat back at the table and let Terry unwrap the sloppy tape job. "I'm sure it's all right."

"Hmm." Terry examined the cut, which actually looked worse now than it did when Katherine bandaged it. Little pieces of bloody tissue were stuck throughout the inch-long slice in her hand, and it was throbbing for the first time. "You should go over to the clinic and see if they can throw a stitch in that. It would probably heal faster if it can't keep opening."

"I'd prefer not to. Can't you just bandage it a little better, and maybe it would stay?"

"Well…I could use some Super Glue."

"What? I don't want Super Glue in my hand."

"You've never used it on a cut?" Terry shook her head, sifting through the first-aid kit until she found a tiny tube. "You stay around the high desert long enough, and you'll figure out what a great thing this is. Hands dry out so badly, especially in the winter, you have to glue them when they split. This stuff works wonders." She examined Katherine's injury a little more thoroughly. "But this cut is deeper than I usually glue."

"Really? Super Glue. Okay. Can't you give it a try?"

"All right, we'll try, but if it opens again, you better go to the clinic." Terry led her to the sink and turned on the water. "Now get that water adjusted, and let the cut rinse for a couple of minutes. I've got some better antiseptic cream up in my bathroom."

She was dutifully holding her hand under the warm water when Terry returned. After drying it thoroughly and putting a tiny amount of cream inside the open cut, Terry squeezed the wound together and laid down a small bead of glue along the line of the cut. "Okay. The trick is to hold it together longer than you'd think. Super Glue works only when you apply pressure to it, so it takes a minute to dry." Terry continued to hold her cut while lightly patting the glue. After a few minutes, she let go. "There. I think it's going to do okay."

She examined her hand and slowly opened and closed it. "Yeah, wow, and it didn't hurt. I thought it'd sting. Thanks, Terry."

"Yeah. Look at that." She started stacking items back into the first-aid kit. "We offer all kinds of services here at Terry and Dick's B and B. How about that sandwich now?"

Chapter Fourteen

Ryan bounced golf balls on the side of her wedge between hitting them at the hundred-yard marker on the range. She'd been out here since eight, even though Terry wasn't supposed to drop Katherine off until nine. It was ten till now, and she kept looking back at the parking lot, watching every car that arrived. She had Katherine's clubs all set up and was eager to see her again today. If Katherine didn't want lessons, she'd call Maggie and tell her to forget it. She refused to let golf be the reason she didn't get to know this amazing woman. She'd let golf interfere with too many things in her life

Finally, at ten after nine, Terry drove her Tahoe up next to the front door of the clubhouse. She raced over to meet Katherine, who was heading to the maintenance shed. She waved at Terry as she drove off and hollered, "Hey, Katherine." She looked great today. Well, she looked great every day, but Ryan seemed to notice more today. Her shiny blond hair was pulled back in a ponytail that bobbed back and forth as she continued toward the shed. She was wearing yet another perfectly matched designer golf outfit with short shorts that made Ryan want to run her hand along those smooth, tan legs.

She started trotting to catch up and called out again, "Katherine."

Katherine spun as she reached her, frowning, and Ryan was immediately discouraged. She'd been looking forward to seeing

Katherine again since the moment she said good-bye. Surely Katherine had enjoyed herself as much as she had. What had happened? "I have your clubs on the range already." She hoped maybe Katherine just wasn't awake yet.

"Sorry I'm late. I got distracted with my writing." Katherine started walking toward the range.

"Hey. I'm starting to think perhaps lessons aren't a good idea. I—"

"What? Why? You and Maggie spent hours convincing me this was what my game needed, and now you're backing out?" Katherine stopped and spun around so abruptly, Ryan nearly collided with her. They were close enough for Ryan to kiss her, but at this moment, that was completely out of the question.

Ryan stepped back. "No. I don't want to quit. It's just…it seems like maybe you'd prefer to write, and that's great. And after yesterday…"

"Listen." Katherine's tone had softened but still had an edge. "We should forget about yesterday and focus on my goal. I've finally accepted that you can help me and have set my sights on the Open. I have four and a half weeks. Can you help me or not?"

"Umm…yesterday never happened?" Ryan mumbled to herself.

"Ryan?" Katherine moved closer. "Are we having a lesson or not? I told you too much yesterday, but at least you understand why it's important for me to win a major. Then I can play golf for fun and write my books."

Ryan nodded and walked past Katherine. "Okay." She worked hard to push her hurt feeling down, which felt like a fifty-pound weight on her chest. She shook her head as she picked up her pace to the range. Why did she care? This woman had shown her only a few kindnesses from the moment they met. She'd be gone in a couple of weeks, and Ryan would never see her again. But damn those few kindnesses had made all the anger and resentment worth it. In fact, when she wasn't focused on her sister's goal, Katherine was wonderful, and Ryan just wanted to be with her.

When she reached the spot she'd picked out at the end of the driving range, she grabbed her wedge—always present when she gave lessons—and leaned on it like a cane. She'd just do this and get it over with as a favor for an old friend. Apparently, as much as she wanted it to be more, it wasn't, so they'd have a lesson.

"Okay. In short, you tense up as the game goes on. Your swing has worked for you for so—"

"Wait. What are you doing?" Katherine asked.

"We're having a lesson." She couldn't quite make eye contact. She hoped her sunglasses were disguising the awkward avoidance.

"You don't have to pretend like you don't know me." Katherine leaned on her big golf bag.

"Are you kidding me?" She bit her tongue to keep from screaming the words. "You…back there…You said you wanted to just have a lesson and forget about yesterday."

"Well, yeah, but you don't have to be mean."

"Me? Katherine, you're confusing the hell out of me." She dropped a ball and swung the wedge with such force the ball soared straight up in the air, dropping only twenty yards in front of her.

And just like that, Mr. Hyde was gone, and the Dr. Jekyll-version of Katherine was back. "You're right. Let's have a lesson."

"Fine." She pulled out Katherine's 7-iron. "Here. I want you to find your target and prepare to strike the ball as soon as I drop it. Don't go through a routine, don't aim, don't take the time for a proper setup. Just hit the ball. And use only your left hand."

Without comment, Katherine stood back and sighted down the range, then took a stance, swinging her club back and forth with only her left hand.

Ryan watched in surprise as Katherine did as she was instructed without comment. "Ready?" She stood back to be out of the path of Katherine's swing and finally looked at her again. She was tuned in and serious, but her eyes were sad. Ryan wanted to wrap her in her arms and take her away from the hurt and the pressure she'd put on herself.

"I'm ready," Katherine said and even smiled a tiny bit.

Ryan relaxed. If she could help her a little, maybe she could win that major she wanted so badly, even if it was a long shot. She could conquer that demon and move on with her life. Even if it meant Ryan wouldn't get to spend more time with her, the poor girl needed a break. "You've done this before."

Katherine smiled. "Drop the ball."

She did, and almost at the same time it hit the ground, Katherine made solid contact, and the ball flew straight out in front of her with a slight draw. "Okay. Nice. Exactly what I was hoping for, but it rarely happens on the first swing. You've definitely done this exercise before."

"Yeah. I know you're right. I start putting more and more pressure on myself, and after six or eight holes, my swing is out of control."

"Your swing works for you most of the time because it's good. You have solid fundamentals, and your swing mechanics are great. Like I said, it falls apart when you start to tense up. So let's see if we can find some physical ways to let go of that tension."

"Mmm-hmm." Katherine bent to set her ball in place.

After nearly two hours of striking balls with only a few wayward shots, Ryan was quite pleased with their progress and was having a nice time with Katherine again. It was like she had an electrical breaker that had to be reset. Ryan wasn't sure how to switch it, but she loved the woman she was with now.

"Do you need a break?" she finally asked.

"No. I'm feeling what you're talking about. Let's stick with it." Katherine swung her driver, and they both watched as her ball passed the two hundred and fifty marker on a straight path. Katherine turned and smiled at her. "I think I've even gained a few yards." She started to set another ball on the tee.

"Yeah. That was awesome."

"Longer than yours?" Katherine asked as she set up to her ball again.

"Actually, yes. Longer than my normal drive," she said and gently touched Katherine's arm to stop her before she could begin her swing. "I have another lesson in ten minutes."

"Oh. Oh…Of course. I forgot you have a course to run." Katherine backed away and stood next to her. "I'll hit the rest of these balls and walk back to Terry's."

"Walk? It's getting too hot." The midday sun was starting to bear down. "I'll have Michael take you back, or Terry would probably come get you."

"No. I want to walk. I like the climb up the hill to her place. She'll scold me 'cause she told me to call, but I want to walk." Katherine turned back to her ball. "I'll see you tomorrow."

And just like that, Ryan was dismissed.

❖

Katherine hit the ball as Ryan walked away. She felt a physical loss as soon as Ryan left. How was she going to keep seeing her and pretending she didn't have feelings for her? She had to. She'd been focused on this goal for too long to give it up for a woman who could so easily abandon her dream.

She hit the next twenty balls with her 7-iron, and all of them landed at the hundred and fifty mark—none more than ten feet from the target. She could hardly believe it. She'd always had an accurate swing, and only recently had it fallen apart, but it had never been as reliable as it had been in the last two hours with Ryan standing beside her. She pulled out her driver again for the last five balls and allowed herself to believe she could actually have a chance at the Open championship.

"For you, Marie," she said as she swung hard. She watched in frustration as the ball took a sharp right turn at its apex. "What the hell!" She reared back to hit her club on the ground, but as she brought it around, she stopped her momentum and set it down lightly. "Tomorrow," she said, leaving the other balls on the ground. She packed up her bag and carried it to Eddie's office.

CHAPTER FIFTEEN

For the next two weeks, Katherine showed up early to find Ryan on the range waiting for her. Most days they hit balls for three or four hours, working on the long game, the short game, and even some putting. When Ryan had time, they would play a few holes and strategize the best course-management techniques, as well as a little anger management. Each day she grew more confident but still occasionally missed an easy shot when Ryan wasn't standing next to her providing words of encouragement. She was able to manage her anger when she missed an easy one, and that went a long way toward success on the next one.

Each day Ryan asked her to go to dinner or have a drink at the pub, but she always had an excuse—her book usually. She even turned her down for Rebecca's breakfast burritos on several occasions. She was pleased that she'd been able to stop blaming Ryan, but as much as she'd love to wrap herself around that hot body, she couldn't forget how Ryan had left the game—while Marie had died for it.

"I'm pretty sure I know what you'll say, but I'm going to keep asking on the off chance that one day you'll change your mind or forget to say no. Dinner tonight? I'll cook on the grill," Ryan asked as she removed Katherine's bag from the cart for her.

"Thanks, but I'm finishing the book. Writing has been good here. I'll see you tomorrow," she called as she walked her bag toward the maintenance shed.

"Good afternoon, Katherine." Eddie met her at the door. "I saw you over on number three today. That was a nice birdie. It's a hard hole, especially where I have the pin this week."

"Right? Are you trying to make this like the Open?" She liked to tease him. They'd become good friends over the past few weeks. She started each day with clean, shined clubs that Eddie had tended to every evening.

"Well…I hear that's the goal." Eddie took the bag from her. "Are you walking back to Dick and Terry's?" It had become Katherine's routine, but occasionally when it was particularly hot, Eddie insisted one of his guys take her back.

"Yeah. I was planning to. It's not too bad today, and you know I like the walk."

"I was wondering if you'd ride with me. I'm heading to Santa Fe to pick up some supplies and thought you might enjoy seeing our capital. You said you haven't been yet. We won't have much time for sightseeing, but I can drive you around a bit. I'll buy you lunch on the plaza. It's swanky."

"Did you say swanky?" she asked.

"Yes. I did." Eddie nodded and grinned.

"Well, how can a girl turn down an offer like that? Besides, it would be a shame for me to have been here three weeks and not see Santa Fe."

"Good. Let me put your clubs in my office, and I'll meet you in the bar. Ask Rebecca to make me a to-go cup of iced tea, and you should get something too."

"Okay." She trotted over to the restaurant. It was right between breakfast and lunch, so it was pretty quiet inside—only a few folks finishing coffee.

She walked to the kitchen, where she knew she'd find Rebecca. "Good morning."

"Well…hello, stranger. I was starting to wonder if I'd done something to offend you." Rebecca looked up from the vegetables she was cutting.

"No. Of course not. Why would you think that?" She approached for a hug. "Congratulations. How exciting." She looked down at Rebecca's belly.

"Thank you." Rebecca returned the hug. "What do you want?" she asked directly.

"Oh. Ahh…Eddie invited me to go to Santa Fe with him to pick up supplies and asked me to get him some tea to go." She repeated Eddie's request and then backed away from the icy feeling surrounding them.

"Where is he?" Rebecca asked.

"He asked me to meet him here."

"Hey, Bec," Eddie said as he walked in behind her. "I'm going to show Katherine our capital."

"The to-go cups are over there. The tea is behind you, and if you want a fountain drink, it's in the dining room," Rebecca said to her. "I need to talk to you." She pointed to Eddie and turned to walk away.

"Okay." Eddie followed her to the back room.

Katherine grabbed the cups and filled them both with tea, put on lids, and picked up two straws. Something was wrong, and she should probably back out of the offer and head back to her book. She'd been doing rewrites in her head all morning, so it wouldn't be a bad thing, but she did want to see Santa Fe. For now, though, she had to wait. She couldn't leave without telling Eddie.

As she was about to dig out her phone and make some notes, Eddie came out. "You ready?" he asked, as calm as ever.

She stayed seated. "Is everything okay? Maybe I should just go back to Terry's."

"Nah. Everything's fine. Come on." He picked up one of the cups and, in long strides, headed for the door. She followed, and within seconds they were on the road.

He began by telling her more history of Los Alamos and Santa Fe than she ever wanted to know. It was interesting, though, and she listened without comment for the forty-minute drive. Then they popped over the mountain onto the far west side of town, and

Eddie weaved his way through small-town streets until they were driving past an ancient church.

"That's the Old San Miguel Mission. It was built in 1610 and is said to be the oldest church in the United States, but it's pretty unlikely that any of the original church remains. Pretty cool, hmm?"

"Yeah. Do we have time to go inside?" she asked.

"I'm going to drop you off here and go load up the gear. Then I'll meet you back in about an hour, and we'll have lunch." He handed her his phone. "Put your number in here, and I'll call you when I'm done."

She did as he asked.

"After you finish in the church, follow this road down to the plaza. You'll find lots of little stores."

"Thank you, Eddie."

"Right. See you for lunch." He drove off, leaving her standing in front of the amazing church with artisan shops all around her.

❖

Katherine managed to make her way through the ancient chapel and walk through a few shops on the plaza before Eddie called. In that short time, she'd purchased enough items that it was getting difficult to carry them from store to store. She'd found several small pieces of jewelry for her mom; the turquoise was gorgeous and impossible to pass by. She also bought a spectacular landscape painting of the red rock she and Eddie had passed on the way to Santa Fe. Her dad would love that. She also picked up a leather bag for Maggie. Her highly paid golf coach carried her things around in a plastic grocery bag most of the time. She had a few other items for friends on the tour, but for herself she bought an amazing piece of horsehair pottery handcrafted at one of the local pueblos. It was wrapped well, but she feared she'd break it if Eddie didn't come soon.

"Perfect timing. I'm loaded down with stuff," she said after she saw the 575 area code pop up on her phone.

“Oh, no. I left you alone too long with too many shops. Where are you?”

“Yes. You did. You should’ve warned me. I’m by this wonderful art studio called Art Exchange. Do you know it?”

“I’ll find it and meet you. We’ll bring your stuff back to the truck. I’m parked down the street from the church, and then we’ll go eat.” She could tell Eddie was walking, as his breathing quickened.

“Okay. Oh, I see you!” She set her packages down and began waving.

“Be right there.”

They carried all the packages to the truck and found a café near the plaza that wasn’t too crowded. The waitress brought water and took their order almost as soon as they sat down.

“Ahhh. That was fun. I needed a little retail therapy—too much golf and not enough shopping.” She wasn’t much of a shopper—that was always Marie—but she did enjoy the diverse culture here, and their art was beautiful, plus buying gifts was always fun.

“I’m glad you enjoyed it.” Eddie fidgeted with his napkin. “I wanted to talk to you about something.”

“I guess I should’ve known you didn’t want to just take me for a ride.” Katherine sat back and stiffened.

“Well, I actually did want to show you Santa Fe. I like you, Katherine, but there’s another reason I brought you here.”

“What is it? Just say it, Eddie.” She felt as though someone had opened a trap door on her perfect day, and she’d dropped into a deep, dark tunnel. She thought she and Eddie had become good friends.

“Okay. Fair enough.” He took a big sip of water. “Why do you keep turning Ryan down when she asks you out?”

“Did she tell you?” She leaned forward and tilted her head. She couldn’t believe Ryan would talk to anyone about what she did or didn’t do. She seemed so private.

“Well, yeah. She mentioned it when I asked how things were going with you two.” He paused, and when she said nothing, he went on. "You see, she's like my niece. Or, no, she's like my daughter. I've known her since she was five, and I care about her a lot." Still, she only looked at him. "I thought you two were having a nice time when I called her to come to the hospital a couple of weeks ago. You know, when we found out Bec and I were going to have a baby."

"Really? She told you what hap—"

"No, no, no. She didn't tell me. I knew you were together, and she was so happy. As soon as we found out Bec was okay—well…Rebecca has a way of getting people to talk, especially Ryan. I might be like a father, but Ryan and Bec are like sisters. Ryan admitted that she'd been with you when I called, and well… it doesn't take a rocket scientist. She was so happy and kept telling us how wonderful you are. At least she was when she wasn't reminding us that the day wasn't about her." Eddie stopped.

"Hmm. Well, okay. She told you I turned her down for a date?" Katherine sat motionless.

"So…I asked how things were going with you two, since she was staying so late at the club every night and coming in at the crack of dawn. Again, I figured that one out on my own. She's used golf and work as an escape her whole life. And if she had a beautiful woman to be with, she wouldn't be spending sixteen hours a day at the course—no matter how dedicated she is to her game." He took another sip and wiped his whiskers. "She said she didn't know why, but you wouldn't go out with her. She assumes you just want to keep things professional, but…well, I figured I'd ask. She'd probably never speak to me again if she knew that I was talking to you about this, but she likes you, and if you like her too, then you should enjoy each other's company. Life's too short. Take it from a man who almost missed out."

Katherine sat for a few seconds without a word and finally spoke. "I can see you care about her very much, and obviously the whole town knows her and loves her. Well, I like her too, but we have different values. I don't really want to get involved with someone so different from me."

"Different values?" Eddie leaned back as if he'd been shocked. "What are they? She's one of the hardest working people I know, and so are you. She cares for her friends like family, and it appears that you do too. She's fun and special and honest and kind and… What the heck, values?"

"She's a quitter, Eddie." She raised her voice but caught herself and repeated more quietly, "She's a quitter."

"What?"

The waitress returned with their meals.

"Wow. I ordered a small salad, hoping not to get too much food, and still…" She marveled at the huge salad in front of her. She put her napkin in her lap and picked up her silverware.

"Katherine." Eddie left his food and silver untouched. "Tell me what you mean."

"She quit after she lost the British Open." She set her own silver on the table again. Suddenly she had no appetite.

"Is that what you think?"

"What else am I to think? She was at the top of her game, and then she was gone." She was frustrated now. She'd have to listen to this man defend Ryan's behavior, so she leaned back, crossed her arms, and prepared for a long story.

"Ryan is one of the most talented and gifted golfers I've ever seen. When she was ten years old, she was striking the ball better than most professionals. She worked every day to become the best."

"That's my point. She gave up her dream."

"You don't know her at all." Eddie stopped and picked up his silverware and started cutting into his steaming-hot enchiladas. "And if you're so quick to judge, maybe you're right. Maybe you do have different values."

"Well, maybe you should explain it to me," she snapped and grabbed her fork.

"Okay. I will." Eddie looked up from his plate. "No one deserves to be on the tour more than Ryan, and no one wanted it more. She should still be there…but she can't."

"Why? That makes no sense." She shoved a fork full of salad into her mouth—still not hungry but needing to do something.

"She won't forgive herself for being in the UK when her mom died."

Katherine put down her fork again. "Her mom died recently?"

"Her mom died two hours after she arrived home after losing the tiebreaker at the British Open."

A huge, heavy weight came down on her. How could she have been so quick to assume Ryan ran away because she lost? "Why won't she go back?"

"That young woman carries the guilt of not being here, and she won't let it go. She once told Rebecca that the best thing she could do was to try to fill her mother's shoes. And that's an impossible goal—Janet was a force. That woman took care of everyone until she couldn't. She practically raised Rebecca, and then Bec took care of her for the last five or six months. She'd been like a mother to Rebecca, and she never felt it was a burden to take care of Janet. She loved her and hurt as much as Ryan did when she passed, and she would've cared for her forever. But…" Eddie took a big gulp of water, clearly pushing down emotions he'd stirred up. "Ryan believes Janet quit fighting because she wasn't there to care for her. So she punishes herself. She doesn't know that's what she's doing, but it is."

"Oh, my…I'm so sorry, Eddie." She was forcing back her own tears as she watched the pain in Eddie's face. "I had no idea." She sniffled and wiped her eyes and nose.

"Well, you couldn't have known, but you shouldn't have assumed. For the first time, she was showing some signs of the old Ryan. You made her happy." Eddie straightened back up and started in on his food.

"I need to apologize to her. I'm supposed to leave tomorrow afternoon, and I've screwed up so badly. Can we go?" She pushed her plate away and waved for the check.

"I guess we can." Eddie took another big bite and then pushed his plate away as well.

Chapter Sixteen

On the way back to Los Alamos, Eddie told Katherine about Tuesday-night karaoke, and she agreed he and Rebecca could pick her up, and she'd see Ryan there. He assured her that no one would mind if she and Ryan took off early.

❖

It was almost seven, and Ryan was still hitting chip shots around the green when Rebecca walked out of the restaurant. "Aren't you going home before karaoke tonight?" she asked as she approached the green.

"First of all, I'm not going tonight, and second, why are you here so late? You're supposed to be working shorter days, not longer." Ryan tapped three balls in a row up on the green. The first two rolled within a foot of the hole, and the last one rolled in.

"You never miss, do you, Ry?" Rebecca crossed her arms and watched as the next ball followed the previous one into the cup.

"I miss all the time. You didn't answer me." Ryan sighed and dropped three more balls onto the ground.

"I came back to do an inventory while Nate was here to help me. I've only been here a few minutes," she said. "Ryan, just come with us. I feel better when you're there."

"I wouldn't be very good company tonight. I'll clean up here and head home. Please don't make me feel guilty." Ryan was practically begging.

"Okay, but can Eddie and I stop by after—to check on you?"

"Bec, really?" She hit the ball too hard, and it flew across the practice green.

"Okay. Okay. I worry, hon." Rebecca stopped Ryan's club in the back swing and pulled her into a hug. "She leaves tomorrow, doesn't she?"

She relaxed into Rebecca's hug. "Yeah. Terry is taking her to the airport after our lesson."

"You like her." Rebecca backed away from the hug.

"Yeah, but it wasn't meant to be. I just need to get back into my groove here and move on." She began collecting all her practice balls.

"Maybe your groove isn't here."

She stopped and looked up at her. "I sure hope so, 'cause this is where I am."

"Do you ever think about going back on the tour?" Rebecca began collecting balls as well.

"You know I'm not going back on tour." Her tone was harsh.

"Okay. I should leave. I'll see you tomorrow. Please think about coming out with us." Rebecca dropped the balls into Ryan's bucket and drew near to kiss her on the cheek.

She leaned forward to receive the kiss and nodded. "Okay, but please don't worry if I don't show up. Where's Eddie? He hasn't been around most of the day."

"He had errands all day. He said he'd meet me there. Good night, Ryan."

"Night, Bec."

❖

Katherine had been sitting outside on Terry's porch swing for nearly an hour when Eddie drove up to give her a ride at exactly the time he told her he'd be there. She'd spent the rest of the afternoon worrying that she'd lost her chance with Ryan.

"Ready?" he asked when she climbed into his big truck.

"I'm nervous." While she'd waited for him, she'd been making herself sit back down on the swing each time she jumped up to pace. "Where's Rebecca?"

"I was afraid she wouldn't be too fond of this idea, so I told her I'd meet her at the pub." He drove off.

At the pub, he led her into the bar and to the regular group table, but immediately she saw Ryan wasn't with the group. She scanned the room, hoping to spot her somewhere else.

As they approached the high-top table, she heard Rebecca speaking to Eddie. "What's she doing here?"

"Bec." Eddie sounded like he was scolding her. "She wants to talk to Ryan."

Rebecca pulled him to the side, where Katherine could no longer hear what she was saying. She was sure it wasn't good. Even though she'd been invited, she felt out of place and started to leave. It would be a long walk back to the B and B, but she couldn't stay here.

"Wait." Rebecca stopped her with a touch on the arm. "She didn't come tonight."

"Oh. I should go. I—"

"Eddie says you want to apologize to her." Rebecca lightly pushed Katherine back to the door, where it was quieter away from the stage.

"Yeah, but maybe it's a bad idea. She probably doesn't want to see me."

"No. It's a good idea," Rebecca said and guided her out the door. "I'll take you."

She stopped and turned to face Rebecca. "You don't like me much, do you?"

"Ryan does, and if you think you can quit hurting her, then maybe I could like you too." Rebecca started walking to her little Honda. "Come on."

They drove in silence around the curvy streets to Ryan's house. She was afraid if she said anything, Rebecca would scold her, so she didn't say a word.

As soon as they got near the house, they both noticed Ryan's truck wasn't in the drive.

"That girl." Rebecca drove right past the little adobe home. "She's still at the course. She hits balls in the dark," Rebecca said, shaking her head.

"Mmm-hmm." Katherine agreed. She was pleased that Rebecca was willing to help her find Ryan. No one knew her better.

"You know she's probably hitting the ball better and playing with more skill than she was when she was on tour? Better than she ever has in her life." Rebecca glanced over at her.

"I know. I can tell she holds back so as not to annihilate me each time we go out on the course." She was in awe of Ryan's skills every time they played. It was like she was throwing darts at a bull's-eye. Katherine had spent so much time pretending it was nothing, she hadn't considered that Ryan could still win tournaments.

"She needs to be back on the tour. She's too good to waste away in this desert town." Rebecca turned into the course parking lot, and Katherine didn't see any cars and specifically no Tundra in Ryan's normal spot. "Dang it." Rebecca spun her tires as she did a full-circle turn in the driveway, throwing gravel behind her.

"What? What is it?" Katherine asked.

"There's only one other place she could be."

"Where?" Did Ryan have a lover or a friend-with-benefits? Her neck and face warmed. She had no right to feel jealous, but that didn't matter. She'd had her chance to be with Ryan, and she'd turned it down even when Ryan was pleasantly persistent. "Is she with someone?"

"Yeah, she is, but not in the way you're thinking." Rebecca sped up, exceeding the city speed limit.

"Ahh…perhaps it's not a good idea for me to show up at someone else's house." Katherine began to squirm in her seat.

"You can drop me off at Terry's. I'll talk to her tomorrow before I leave."

"No. You need to come with me." As Rebecca was about to make a turn, sirens sounded behind them. "Oh, for the love of all…" Rebecca slowed and pulled to the side of the road.

"Will he give you a ticket?" Katherine asked as she turned to look behind them at the officer still sitting in his cruiser.

"He's bored," Rebecca said and sighed heavily.

Finally, after what seemed like forever, a short, stocky man who appeared no older than a teenager strolled up to the car. "Rebecca Sanchez, what are you doing? You haven't been drinking, have you?"

"Wally, you know I'd never drink and drive. I need to get over to Guaje's."

The officer tipped his head to look in the car window. "Ryan?"

"Yeah. I'm sorry. I shouldn't have been speeding, but I was worried about her."

"I'll escort you over there." He turned to walk back to his car without another word.

"No. Wally. No. I'll go slower. She'll be so embarrassed if you do that."

He took two long strides back and nodded at her. "You're right. I'll be nearby, though, if you need me. Go get her." He leaned down again. "A little slower, please. Tom's out here tonight too, and he might not be so understanding."

"Thanks, Wally." Rebecca put the car in gear, then turned back to the officer. "Eddie's at the pub. Could you stop by there and let him know where we are, but tell him not to worry."

"I'll stop in, but when it comes to you and Ryan, not much can stop Eddie from worrying." Wally walked away as Rebecca drove away.

"I continue to be amazed at how small this town is," Katherine said. "And was that guy old enough to be a police officer?"

"Yeah. I babysat him as a kid. He lived two houses down the street from us. He and Ryan went to school together." Rebecca focused on the road.

After a few miles from where they'd been stopped, Rebecca turned into a cemetery with a big sign above the gate that read "Guaje Pines Cemetery."

"Cemetery? Her mom. Her mom is buried here." Katherine finally realized who Ryan was visiting.

"Yes, and she comes here by herself way too often. She can't forgive herself," Rebecca said as she made several turns down the one-lane gravel roads.

Finally, Katherine spotted Ryan's red truck. "Can I go talk to her by myself?"

"Well. I guess. She's not going to be happy that we found her here."

"I understand, and if she doesn't want to talk to me, I'll come back and get you." She reached for the door after Rebecca parked next to Ryan's truck.

"Okay, then. Walk straight back until you get to the last row, and she'll be on the right about two or three stones down. There's not much else out there."

She started walking down the path with headstones standing like sentries on both sides of her. She wasn't fond of cemeteries, so she was glad it was still light out, but the sun had already dropped behind the mountain, creating an eerie flat light. As she crested the small hill near the back of the cemetery, she could see Ryan leaning against a stone exactly where Rebecca said she would be. Ryan was facing it, and Katherine didn't want to scare her, so she called out softly as she approached. "Ryan."

Ryan spun around. She was prepared for anger, but Ryan simply said, "Hi."

"Hi. Are you okay?"

"I think so, but I'm sure my nosy friend, who probably brought you here, would say otherwise."

Ryan's face was flushed and her eyes a little bloodshot. She'd clearly been crying but wasn't now. Katherine approached the stone. "May I sit with you?"

"Sure." Ryan scooched over to make room for Katherine to lean on part of the stone.

"I'm sorry about your mother. I had no idea she died so recently. I'm a horrible person for being so mean to you." She looked Ryan in the eye. They were only inches apart. "I'm sorry."

"How could you know?" Ryan turned back forward. "I miss her so much." She heard in Ryan's voice that she was forcing down the tears that were so near the surface.

"Oh, my gosh, Ryan." She took Ryan's hand. "I can't imagine the pain you must feel."

"I should've been with her. She died in Rebecca's arms. She was a far better daughter to her than I ever was, and she wasn't even blood kin. I'm so grateful for her and that she was here with my mom."

"She's a wonderful person." Katherine was searching for some comforting words, but she felt like a child. Nothing was coming to her.

Ryan nodded and then just sat. After what seemed like several minutes, Katherine couldn't stand the silence any longer. "She brought me here to see you."

"Yeah. She worries." Ryan was so calm that Katherine worried too. "You're leaving tomorrow." It wasn't a question.

"Yeah. I guess I'll play in Arkansas next weekend to prepare for the Open." Katherine laughed. "I don't know if I could ever win a major." *Or if I want to anymore.* She couldn't say the words out loud. At least not yet.

Ryan turned to her again, and she felt like those eyes were drilling into her. "You can, but you need to want it for you, though, so you can see yourself winning it."

Katherine was sure Ryan had read her mind. It was probably written on her face.

"You should play it!" she shouted, but before she went on with such excitement, she checked herself, realizing where they were. She wasn't sure why she needed to be quiet since she was sure no one else here would mind. "Ryan, you would be eligible because of your last professional tournament, and you're playing better than I've ever seen you do. It's like you can't miss."

For a second, she thought Ryan might be considering the idea, but then she spoke. "No. I'm not playing the tour again. I lost too much being gone all the time. I won't do that again. Especially not now. Eddie and Rebecca are going to have a baby. They'll need me."

"Okay."

"Rebecca's waiting to see if I'm okay, isn't she?" Ryan asked and looked in the direction of the parking lot, even though she couldn't see the cars from where they were sitting.

"Yeah. I'll go tell her." She started to get up.

"Nah. Let's go together." Ryan jumped up and held out her hand to help Katherine up.

Katherine looked at the headstone when she stood. "It's beautiful."

"Thanks. I don't know why I come here. She isn't here. She's on the course with me every day. That's where I feel her, but…" Ryan rubbed her fingers against the top of the smooth stone. "Come on. Rebecca will be walking down here to get us in a minute." They both turned toward the cars.

"Yeah. I think she was afraid you might send me packing."

"Why would I do that?"

"I've been so mean to you. I'm really sorry. I thought you quit the tour after losing the British Open. I never even considered that you had a reason. I was only thinking of me and finding someone to blame for Marie's accident."

Ryan reached for her hand. "I guess we've both had our share of loss. You weren't that mean. You let me know you weren't interested. I understand."

"No. That's just it. I like you. I want us to get to know each other. I wish I'd gone out with you. I had such a great time when we were together."

They were approaching the cars, and she could see Rebecca's expression of concern.

"Well, I guess it wasn't meant to be," Ryan said. "You're back on the tour next week, and I have a course to run—something I haven't been doing too well lately."

Rebecca got out as they approached. "You okay?" she asked Ryan and glanced over at Katherine.

Ryan walked into Rebecca's hug. "Yes. You worry too much."

"Hey. It's my right as a big sister." Rebecca finally released Ryan. "If you two are okay, I'll head back to the bar."

"Yeah. I'll take her back." Ryan motioned toward Katherine.

"Okay. Eddie will be worried. I sent Wally over to tell him where we were."

"Wally? Why?"

"Long story. I'll see you both tomorrow." Rebecca climbed back into her Civic and drove away, leaving Ryan and Katherine standing in the dusk.

"Let me get you back to Terry's place. You still want one more lesson tomorrow? I'm not sure I can teach you anything else." Ryan was still somber but no longer on the verge of tears.

"Perhaps we could talk some more about maybe getting together some time." She squeezed Ryan's hand.

"Hmm…" Ryan finally smiled. "Maybe we could have a drink on my patio."

"That sounds perfect."

CHAPTER SEVENTEEN

It was almost completely dark when Ryan pulled into her drive. She got out and went around the truck to meet Katherine. "I have some white wine."

"Nice."

Ryan let Katherine go ahead of her to the door, partly because she was being polite, but mostly to watch Katherine walk to her door. She had a beautiful body.

In the kitchen, Ryan poured two glasses of a local New Mexican pinot grigio and passed one to Katherine. "This way." She walked toward the patio and motioned to a redwood deck chair for Katherine, and she sat in the other.

They both stared over at the mountain at the same time. The neighbor's house partially blocked it, but the view was still nice. Neither of them spoke for a moment.

"So you wanted to talk," she said and took a sip of her wine.

"Um…well…I was hoping we could pick up where we left off here a couple of weeks ago," Katherine said.

Ryan laughed a little, but the warm feeling in her middle emphasized how much she wanted that too. "Mmm. You know you're blushing."

Katherine covered her face with her hands, then finally peeked through her fingers. "I'm not usually so forward."

"You know what you want. It's a good thing." She sipped again. Should she get up and take this beautiful woman to bed like she'd asked, or should she avoid making her desire to be with her even worse since she was leaving in a few hours?

"Yes."

Katherine's honest, confident tone was all it took to get Ryan moving. "Follow me." She stood, picked up Katherine's wine, and walked straight to her bedroom. "I think we were here."

"Mmm-hmm." Katherine took a step closer.

Ryan inhaled deeply and willed her pulse to slow. "Damn."

Katherine's smile wavered. "What?"

"You are so…" She swallowed hard, unable to find the words to tell Katherine how absolutely stunning she was. Instead, she pulled her through the door and kissed her. When she stroked Katherine's tongue with hers, she had a flash of the fantasy she'd been running through her head since she'd left Katherine in her house thirteen days ago. In her fantasy, she took Katherine to her bedroom and made love to her before they said another word. She wanted the fantasy, but at the same time, she wanted to slow down and just be with Katherine. With an audible groan, she took a step back.

Katherine groaned too and leaned toward her, but finally the kiss was broken.

"Ahh…Maybe we should slow down," she said.

Katherine shrugged and began looking around the small, neat bedroom.

She quickly filled the silence "It's the same room I used to sleep in as a kid. I can't bring myself to move into Mom's. It's bigger though. I did manage to take down all my posters of Anne Hathaway." She laughed.

"Nice choice," Katherine said and winked. Then she walked over to the dresser, where she lingered on some family photos—mostly of her and her mother playing golf. "May I take a look?"

She nodded and followed Katherine across the room, where she leaned closer to Ryan's favorite picture of her mother.

"You resemble your mom," Katherine stated. "She's…what's the right word…glamorous." Katherine turned and looked at her.

"Glamorous!" She burst out laughing. "She'd have thought that was the funniest thing ever. The most glamorous thing she ever wore was last-year's golf fashions. She would never have bought them unless they were on sale from the previous season." She laughed again.

"Clothes. No. That's not what makes her glamorous. Look at her." Katherine pointed back at the picture. "She emanates beauty and confidence and love and kindness."

Ryan stepped closer. "I guess. I knew she was beautiful, but her looks didn't mean anything to her, so I didn't give it much thought. But yes, she was the most confident person I've ever known, and truly kind."

"Oh, this is cute of you, Eddie, and Rebecca."

"Mom took that and told us it was a picture of her kids. Eddie was a few years younger than her, but she took care of all of us."

Katherine smiled and then pointed at Rebecca. "Rebecca plays golf?"

"Are you kidding? Yeah, and she's pretty dang good. She used to win local tournaments." She pointed at a second-place trophy on a shelf above her bed. "She was first place in that tournament."

"Oh, my gosh. She beat you?"

"All the time. Mom was always making me work on something new, and I'd mess up pretty badly while I was adjusting. Bec loved it and would kick my ass. I think she conspired with mom so she could beat me." She looked at the picture more closely. "You had to play golf if you wanted to spend time with her. Bec figured that out and started hitting balls one day. She doesn't play much anymore. We knew Mom was sick when she took that picture, but I think only Bec knew how sick. I was home on an off week and spent every day on the course with her." She sniffed back a tear. "I'm sorry."

"Don't be. I wish I could've known her." Katherine pointed to the last picture in the row. "Who's this?" It showed a tall, lanky man wearing a white, starched shirt buttoned to the neck and a pair of black slacks standing next to a missile. "He's handsome."

"My dad. Mom took that the day we arrived here. I was pretty young, so I don't really remember. He died soon after we got here. I don't have many memories of him, but in the ones I do have, he's always wearing a white shirt and black slacks." She wasn't sure they were real memories or had come from the photo and stories she'd heard her mom tell.

"I'm so sorry, Ryan." Katherine turned to her.

"I didn't know him, but I did get his long legs." She laughed. "So, I have that."

Katherine pulled her close to her and kissed her, but Ryan stopped before the passion could suck her in.

"I'm scared of what will happen if we go further, and I'm scared that if we don't, I'm going to regret it," she said.

"I know." Katherine took a tentative step closer, reaching for her. "But I want to see what happens. I want to give us a chance." Katherine paused. "I want you, Ryan."

Behind her whispered confession was a hunger that she felt herself. Then Katherine's mouth was on hers, her tongue parting Ryan's lips, and she couldn't back away again. Katherine pressed tight against her, and between kisses along Ryan's neck, she whispered what she wanted, telling her exactly what she needed. She grasped Ryan's hair, tugging it lightly, and Ryan couldn't help but think of how perfectly they fit together—molding into one, like they were meant to be together. She slid her hands around Katherine's trim waist and began to slowly push her toward the bed.

She removed Katherine's designer shirt, and Katherine immediately did the same to her. She was desperate to touch Katherine's skin but trying hard to take her time. When Katherine pulled her sports bra over her head, she began to feel a little awkward as Katherine's gaze lingered on her breasts, but this discomfort fell away when she saw the pleasure in her eyes. Katherine lightly traced the tattoo on Ryan's left side below her breast. It was over a year old now—an image of her mother's hands resting on the top of her Big Bertha driver. Ryan had hung the complete full-length photo of her mother looking over the ninth hole in her office at the club.

"Your mother's hands?" As Katherine gently kissed the bright ink not yet faded with time, Ryan felt a tingle of sensation with each light touch of her lips.

"Mmm-hmm." Ryan mumbled agreement. She gently pulled Katherine back up to eye level and took a small step back. She wanted to see all of her, to study every line and curve until she knew she'd never forget. After a few seconds Katherine pushed her shorts and underwear down, seeming to know what Ryan wanted. She stood there motionless and confident as Ryan admired her. She gazed at the path of her fingers as she let them wander over Katherine's soft skin. She couldn't help it. Katherine was truly amazing unclothed—thin but indisputably feminine, with large, firm breasts and a neatly trimmed patch at the junction of her thighs. It seemed to be begging for her touch.

Her throat tightened at the thought of the last time she and Katherine had been together. It had been too fast and over too quickly, but the memories were still detailed and vivid. "Katherine, you're so beautiful."

Katherine smiled, and her breathing was short, her eyes heavy with desire. "As are you—so, so sexy. I could come just looking at you." Katherine gently thumbed her nipples, slowly swirling around the hardening tips. She moved her hands down Ryan, past her stomach, exploring more of her.

She jerked involuntarily when Katherine touched her sensitive clit, but she didn't move away. Katherine's touch was incredible, firm against her. She wrapped her other arm around Ryan's neck, pressing herself into her. "Mmm." Katherine's voice was audible before her tongue made its way over the earlobe.

She turned her head to join Katherine's lips again, the kiss building until a wetness began to form between her legs. She guided Katherine to the bed, laid her down, and took a second to admire her beauty. She'd have this memory of Katherine in her bed even if she had nothing else. She bent down over Katherine and began exploring every inch of her with her tongue. She kept attending to every curve and valley until Katherine began quivering underneath her. She experienced the same intensity as Katherine begged for more and insisted that she not stop touching her. Finally, she settled over Katherine's hard clit, circling lightly and then slowly dipping inside her.

Katherine's back arched, and she called out. "Oh. Wait. Please. Wait. I don't want to come yet. Not before I've touched you." To Ryan's surprise, Katherine rolled her over effortlessly, her thigh gliding between her legs like it belonged there. She felt a great sense of pleasure, wanting her so badly. They kissed—soft and sweet, hot and passionate. Ryan was wet from the moment Katherine touched her nipple, and now she was nearly ready to explode.

Despite Katherine's continued refusals over the past couple of weeks, Ryan's desire hadn't waned. And now being exactly where she'd wanted to be for weeks, she felt her control failing. She desperately wanted to consume Katherine. She could tell Katherine felt the same, based on her intensity and incoherent but pleasant sounds.

Katherine sucked her nipple, tugging gently with her teeth. An incredible tingle spread from her nipples to her stomach, and when Katherine bit harder, she flinched at the pulsing of her clit. "Oh my God, Katherine."

"Mmm?" Katherine mumbled but didn't stop teasing her nipple.

"You have no idea what that does to me," she breathed. Katherine bit down a little harder. Ryan bucked beneath her, panting and asking for more.

"Hmm. I think I have a pretty good idea." Katherine reached between them and glided her fingers over her skin, making her shiver. Finally, Katherine reached her clit. With Katherine's first light touch, she quieted and waited for more. Katherine continued, but only briefly.

"Katherine, more…please…I want to come."

Instead of complying, Katherine withdrew completely from between her thighs. Ryan squeezed and tugged at her down comforter in frustration. When Katherine moved to straddle her while continuing to attend to Ryan's breasts with her tongue, the frustration melted away, but her arousal deepened through every cell, spreading heat through her.

Soon it became clear Katherine wouldn't give in too quickly. Every time she moved to grind against Katherine, she was met with disappointment, and then Katherine giggled. Finally, when she wrapped her arms around Katherine's waist and sat up, Katherine's little chuckle turned to a surprised gasp.

She tongued a taut nipple, sucking gently until Katherine grabbed the back of her neck and a fistful of her hair as she ground herself against Ryan's thigh, Katherine's wet arousal covering Ryan's skin as she pleasured herself. The throb in her clitoris built almost to a breaking point. She was so close, but no…not yet.

As she bent to slowly drag her teeth along Katherine's neck, she reached between them to lightly circle Katherine's clit, giving her what she'd given Ryan. But she was only teasing herself as well.

Katherine groaned, sucking her ear. "Please," she begged. "Fuck me. I want you to—"

She entered Katherine in a single smooth motion. She was so wet, Ryan glided her fingers effortlessly through her soft vagina, exploring all of her. They were slick with sweat, Katherine's breasts sliding seductively against Ryan's. Katherine rocked hard in sync with Ryan's movements. Katherine's arms were wrapped around Ryan's neck, and she panted in Ryan's ear, begging for more while nipping and sucking her neck. Every sound and twitch

Katherine made added another layer to her intense arousal until pleasure shot down her legs, up her spine, through her stomach.

When Ryan curled her fingers against Katherine's inner walls, Katherine bit down hard on Ryan's shoulder. Katherine called out almost incoherently, "Oh God, I'm gonna come…I'm coming. Don't stop. Please don't—"

"No," Ryan rasped, withdrawing abruptly. "I want you in my mouth."

"Ahhh." Katherine sighed.

In Katherine, Ryan had found what had been missing for so long. In Katherine's pleasure she'd found her own. She wanted to taste her so badly. Katherine held on to her, begging, her face pressed against Ryan's neck and her legs wrapped around Ryan's waist as Ryan gently tilted forward to lay her down. She slid down between Katherine's legs and spread them apart.

Katherine cried out hoarsely at the first touch of her tongue and again when she delved deep inside her. Katherine called out, "Ryan, Ryan, Ryan," the volume rising with each strangled word. Katherine hardened and swelled, her clit pulsing against Ryan's tongue as she arched off the bed. Suddenly, with one final call of Ryan's name, Katherine tightened around Ryan's fingers as she came in her mouth, clutching Ryan's hair. Ryan stayed with her as she rode the climax, enjoying her desire until she finally lay still, her breathing loud and erratic.

She rested her cheek against Katherine's belly, also needing to catch her breath. "You taste so good." Ryan's voice sounded strange in her own ears. Pressing kisses to Katherine's skin, Ryan slowly made her way back up Katherine to kiss her, but Katherine stopped her and ran her tongue over her lips and probed her mouth.

Ryan's stomach clenched, the pounding between her thighs nearly unbearable. She could feel the edge of her orgasm, just out of reach. She was almost there, and the moment Katherine touched her she would explode.

Katherine hooked her leg around the back of Ryan's and rolled her over, lying on top again. For the longest time, Katherine did nothing but look down at her, and for the first time in a long time she had a feeling she was truly being seen and understood. She breathed heavily—wanting. She wasn't afraid of being laid bare for Katherine but feared the intensity of her desire would frighten Katherine. She tried to swallow it but couldn't hide her feelings.

Katherine's breasts rose and fell with each inhalation, her expression a mix of anticipation and desire. It had to be mirrored on her own face. She still didn't quite believe she was here, but even if only for today, Katherine was hers. Katherine finally ran her fingers over Ryan's stomach, making her tense and twitch as Katherine moved her hand lower, skimming her flesh. The tingling sensation made her shiver. Katherine was so close to where Ryan needed her to touch, but she seemed to still be deliberately staying away. The teasing was making Ryan crazy, but she loved it.

Katherine's lips moved, and Ryan barely heard the whispers of her desire. "God, you are unbelievable." Her tongue swept over her lower lip. "Can I taste you?"

Ryan nodded, and Katherine slid down between her thighs, pushed her legs apart, and lowered her mouth to Ryan's clit. At the first touch of Katherine's tongue on her most sensitive spot, she couldn't stop herself from crying out, and then again as she slid inside. Katherine reached up and teased her nipple, and that sent her over the edge. Her climax came swift and hard, cresting in intensity and then lowering her back down.

Katherine didn't stop licking. Instead, she slowed to long, light strokes. With an unexpected rush, Ryan came again, harder this time, clutching the sheets, Katherine's hair, and anything else she could grasp. Her second climax spread like lava across her body, leaving her jerking and squirming under Katherine's continued touch.

When she could move again, she lifted Katherine's head to look at her. If she lived another hundred years, she still wouldn't have enough time to tell Katherine how she felt, but she tried, her voice rough from crying out in pleasure. "Katherine, you're incredible."

Katherine smiled, kissing the inside of Ryan's thigh. "You're only saying that because you just came."

"Not true, though it was pretty spectacular. Both times."

Katherine shrugged, looking self-assured. Ryan reached for her, and she moved back to her arms. Lying half on and half off Ryan, Katherine traced the outline of her tattoos again. The sensation was soothing.

Katherine didn't say a word, but she kissed lightly where Janet's inked hands crossed. Then she started tracing Ryan's skin again, running her hand down her leg. She paused, stretching, but couldn't go lower unless she moved. And Ryan had a feeling she couldn't.

Chapter Eighteen

Katherine woke at five in the morning, curled in the crook of Ryan's arm. She hadn't felt that safe since before Marie died. Ryan's breathing provided a soothing comfort. She desperately needed to move her right arm that had lost all feeling, but she didn't want to wake Ryan and lose this sense of security. If only she could lie here with this amazing woman forever. But her flight left Albuquerque in the afternoon.

If only she hadn't wasted so much time pushing Ryan away—blaming her. She couldn't blame anyone else any longer, but could she stop blaming herself?

Until she figured things out, she couldn't back away from her goal to win a major—not now. Too many people were counting on her to represent her sister. If she could just win the Open in two weeks, she could be done with this charade. But could she? A year ago, two strokes off the lead and tied for third place, she'd believed she could. But now, even with all Ryan's help, she wasn't back at the top of her game. Would she ever be? And did she care?

"You're awake." Ryan's voice was raspy from sleep.

"Oh. I'm sorry. Did I wake you?" She snuggled closer, tightening her grip around Ryan and releasing her arm from its locked position.

"No. I don't think so. Are you okay?"

"I'm more than okay." She leaned up to meet Ryan's lips.

"Mmm. This was better than every one of my fantasies," Ryan said.

"Oh, so you were fantasizing about me?"

"Every day."

"Honestly, I had a few myself."

"Really? Even when you were telling me no and crushing my confidence?"

"Yes." She pushed against Ryan's chest. "I've been attracted to you since the minute you walked out to the range the day we met. I was so in my head I couldn't let go. But you probably knew that."

"How could I? I was sure you hated me from day one. Well, there was that one moment you changed my mind briefly." Ryan smiled down at her.

"I'm sorry. I owe you a big apology."

Ryan tilted Katherine's head up. "I accept your apology."

"Thank you." She kissed Ryan again before burrowing back down in the bed and laying her head on Ryan's shoulder. She began to play with the small ring on Ryan's left ring finger, holding it up to look at it.

"It was my mother's," Ryan said.

"It's beautiful." She stroked the small diamond and the decorative design on the gold band.

"It's small, but my dad gave it to her, and she cherished it." Ryan squeezed her hand and changed the subject. "So are you ready for the Open?"

"Yeah. I have to give it a shot, and I have my confidence back—mostly."

"Yes. You do. You could win it," Ryan said.

"Will you come with me?" she asked, but didn't move from her position because she was afraid of Ryan's expression.

"Ah…I…I'd rather not. You don't need me. Listen to Mags. She's good, even if she's a bit of a womanizer. She knows golf."

"I'd like you to play with me, compete too." Since she'd started, she figured she'd keep going. Ryan was at the top of her game, and she was a professional golfer. She needed to be playing on the tour.

"No."

Ryan seemed to pull away a bit, so Katherine said, "It's just… no, you're right. You can't play until you're ready."

"Listen, Katherine. Maybe I could come up and watch a couple of rounds if you'd like."

"Yeah?" She propped herself up on one elbow.

"Yeah. If you'd like to see me again. I'd try not to distract you."

She wrapped her legs around Ryan's and pulled herself on top of her. "I might need a distraction." She leaned down and kissed Ryan.

"Mmm."

Chapter Nineteen

As soon as Ryan dropped Katherine off and kissed her good-bye, she quickly returned to her house and showered. They'd discussed continuing to see each other and even had a tentative plan for her to meet Katherine at the Open in a couple of weeks, but their last kiss still felt like an ending instead of the beginning Ryan wanted.

She wasn't late to work, but the last few minutes with Katherine had delayed her from her usual early hour. Rebecca already had coffee on when she arrived and of course gave her a hard time.

"Mmm. That smells good," she announced as she entered.

"Well, good afternoon." Rebecca came from around the corner of the kitchen door and stood with her hands on her hips, staring at Ryan.

"Stop that. I'm only twenty minutes later than normal, and I'm still here before the first tee time." She walked over and gave Rebecca a quick hug.

Rebecca stood stiff. "Two foursomes have teed off already." Finally, she gave in and returned the hug. "Based on your goofy grin, you had a good night. We missed you at the pub."

"Bec, she's amazing." Ryan leaned against the wall and spread her arms.

"Be careful, li'l sis." Rebecca turned to go back to the kitchen. "She hurt you before," she called out over her shoulder as she walked away.

"I know, and she's leaving, but I can dream for a minute, can't I?" She walked away toward her office.

"Ry, wait. I'm sorry. You're right. She did seem sincere last night. If she hadn't, I wouldn't have taken her to you. I'll get coffee, and you can tell me about it. You don't have anything on your schedule except the airport." Rebecca grabbed two cups and headed to the coffee pot.

"How do you know I'm taking her to the airport?"

"Well, I figured you would after last night, and you just confirmed." Rebecca smiled as she walked to her table with coffee. "Now I want to hear all about it, but leave out the details, 'kay?"

She took the coffee and sat across from Rebecca. "She was so kind and finally realized how she was blaming me. She kept apologizing. Well, she stopped now and then so we could do some other things." She smiled.

"I said no details." Rebecca thumped the back of Ryan's hand with her coffee spoon.

"I think she recognized she'd built some big walls, and she may have started to break them down."

"Great. I've thought the two of you looked good together. Very tall." Rebecca laughed and took a slurp of hot coffee.

"She's gorgeous, isn't she, and amazing?"

"Yes, she is gorgeous. Between the two of you, I was afraid some of the old men around here were going to have a heart attack. But amazing…I told you no details." Rebecca chuckled again. "Are you planning to try to see her again, or are you going to be okay with the time you've had?"

"We did talk about it, and I would like to see if we could have more, but…"

"What? What's the *but*?"

"It's so hard when someone's on tour. I'm not sure I could handle it."

"Why?" Rebecca stared at her. "What would be so hard? You could meet up at the beginning of each week. And you could spend the off-season together. Why not try?"

"I don't know about being that close to the tour. I gave it up."

"That might be another thing for me to ask why about, but I know you don't want to talk about it. I just want you to be happy."

"I'm happy."

"I would like you to have what Eddie and I have. And you're too big for this town. Too good."

"What's that supposed to mean? It's my home!"

"Ry, it'll always be your home, and you know we love having you here. Janet wanted you to be happy, and she always talked about how happy you were when you were competing every week. Even in her darkest days, watching you play lit her up, because she knew you were doing what you loved."

"And I missed all those moments with her. I could only see the next tournament. Even when you called and told me I should come home, I was too focused on golf to do the right thing. You spent nearly a year of your life caring for a woman who wasn't even your mother, and I was hitting golf balls around England, only to leave with nothing to show for it." Tears streamed down her face.

"Oh, Ryan. I'm sorry. Please don't cry." Rebecca stood and wrapped her arms around her shoulders. "Please never think caring for Janet was a burden. She was the only real mother I had, and she'd have been so disappointed if you'd left that tournament. You knew that."

"Why? Why did she have to die? We loved her so much." She sobbed in Rebecca's tender hug.

"She gave us all we needed, and then she left. I believe she's watching us, and I believe she's as worried about you as I am."

"So I go play golf for a living, and you'd stop worrying?" She backed away.

"No. It would make me happy for you to stop worrying about losing the other people you love and live your life. Eddie and I and the course will be fine, and we'll be here with open arms anytime you want to come *home*." Ryan started to interrupt, but Rebecca continued. "But if you're happy here, we'll continue to enjoy being together as a family." Rebecca sat back down and took her hands. "Just know you'll be on auntie duty in about five months." She laughed again.

"I can't wait." She relaxed a bit and squeezed Rebecca's hands. "How can I leave when I'm about to be the best aunt on the face of the earth?"

"Well, you'll be that, no matter where you are." Rebecca smiled. "I want you to be happy, and if that's here, then even better, but if it's not, that's okay too, because you haven't been. I know, so don't try to convince me otherwise."

She nodded. "I love you, Bec."

"Of course you do." Rebecca looked at the big clock on the wall. "Now what time do you have to get that hot, amazing chick to the airport?"

"Oh, shit. What time is it?" She spun around. "Oh…I have time. We have to leave here at ten."

"Okay. Let me make you some breakfast, and you think about what I said."

Chapter Twenty

Katherine opened the front door of the bed-and-breakfast as quietly as she could, but the heavy oak door creaked with such a squeal, it was like an alarm alerting residents of her arrival. It was almost six, and since she hadn't had breakfast there during her entire visit, she had no idea what time Terry got started each day. Before she could close the door, she heard Terry's voice.

"Is that you, Katherine?" Terry peeked around the kitchen door.

"Yes. How did you know?" She walked toward the kitchen.

"Oh, I hear things." Terry went back into the kitchen but kept talking. "There was much ado about Ryan not being at karaoke last night and Rebecca leaving early to take you somewhere."

"You figured out I wasn't here last night from that information?"

"Oh, yeah. Plus, I talked to Rebecca first thing this morning." Terry laughed, apparently quite tickled with herself.

"Oh my gosh. You talked to Rebecca already. It's barely six." She shook her head. "This town! I can't decide if I love it or hate it."

"Most people feel that way." Terry turned around with a cup of coffee in her hand and passed it to her. "Here. Maybe this will make you feel better about it. Rebecca and I walk every morning at five."

"That's crazy. Thank you for the coffee. It smells amazing." She took a tentative sip.

"So do I finally get to make you breakfast?" Terry gave her a hard stare. "You're the only one here this morning, so I'll take particular offense if you don't eat."

"Okay. Yes. Please make me breakfast."

"Now, your friend, Maggie, that's her name, right?" Terry asked, and she nodded as she finished another sip. "Yeah. She loved the works—full Western breakfast, but I hear you're a minimalist. Probably worrying about your cute figure. So what can I make? Please don't tell me to toast a bagel. I might make you do it yourself."

"I think I'll go for that full Western breakfast," she said.

"Okay! You must've worked up an appetite." Terry laughed and reached for the refrigerator door. "You take that cup upstairs and enjoy it. I'll call when it's ready."

Katherine nodded and climbed the stairs to her room.

She hadn't packed anything before she ran off to find Ryan last night, so as soon as she walked in, she began throwing things into her bags. She was able to get most of her stuff packed before she heard Terry yell. After two years on the tour and living in hotel rooms most of the year, she was pretty good at getting ready to leave.

"Oh," she said as she approached the dining-room table filled with bacon, eggs, hash browns, biscuits and gravy, and about six different jars of jam. She spotted orange and apple juice in pitchers and a carafe with more coffee. And right in the center of the table sat a full plate of fresh fruit. "How much did you think I could eat?" She stood staring at the spread.

"Oh, only what you want. Dick will be here in a few minutes, and he'll take care of what's left." Terry poured another cup of coffee and started back to the kitchen.

"You're not going to make me eat by myself, are you?"

"Well, I usually like to let my guests have some privacy, but if you're asking me to stay, I'll eat with you." Terry smiled. "Plus,

I'm sure Rebecca is getting the full story from Ryan right now, so I need some good stuff too."

"What?" She stopped filling her plate and looked over at Terry.

"She always gets the best gossip."

"You want me to tell you what happened last night?"

"Well, yeah." Terry started filling her own plate.

"Um. I…"

"No. I'm teasing, but I do want you to feel comfortable talking to me. Rebecca and I might share some gossip between the two of us, but we love Ryan, and we've been hoping you two would get together. We'll have fun being happy for you two."

"Again. This town!"

"Oh, now, you can't blame the town on our need for some good stories." Terry sat and started eating. "Dig in, honey. Isn't Ryan going to pick you up pretty soon?"

She quickly glanced at her watch. "Oh. I have plenty of time. She's coming at ten. I need to shower, and I have to finish packing."

The two of them sat silently for several minutes. She was eating heartily but was so lost in her thoughts of the night before she barely noticed the food and had no idea she was shoveling it in so quickly.

"I won't take it away from you." Terry was staring at her.

"What?" Katherine stopped long enough to look over at Terry.

"You're eating so fast. I thought maybe you were worried I'd take it away."

"Oh, wow." She looked down at her plate. "I'm sorry. It's amazing. I think I went to my happy place there for a moment."

"Yeah." Terry nodded. "You really like her, don't you?"

"What's not to like? She's amazing and kind and so easy to talk to and smart and strong and…"

"Well, yeah, and…"

"Gorgeous and sexy." She actually let a soft moan escape.

"Hmm…well, okay then." Terry flushed a little. "So we'll be seeing you back here in our little town soon?"

"I don't know." She stopped eating again and took a sip of coffee. "I mean…I hope so. It's just…I'm not sure what Ryan wants. She doesn't want anything to do with the LPGA tour, but I'm not sure I do either."

"What do you mean? I thought you were here to get lessons from Ryan so you could go win a major."

She shook her head, starting to realize not much happened at the golf course that Terry didn't know about. Probably the whole town knew too. "That's how it started. Maybe I've realized a lot about myself these past few weeks, and maybe I don't want that anymore."

"Oh," Terry said.

"I know that sounds weird, and I'm not sure I fully understand it myself, but…" She stared at the large grandfather clock against the wall as it struck half past eight. "I need to go pack and get ready. Thank you for breakfast and for being so kind and hospitable during my entire visit. If I do come back, I'll be staying here."

"Well, I doubt that." Terry winked. "But you're always welcome. Now you get upstairs and get ready. I'll send Dick up to bring your stuff down in a while."

Chapter Twenty-one

Ryan was struggling with the rate at which time was moving. She didn't want it to pass because that meant Katherine was closer to leaving, but she also wanted to see her and spend time with her, even if it was only for a couple hours on the drive to Albuquerque. She wanted to talk to Katherine about so much, but she wasn't sure she could say all that was on her mind.

She mostly felt like this affair needed to just be over, since it probably couldn't be more than that anyway. Rebecca had told her not to be so negative. She didn't want to be. She truly wanted to be hopeful that somehow this could be something. She liked Katherine, but she was also a realist. If she gave herself some hope, then she'd be disappointed and heartbroken when things didn't work out. Or perhaps she'd see her again, but it would be weird between them. She couldn't handle that either.

As soon as Rebecca had stopped grilling her for information, she went to her office, hoping to clear some of the paperwork off her desk. It had been piling up over the past few weeks, but the minute she sat down, her mind went to better times—only a short time before, when she'd still been curled up next to Katherine. It felt so natural to be with her.

After what seemed like hours but had been only fifteen minutes, she walked to the starter booth to see if they needed help keeping the course moving. It was a beautiful day, and all the tee times had been booked. If they got even a few minutes behind, the whole day could be backed up. But as soon as she arrived, she saw Tiffany in the booth calling off names and hustling guys down to the first tee box. And when she walked in, Tiffany waved her away. If you had a good system going, the last thing you needed was someone to come in and try to help, and Tiffany was good. This was her third summer, and with her at the helm, only when golfers didn't arrive on time did things get behind. Everyone seemed to be punctual today, so Ryan didn't have anything to do.

She stopped by the pro shop to say hi to Patty, but she was juggling three customers wanting to test gear, try on shoes, and compare premium golf balls while also taking payment from players for their round of golf.

"Need help, Patty?" she asked as she entered.

"No. Go on. I got this." Patty waved her arm for her to get out of her hair.

The course ran like a perfectly maintained machine most of the time, due to her mom's hard work in getting the perfect staff to stay on board season after season. She'd taken care of them like family, and it had paid off. Ryan wanted to think she was filling her mother's shoes, but the staff her mother had trained was mostly taking care of her and not the other way around. She strolled back through the restaurant, and it was hopping too. Mostly folks were getting their morning coffee, but a handful were eating breakfast. Rebecca was busy at the grill, while two high school students worked the tables.

"Need any help?" Ryan called back into the kitchen.

"Do we look like we need help?" Rebecca snapped as she rolled three burritos one after the other.

"Ah…" She wasn't sure what the right answer was since Rebecca looked so busy.

"No! We don't need help. Go do some of your golf stuff," Rebecca said. "Order, Jenny," she yelled out the small window to the dining room, then waved good-bye to Ryan.

She looked at the clock above the bar, hoping it would say it was close enough to ten for her to drive over and get Katherine, but it showed eight thirty.

"Hey, Ryan. Aren't you teaching lessons today?" Dr. Murphy called from across the room.

"Not today. I'm heading down to Albuquerque."

"Why would anyone do that?" Doc laughed as he refilled his coffee.

"Right!" Ryan nodded, then walked over closer so she could talk to the doctor more privately. "Hey. How's Rebecca doing? I can't get her to slow down."

"I can imagine that would be a hard thing to do. Do the best you can, and as she gets farther along, we'll tag-team with Eddie."

"Okay. I worry."

"Don't." Doc patted her shoulder and slid past her, leaving her with time on her hands yet again.

Finally, she strolled out to the maintenance shed, which was empty except for Eddie clinking around in the back under an old mower. All the other guys were taking care of carts or mowing the back nine before the golfers made it to that side.

"Hey, Eddie," she called out as she approached the back of the shed.

"Ryan? Shit. You scared me." He pulled himself up from under the large mower. "What are you doing here? I thought you'd be on the way to ABQ by now."

"We don't leave until ten." She hopped up onto the red toolbox next to the mower.

"Oh, well, then." He wiped his hands on a greasy rag that probably left more dirt on them than he was able to wipe off. "Is everything okay with you and Katherine?"

She was sure by now that Rebecca had filled him in when she took him a cup of coffee, but she answered anyway. "Yeah. All good."

"Hmm…" He climbed up in the seat of the mower and waited in the silence for her to speak. He'd been using this tactic on her since she was a kid. If he waited long enough, she would start talking.

"I like her, Eddie."

"Well now, there's some news." He laughed.

"It's just…I don't know if it's a good idea to try to be in a long-distance relationship with someone on the tour."

"Why's that?"

"Come on, Eddie. I'd hardly see her, and if she's serious about winning a major, she's going to be putting in some long hours that probably won't include too many days in New Mexico." Ryan spun a socket wrench around in her hand.

"Well…she might need a full-time swing coach to travel with her."

"I have to work, and this is where I live." She dropped the wrench back onto the top of the toolbox with a clank. "Are you and Rebecca trying to get rid of me? Shit!" She let her voice rise.

Eddie said in a calm, low voice, "Ry, we want you to be happy."

"And you've both figured out leaving here will do that." She jumped off the toolbox and headed toward the door. "I'll see you tomorrow."

"Ryan, wait."

She stopped and turned back toward him.

"Don't close any doors." He approached her and carefully gave her a one-armed squeeze so he wouldn't get grease on her clothes.

She leaned in to receive his hug. Her mom had said those words to her a hundred times. "Right. I know." She squeezed back and walked away.

CHAPTER TWENTY-TWO

Ryan drove up in front of Terry and Dick's ten minutes early, certain she would've exploded if she'd stayed at the course even one more minute. She thought she'd be able to catch up with Terry for a few minutes while she waited for Katherine, but she was sitting on the porch with all her bags surrounding her except for her clubs.

"You're ready?" she asked as she climbed out of her truck.

"Yep. We need to go get my clubs."

She smiled. "Do you think I'd forget golf clubs?"

"I guess not." Katherine met her at the bottom of the steps and kissed her. "It seems like it's been forever since I last saw you." Katherine kissed her again, pressing her lips hard against Ryan's.

She growled deep in her throat and pulled Katherine closer, entangling their tongues.

"Okay. Want me to put…" Dick stuck his head out the door, then stopped and let the door slam as he headed back into the house.

"Hey, Dick." She backed away and took Katherine's hand.

"Hey, Ryan. Sorry to interrupt." His face had flushed a bright red.

"No worries. How are the grapes?" she asked. Dick and Terry had one of the largest vineyards in New Mexico, and their wine was well known.

"Pretty good. Hoping for a bit of rain soon though." He stepped out onto the porch again and grabbed Katherine's two bags. "I'll throw these in the back."

"Thank you," Katherine said.

"Oh, ah, throw them in the backseat." Ryan chimed in. "You know, in case that rain you're wanting shows up."

"Course." Dick turned back to Katherine. "You better go tell Terry good-bye."

"I wouldn't dare leave without saying bye," Katherine said, and led Ryan up the steps.

Before she could get to the door, Terry was opening it. "Hey, Ryan."

"Good morning, Terry."

"Well, I guess you're going to take this one away from me now." Terry nodded toward Katherine.

"Unfortunately."

"Terry, thank you so much for having me and taking such good care of me. Can I stay again?" Katherine asked.

"Of course you can. If she won't let you stay with her, I'll keep the light on for you." Terry laughed and gave Katherine a big hug. "Even if you don't, you better come over for breakfast."

"Thank you." Katherine smiled and reached out to hug Dick as he came up the stairs.

"Oh…" Dick backed away in clear surprise but quickly returned the embrace.

"Okay. Now you girls get on the road," Terry said. "Drive safe, Ryan. We'll see you in a few hours."

"Yep. Be right back," she said.

"Bye. I'll see you soon," Katherine said as Ryan led her to the truck.

❖

Katherine jumped up into Ryan's big truck and took a last look around at Terry and Dick's large house. Too bad she hadn't taken advantage of everything this small New Mexico town had to offer. She'd been so busy being angry that she'd missed an opportunity. She turned back to Ryan. Her biggest regret was pushing her away for so long. They could've spent nearly three weeks getting to know each other, instead of having just the past forty-eight hours. She wasn't going to give up on this relationship though.

After they rode the few miles to the edge of town in silence, Katherine reached across the console and took Ryan's hand. "I want to see you again." She waited a few seconds, but Ryan didn't respond "Would you like that, or have I completely misread this?" A pressure began to build at her sternum as she waited for Ryan to say something. Finally, she started to release Ryan's hand, but Ryan held fast.

"Katherine, I would like that more than anything, but…"

"But what?"

"I guess I'm scared. I mean, how can this work? I have a course to run, and you have a tour to follow. We'd hardly see each other."

"Isn't it worth trying?" Tears started building in her eyes. They barely knew each other, but she couldn't discount her strong feelings for Ryan. Almost from the first moment she let Ryan in, even a tiny bit, she had feelings for her.

"I…I guess we can try."

She did pull her hand back this time, with force. "You guess?"

Ryan reached back across the large expanse of her pickup's front seat, but Katherine kept her hands in her lap. "I want to. Yes, Katherine. I want us to see each other. But I'm scared."

She sat quietly for a long time. They were only a few miles from Santa Fe before Katherine finally reacted. She took Ryan's hand again. "Well…you have to try not to be scared. We can do this if we want."

Ryan gripped her hand. "Yes, we can. I'm sorry. Can we make a plan?"

"I'd like that."

During the remainder of the drive, they came up with a plan. She would initiate a daily phone call each day when practice or tournament play was over. Ryan assured her that she would make herself available whenever Katherine called since her schedule was much more flexible. Daily contact sounded great, but the fact that they wouldn't see each other again until the week of the Open disappointed her. Yet she understood that Ryan took great pride in her course, and she couldn't expect her to follow her from tournament to tournament. Besides, Ryan had made it quite clear that she wanted nothing to do with the LPGA tour.

"It might be the longest two weeks of my life," she said.

"No. Now listen to me. You need to concentrate on playing golf. You're ready for this, but don't lose focus." Ryan glanced across the truck before she turned off on the exit to the Albuquerque International Sunport, the name given to the airport in 1963. As funny as it sounded, it had stuck, and even the old-timers called it that now.

"Oh, so now you're my coach? If you switch from girlfriend to coach so quickly, you're going to spin me all around."

"Girlfriend?" Ryan asked and raised her eyes.

"Yeah. Is that okay?"

"I like the sound of it." Ryan slowed to fifteen miles an hour toward the airport parking garage.

"No. Don't park." She spoke sharply.

"What?" Ryan jerked the wheel to drive through to the terminal. "Why?"

"This good-bye is going to be hard enough. I'd rather not make it longer and more painful. Drop me off and give me a kiss I won't forget, and I'll call you when I get to Des Moines." She started to reach for the door handle as Ryan pulled up to the American Airlines terminal doors.

"Okay." Ryan nodded and stopped the truck. They both started jerking items out of the backseat, and Ryan waved over a skycap. A young man who looked to be no more than fifteen rushed over to her. Ryan helped him pack the bags on his cart and then pushed a twenty-dollar bill into his hand. "Take these over. She'll be right there."

"Yes, ma'am."

"Damn. I don't want you to leave." Ryan hugged her close.

"I know. I don't want to." She leaned into Ryan and held her tight. "Two weeks. That's it," she whispered in Ryan's ear.

"Right. Now for that kiss." Ryan gently placed her hand on the side of Katherine's face. Their lips brushed against each other, and she leaned her forehead against Ryan's.

"I knew this was going to be hard." She began to cry and watched tears slowly slide down Ryan's cheeks as well.

"Nah. It's fine." Ryan sniffed. "I'll be in North Carolina before you get there—only a few short days." She smiled and then kissed her passionately. She pulled Ryan into the kiss again when she felt her backing away.

Finally, they broke apart, breathing heavily. "Well, it worked. At least for a few minutes I wasn't thinking about missing you," she said and winked.

"For sure." Ryan backed away and gently pushed her in the direction of the terminal. She watched Ryan wipe tears from her face at the same time she did.

"I'll see you soon," she said and backed away while still grasping Ryan's hand. She held on until she couldn't stretch their arms anymore.

"See you," Ryan said and turned to her truck.

Chapter Twenty-three

"Come on! Get in the hole." Ryan yelled at the TV above the bar. "Get. Get. YES!" She jumped from the bar stool and slapped Eddie and Michael on the back as she jumped around.

"Did she birdie?" Rebecca yelled from the kitchen as she ran in to see the TV.

Ryan grabbed her, lifted her in the air, and spun her around. "Yes! She's tied for the lead."

"Put her down," Eddie said.

"Oh my gosh. Is she trying to kill us?" Rebecca said as Ryan put her feet back on the floor. "She just needs to get this over with."

"She's got this. She's got this, Bec." Ryan squeezed Rebecca, struggling with limited success to hold back her excitement. "Sit with us and watch the rest." She led Rebecca to the bar stool, where she'd been sitting next to Eddie.

"No. I'm going back to the kitchen. I can't stand it." Rebecca rushed away as Ryan watched Katherine walk to the seventeenth hole, while the leader she was tied with walked to number eighteen. She looked amazing. Ryan wanted to pull her out of the television to have her there with them.

"Can we turn it up now?" Michael asked. The bar TV played golf twenty-four seven, but it was rare that anyone actually wanted to have the volume up.

"Yeah." Ryan reached for the remote and hit the unmute button.

"...haven't seen that level of play in over a year." The TV announcer blared obnoxiously until Ryan got the volume adjusted. At a more reasonable tone, they all listened to him say, "What are your thoughts on this, Judy?"

"Word from her coach is she took a little break. As you know, she hasn't played the last three tournaments."

Ryan talked back to the screen. "Stop speculating! She's that good."

Eddie patted her shoulder. "Yes, she is."

The TV went back to the camera on the eighteenth tee, and the announcer started in again. "If Kamerin can take the lead back and keep it, this will be her third win this season."

"She's not going to be at the top of the leaderboard by herself again," Ryan said and jumped out of her chair and paced to the kitchen door. "At least not today." She rushed back to the bar seat as Kamerin Kim hit a perfect drive to the center of the eighteenth fairway.

"Awww." Ryan growled and slapped the bar with her palm.

"Easy now," Eddie said.

The camera was on Katherine, now standing on the seventeenth tee box sighting down the fairway.

"Damn, she looks good," Michael mumbled.

"What did you say?" Ryan glared at the young man.

"Ahh..." He tried to speak but was stopped with an arm across his wrist when the sound of Katherine making contact with her driver caused Ryan to refocus.

As the camera followed the tiny white speck through the air, Ryan mumbled incoherently. Finally, the ball dropped perfectly, less than ninety yards from the green. Katherine was set up for a textbook up and down—chip and putt—on the short par four. If she could stay focused, she'd birdie the hole easily.

"She's got this." Michael tried to engage again.

"Damn right," Ryan said, but continued to stare at the screen.

After the commercial break that lasted way too long, the TV screen was filled with Kamerin Kim holding a long iron. Her drive, while perfectly on line, had fallen short, and she had one hundred and fifty yards to the green.

"Okay, Kamy. Time to shank it," Ryan said. She'd played with Kamerin Kim when she was on the tour and liked her, but not today. Today all she wanted was to see Katherine at the top of the leaderboard.

Miss Kim did not shank it. She hit a perfect line drive that bounced onto the green and inches from the hole. It was pretty much a guaranteed birdie for Kim, but Ryan would have to wait to see, since the network immediately went to another commercial break.

"Oh My F-ing God." Ryan jumped off her stool yet again.

"Did she win?" Rebecca yelled from the kitchen.

"Not yet," Eddie called back.

"Would someone just tell me when she wins?" Rebecca asked.

"Come watch it with us." Ryan stuck her head around the corner into the kitchen.

"And go as crazy as you are?" Rebecca stepped into the dining room. "No, thanks. I have food to prepare."

While the commercial continued, Ryan leaned on the door frame, waiting. "Did you ever watch me play?" she asked Rebecca.

"Not when it was close. I was here watching your mom do the same thing you're doing right now. My nerves couldn't handle it. I'll just wait for the results."

Before Rebecca finished, Ryan was rushing back to the TV, because the first scene after the commercial showed Katherine throwing a few pieces of grass in the air to judge the wind.

"Good girl," Ryan said as she sat back down. "Watch what you're doing. Don't let that drift too far to the left, or you'll be in the sand."

"Um…so you know she can't hear you, right?" Michael stared at her.

"She hears me." Ryan spoke with enough confidence to make Michael tilt his head to question her.

Without a practice swing, Katherine swung her 9-iron, putting her ball high in the air.

"Hold on, turn, turn over, TURN!" Ryan yelled at the TV.

Katherine had misjudged the wind enough to leave the ball nearly twenty feet from the hole.

"Can she make that?" Eddie looked at Ryan.

"Yeah. Yes. Yes, she can make it. We gotta believe."

The TV flipped back to Kamerin Kim tapping in an easy birdie to move to the top of the leaderboard alone once again.

"She can still tie even if she doesn't birdie this hole," Michael said almost as quickly as Kim's ball clanked on the bottom of the cup.

"Dang it." Ryan stood up, anticipating a commercial, but the programming was focused on Katherine yet again.

"Ry." Eddie called her back.

Ryan turned to the screen as Katherine's putter made contact.

The entire bar, which was previously full of murmurs and random conversations, went completely silent. They all watched as the ball moved toward the hole, quickly at first.

"Okay," Ryan whispered.

Then almost as quickly as it shot from her putter, it slowed to barely moving.

"No, no, no, no." Ryan spoke louder and moved closer to the TV. As she was about to turn away to avoid seeing the ball come up short, it picked up speed and made a slight turn toward the cup. "Okay. Keep moving!"

But the ball nearly stopped.

"Oh my God. Are you kidding me?" Rebecca said from right behind Eddie. She'd snuck in when she heard all the excitement but quickly returned to the kitchen.

"Woo. You scared the crap out of me, woman," Eddie said. He put his arm around her and pulled her close to him. Ryan turned to pace back toward the kitchen.

"Look." Michael yelled and pointed to the TV.

They all watched as the ball slowly crept toward the hole and finally…dropped over the edge.

"She's tied." Eddie was the one to jump off his chair this time. "Easy birdie for the win."

"Okay, all right." Ryan nodded and began jumping around with Eddie.

"She won?" Rebecca yelled.

"Almost," Eddie and Ryan called back in unison.

"Would you two stop hopping around and just tell me when she wins." Rebecca said.

"Another commercial!" someone in the bar called out, clearly as excited and frustrated with the network TV as Ryan was.

"This place hasn't been so packed watching a tournament since you played, Ryan," Charlie Parker said.

Ryan smiled and nodded. The last thing she wanted was for this to be about her. The woman she was in love with was about to win her first tournament in months. This was all about Katherine.

Finally, the commercial ended, and the TV was filled with a close-up of Katherine walking to the eighteenth tee. She had on her white ball cap from the Los Alamos course, with her silky yellow hair pulled through the hole in the back. Since her sponsors had left her, she could wear whatever she wanted. Ryan was pleased to see her in the hat she'd given her. Not because it was going to bring any business to New Mexico, but because most players would've continued to wear their sponsor's gear in hopes they'd take them back after a good round. Ryan knew there were golf companies out there regretting the decision to pull their contract with Katherine Reese. That made her happy because she hated how fickle they were and how easily they'd drop you if you struggled through a tough season.

"Has she hit her drive yet?" Rebecca yelled again.

"No. Dang it, Bec. Get out here and watch it with us." Ryan backed up to the kitchen so as not to turn her back on the screen, but before she could get all the way to the kitchen, Katherine hit a long, perfect drive to the center of the eighteenth fairway. Ryan screamed with several others in the bar, including Eddie and Michael. The entire room was cheering for Katherine to win.

"No commercial!" Michael yelled at the screen.

His command appeared to work, because instead of seeing a golf-ball advertisement, they all watched Katherine walk down the fairway. One of the cameramen was right next to her, and she asked her caddie, "One twenty to the pin?" But before her caddie answered, she turned to the camera and said, "This is for you, Ryan."

She couldn't help but smile as tears rolled down her cheeks and the announcer began to speculate. "I'm not sure who she's talking to, but perhaps she's referring to Ryan Gibbs, who played exceptional golf for nearly three seasons and then disappeared."

"Yes, she is, you idiot. Stop talking." Ryan scolded the announcer as if he could hear her.

She watched Katherine reach for an iron, unsure from the angle, but she thought it was a 7-iron. "That's too much club, Katherine. Use your eight. What the hell's her caddie doing?"

"It *is* an eight," Michael said.

"Are you sure?" Ryan asked as Katherine made contact with her iron. The camera followed the ball straight up in the air, and the whole room stared at the TV as it landed so softly on the green it looked like someone had placed it on a pillow.

"Look." Michael grabbed Ryan's arm. The ball was less than six inches from the edge of the hole.

Ryan nodded and sat in her seat. "Bec, you can come out now. She's won!"

"Really?" Rebecca trotted in from the kitchen and stood next to Ryan and Eddie. They all watched as Katherine's playing partner finished the hole so she could tap in her putt for the win. And she did exactly that, finishing four under par and winning outright by one stroke.

❖

"Did you see it?" Katherine practically yelled into the phone as soon as Ryan picked up. "I felt like my old self again. I enjoyed every single shot. I had so much fun. I owe it all to you."

"Katherine, I had nothing to do with it. You did this. You played amazing golf. I can't wait to see you win the Open next week."

"I can't wait to see *you*." Katherine started firing questions. "Do you have your tickets yet? Are you bringing your clubs? Oh my gosh, when do you arrive? I can't wait. I'm so excited."

"I finalized the purchase before you started playing today. No, I'm not bringing my clubs, and I should arrive around three in the afternoon."

"I'll be there to pick you up."

"You don't need to do that. I'll meet you at the hotel. You'll be practicing. Just send Mags."

"I can take a break to pick you up, and I'm not sending Maggie to pick you up by herself." Katherine laughed. "I don't trust her."

Ryan changed the topic. "I'm so proud of you. That was amazing golf today."

"Thanks to you. I don't think I've ever felt so confident on the course and so relaxed. You know I didn't care one bit if I won or lost," Katherine said. "But enough about golf. I miss you so much. I can't wait to wrap my legs around your sexy body."

"Stop that. You'll drive me crazy."

Chapter Twenty-four

Ryan felt the humidity as soon as she exited the tiny airplane. It was so small they had to disembark from stairs on the tarmac. The air was like a weight compared to the low-humidity, high-altitude air in New Mexico. She was beginning to sweat even before getting inside the terminal. Despite the size of the plane she'd flown in on, the airport was pretty big, and Ryan entered from the last gate in the terminal. The long walk allowed her plenty of time to grow nervous.

She hurried down the hallway, watching familiar airport shops pass by: Hudson News, Brooks Brothers, The Body Shop. Weaving through passengers focused on their phones or their kids was a bit like being on an obstacle course. Ryan was so anxious, almost sick to her stomach at the anticipation of seeing Katherine. It had been only eleven days since she'd left her at the Sunport, but it felt like so much longer. Each day had crawled like the end of a long workday. She felt a little like Fred Flintstone waiting to slide down the dinosaur.

She forced herself to walk; it wouldn't be a good idea to run through the airport. She didn't want to freak out the TSA agents, but as she approached the exit and noticed the overweight woman bursting out of her blue uniform, staring into space, she was sure she could've run through with guns hanging on both hips. That barely present woman wouldn't have noticed.

As she crossed through the security gate, she saw Katherine standing at the dotted line waiting for her arrival. She looked so radiant, Ryan actually paused for a second to admire the tall, athletic woman she'd fallen in love with. Her blond hair hanging loose around her face highlighted her tanned skin. It was normally in a ponytail to be out of her face when she played golf, but Ryan loved seeing it down. She looked casual and relaxed, not the intense golfer who had won an LPGA tournament last week.

Without a word, Ryan walked into Katherine's arms and they kissed—casually at first—but when she felt Katherine's tongue along her lower lip, she was all in. She pulled Katherine to her and felt her warmth and curves. If they'd been in a private room nearby, she was sure she could've had Katherine undressed in three seconds.

Finally, they both backed away, making every effort to control their breathing. Perhaps they both realized where they were and the futility of driving each other crazy in the middle of the airport. They'd drawn a bit of attention with their obvious public display, but most people were moving on. "You look amazing. I can't wait to get my hands all over you." Ryan spoke softly in Katherine's ear.

"Stop that. It's hard enough to control myself." Katherine leaned in for a quick kiss. "I'm so happy to see you. I've missed you so much."

"Me too. Can we get out of here?" Ryan gently turned Katherine toward the exit.

Before they even started moving, a man spoke to her. "Ryan Gibbs! Can't wait to see you play this week."

Ryan started to speak, but Katherine moved her away. "Do you have bags?"

"What? Oh, no. Just this carry-on." She followed Katherine. "What was that all about?"

"What?" Katherine asked.

"That guy."

"Oh, he probably just recognized you." Katherine sped up, forcing Ryan to increase her pace.

"Hey, slow down. Is something wrong?" She stopped Katherine.

"Well… Ahh… Follow me. We need to talk to you."

"We? Do you have a mouse in the car?" She held on to Katherine's arm and wouldn't let her move.

"Not exactly a mouse."

"What the hell are you talking about?"

"Please, Ryan. Just follow me, and we'll explain."

"Who's we?" Ryan continued to stand still.

"Please," Katherine said and lightly pulled away.

She finally acquiesced and followed Katherine through the parking garage, then watched as Katherine walked toward a white Escalade. As they got closer, she could tell the engine was running and could even see someone in the driver's seat, but she didn't know who it was until Katherine opened the passenger door and held it open for her. She looked at the driver, then back to Katherine for an explanation, but no one spoke.

"Mags?"

"Hi, Ryan."

"Hi. Umm… Does someone want to tell me what's going on?" She looked back to Katherine.

"Aren't you glad to see me, Ryan?" Maggie finally got out of the vehicle and walked around to give Ryan a hug.

"Well, Maggie, to be completely honest, I was hoping for some time alone with my girlfriend." She turned back to Katherine again, who'd managed to slink in behind Maggie. "Katherine, I thought we'd have a few hours together."

Maggie spoke quickly. "I'm here, so don't get mad at Katherine." She started to respond, but Maggie went on. "While we both agreed, I'm the one who asked her to keep it a secret."

"What the…? What are you talking about?" She put her palm on the door frame and stared down at Maggie.

"I registered you for the Open." Maggie paused for a minute, but before Ryan could gather her thoughts, she went on. "It's all done. You tee off at ten fifteen tomorrow morning. You were exempt from qualification rounds due to your previous pro-tournament success and LPGA tour card. You know you're ready. You—" Because of her pro status she didn't have to play in any qualification rounds like other players since the tournament was open to anyone who qualified, not just professional golfers.

"Wait, wait, wait. I'm not playing in the tournament. I'm here to watch Katherine." This time she physically moved Maggie out of the way so she could see Katherine.

"Maybe we should drive to the hotel and talk there. We can sit down and get out of the heat." Katherine gently pushed her into the passenger seat and nodded at Maggie, who took the hint and went back to the driver's side.

Inside the car, she sat quietly for a few minutes until Maggie left the parking garage. When they were driving down the highway, Ryan finally spoke. "This is ridiculous. I haven't played tournament golf in over two years. I can't play in the Open. I'd make a fool of myself."

Katherine started to speak, but Maggie interrupted. "A fool? Seriously, you're at the top of your game, and you've played Pinehurst before. It's the perfect time for you to compete. You can win."

"Let's assume that BS is true, but I'm not playing against Katherine. She's ready to win her major."

"I'm not playing."

CHAPTER TWENTY-FIVE

Ryan spun around in her seat. "What? This is it. It's what you've wanted."

"No. It's what Marie wanted. I want to write books and play an occasional round of golf with my amazing girlfriend and watch her win the major *she* deserves."

Ryan began to finally understand everything they'd been saying to her. "Wow. I don't know what to think. I'm not sure if I'm mad or interested."

"I know. I'm sorry we surprised you with this, but I knew you'd say no if we told you about it in advance." She touched Ryan's shoulder.

"And what's to keep me from saying no now?"

"Nothing." She paused and then leaned forward and spoke softly in Ryan's ear. "But would you do it for me?"

"I don't have my clubs. This is crazy. I can't play in a major tournament without training and with unfamiliar clubs and…it's not real."

Maggie spoke up. "We have your clubs." Before Ryan could ask, she went on. "Eddie sent them on the flight you just came in on."

"Seriously!"

"Yeah. Apparently he knows someone. He took them to the airport, got them tagged as yours, and I just picked them up. Anyway, they're in the back, and you've trained every day for the last two years. You're as prepared as you ever were. You're ready."

❖

The two-hour drive from the airport passed quickly, with Katherine and Maggie assuring Ryan that she could win, but when Maggie admitted that she'd told a sports commentator, the last few minutes of the drive had crawled by in silence. Katherine was beginning to worry that they'd miscalculated.

As they were pulling into the Hilton parking lot, Ryan finally spoke—short and to the point. "So this is all settled then. I don't get a say." And Katherine knew they'd made a mistake. Ryan jumped out before Maggie had completely stopped the vehicle and grabbed her carry-on. She practically ran toward the doors of the hotel.

"Ry, wait!" Katherine caught up to her.

Ryan stopped but didn't turn around. When Katherine reached her, she just stared at her.

"I'm sorry. This was a mistake."

"Yeah, it was. I can't believe you would do this to me. You know how I feel about the tour." Ryan started walking again.

"I do, but I thought…" Katherine stopped herself. "Then don't do it. I'm sorry. I…"

"Don't do it? Just like that? My name is mud on tour as it is. Now, I'm just not going to show after the LPGA world has been told I'll be there. So how does that work?"

She stepped up beside Ryan. "If you don't want to have anything to do with the tournament, then who cares what they think?"

Ryan shook her head, then pushed the revolving door and kept walking. She followed and made it through the door herself in time to hear her ask for a room.

"There are no more rooms, Ryan." She stood next to her by the counter.

"She's right, ma'am," the receptionist said. "I'm sorry."

Katherine guided Ryan away from the counter for some privacy. “You’re so mad, you don’t even want to stay with me?” She fought to keep from crying, but little pools of tears built in her eyes.

Ryan looked away. “I need some time. Apparently, I need to be ready to tee off at ten in the morning.”

Maggie came in and walked up to them. “Listen, Ryan. Don’t blame her. I did this.”

Katherine turned to place herself between the two women. “Mags, please just go.”

“Yeah. You’ve done enough.” Ryan reached for her phone. Maggie stopped talking but didn’t leave.

“What are you doing?” Katherine took Ryan by the shoulders and turned her toward her.

“I need some time.” Ryan headed to the door.

“So we’ll see you tomorrow?” Maggie called out.

“Mags! Enough!” Katherine cried and chased Ryan. “Stay in my room. I’ll stay with Maggie. There’s no rooms this week. You know that.”

Ryan turned back around but said nothing.

“Please.” Katherine took the handle of Ryan’s bag and started tugging it toward the elevators.

Ryan followed, with Maggie behind her, and they all got into the elevator and rode up in silence.

“Just take my room. I have somewhere I can go,” Maggie said to Ryan, then rushed out of the elevator and swiped her key on the third door from the end. “I’ll get my stuff out of here.” They all walked in, and Ryan and Katherine stood by the door while Maggie threw her items into a large duffel bag. As she walked past them, she said, “Ryan, don’t make the mistake of ruining what you have with Katherine over this. I hope I see you in the morning.”

They watched her leave. “Here’s your bag. I guess I’ll see you…well…when I see you. I’m right there.” Katherine pointed to the door across the hall. “In case you change your mind and want to be with me, I’m sorry.” She turned and swiped her own key.

CHAPTER TWENTY-SIX

Ryan stood in the empty room. She could faintly smell Maggie's cologne, which had a little hint of bergamot. She remembered it from when they were on the tour together and when they were more than coach and player. If she hadn't been so angry, it would've been comforting.

"What the hell am I supposed to do now?" She plopped down on the king-sized bed and found herself face-to-face with her image staring back at her in the full-length mirror.

After only a few minutes, the walls started to close in, so she grabbed her wallet and phone and ran out. She rushed down the hall so Katherine wouldn't see or hear her. The Uber driver was there within minutes of requesting a car. He dropped her off at a place called Drum and Quill, but it was so packed, she just kept walking. A couple of blocks later, she was seated at an equally crowded place, Dugan's Pub, but she was able to find a seat, and the ale was smooth—even a little relaxing—until someone recognized her. It would only happen when the few diehard LPGA fans were all in the same place together. She smiled and nodded as the guy explained to his friends who she was, but when he offered to buy her another beer, she excused herself and continued to walk around the quaint little town. Somehow before she finally pushed the Uber app again to go back to the hotel, it was dark. If she intended to play tomorrow, she should've spent the daylight hours familiarizing herself with the course.

Back at the hotel she convinced herself that she could sleep, but after several hours of flopping around restlessly on the bed and pacing the few feet from the door to the window of the hotel room, she finally put on a pair of jeans and walked across the hall. She was knocking lightly on the door before she glanced at her watch and realized it was almost two in the morning. After waiting a couple of minutes and realizing it was too late, or was it too early, she started to return to her room.

But the door opened, and Katherine spoke before she could get back into her room. "Hi."

"Hi. I didn't realize what time it was until after I knocked." She noticed immediately that Katherine's eyes were bloodshot, and her face was flushed. "You've been crying."

"I'm fine."

Ryan gently stroked the side of her cheek. "I'm so sorry. I may have overreacted."

"No. I was wrong. I thought I knew what was best. I'd like to blame it on Maggie, but I could've told you—should have." A tear slid down her face.

She pulled Katherine into her arms. "Can I come in?"

"Mmm-hmm." Katherine held her close and walked them together back into her room. Ryan kicked the door closed with her heel and continued to hold Katherine. "I don't even know what to say." Katherine spoke softly in her ear.

"Nothing needs to be said." She began to back her toward the bed. As she did, she noticed that the blankets and sheets looked a lot like the ones on the bed she was trying to sleep in, all wrinkled and crumpled. In the background, she heard CSPAN droning on.

Katherine let go and bent to straighten the blankets and pillows. "I couldn't sleep." She pushed the button on the remote, and the monotone voices halted. "Here, sit." She backed out of the way.

"I'd rather lie here and hold you," she said, and the corners of her mouth tipped up a little. This was where she'd wanted to be all day. "Maybe we can at least rest. Tomorrow will be brutal if I don't get any sleep." She sat down, pushed herself up to the head of the bed, and moved a pillow under her head before she reached out for Katherine to join her.

"You're going?" Katherine climbed in and laid her head on Ryan's shoulder. "Oh my gosh, Ryan. You feel amazing. I've missed you so much, and all I wanted was for us to be together, and I was such an idiot. I shouldn't—"

"Stop. I just want to hold you. I've missed you too." She squeezed Katherine to her.

"Can I say one thing, and then I'll stop." Katherine looked up at her.

"Okay." She didn't want to talk at all, but Katherine obviously needed this.

"I thought you were blaming the tour for your loss. I thought if you played again, you'd want to come back. Ryan, I've watched you play from the minute I found out who you were, and I've been in awe."

"Aw. I thought all you wanted to do was beat me." Ryan laughed.

"Okay, yeah. I was struggling with my own loss, but there was never a question of your natural skills. And you love the game. I thought I knew best, but more than that, I'm in love with you, and for most of the day today, I was sure I'd lost you, and I never want to feel that way again. I just…"

"Wait. You said you love me."

"I do love you."

"I love you too." She pulled Katherine up to her and kissed her. "No more talking."

They made love—soft and tender. It wasn't the hot passion Ryan had imagined, but it was better—gently touching and loving every inch of Katherine's sexy body and expressing deeply how she felt. Sometime soon after their lovemaking, they both fell asleep.

When she finally heard Katherine's phone buzzing on the dresser, she could tell it was light outside and started to run and get dressed and find a way to the golf course. Instead, she slowly slipped out of bed. However, she couldn't manage to get up without waking Katherine.

"Where are you going?" she asked.

"Your phone."

"Leave it. Come back to bed." Katherine held out her bare arm and exposed her full breasts.

As tempted as she was to lie back down with Katherine, the realization of the looming tournament wouldn't allow her to. "Shit. It's Maggie." She answered it. "What time is it?" She started grabbing clothes they had discarded one by one around the bed.

"Ryan, holy shit. I didn't believe you wouldn't show. Seriously." Maggie was actually calmer than Ryan expected.

"Is it too late?"

"No." Maggie's excitement returned. "It's eight o'clock. I'll be there in fifteen minutes. You still have time."

"Okay." She clicked off, surprised at her own calmness. She'd expected to have already been on the course hitting balls and putting for a couple of hours by now but wouldn't have exchanged the last two hours with Katherine even for a guaranteed win. Yet all of a sudden, she was feeling the pressure. She had a love/hate relationship with that feeling. Right now, it was mostly hate because she was about to run to hit golf balls instead of being with the woman she loved.

She finished dressing—more quickly now—and reached down to kiss Katherine. "You got me into this. You have to watch me play."

"Only if you're doing it because you want to."

She nodded. "I'll see you in a couple of hours. Oh, and there's a voice mail on your phone." She handed Katherine her phone before she rushed out.

CHAPTER TWENTY-SEVEN

Katherine sat up and pushed the voice-mail button and listened to the deep male voice on the recording. "Ms. Rivers…oh, I mean Ms. Reese. I forget that's your pen name. This is Jacob Mathers of HarperCollins. I talked with your agent this morning, and she asked me to call you directly. We're sending over a contract tomorrow for your current book, with an option for three more. I'm excited to work with you. You have my contact information if you have questions. Your agent will be in touch. Congratulations."

Katherine couldn't help but smile. She'd hoped for one of the big five but would've been happy just to get it published. She knew it was good. A part of her wanted to call Teri, her agent, and find out the details, but it wasn't about the money, and she had some golf to watch. Today was going to be a great day after all.

After showering and dressing, she rushed out to drive to the course. Even though she'd dropped out of the tournament, she still had her pass. Despite the late hour, she was sure she could get in the venue and park with plenty of time to reach the first hole before Ryan teed off. But she hadn't considered how heavy the traffic would be. Most of the big names wouldn't tee off until afternoon, so the crowds had delayed their arrival, and now it seemed they were all trying to get in at once.

❖

"Where is she?" Ryan tapped her new Titlist on the handle of her driver. "Something's wrong. She said she'd be here."

"They're going to call your name in a minute. You need to chill out." Maggie stood next to her. She'd insisted on caddying for her, even though Ryan put up a bit of a fight, insisting she didn't need a caddie.

"If she doesn't show, I'm not teeing off. I'm going to find her." She started to pull her head cover back over her driver as the announcer called the first name in her threesome.

"Seriously, Ryan! She'll be here." Maggie took the driver and removed the cover again.

Ryan was walking in circles to the left of the tee box. "Mags, get your player in line." The caddie for Jennifer Sawyer, the golfer who was about to tee off, scolded Maggie.

"Ryan."

She spun at the whisper of her name and saw Katherine nudging her way up to the yellow nylon rope.

"Oh, thank God." Ryan reached for her.

Katherine bent over the rope and kissed her. "Good luck. You got this."

She nodded and took her driver from Maggie as the announcer called her name. "Teeing off at 10:10 is Ryan Gibbs of Los Alamos, New Mexico. Twelve-time LPGA tour champion."

Ryan placed her ball and sighted down the long, straight par four. She set up to it, and without a practice swing or the slightest hesitation, she swung away. The bright-white Titleist launched into the air.

"In the hole," someone yelled as soon as her club made contact with the ball, and then the rest of the crowd responded with obnoxious cheers. Ryan watched the ball draw slightly at the exact curve of the number-one dog leg and roll past her competitor's ball in the center of the fairway.

Ryan heard above the other cheers, "I love you, Ryan Gibbs." She smiled and handed Maggie her driver and walked toward her ball like she'd done a thousand times before. The ease and familiarity with which she fell into the groove surprised yet comforted her.

After nine holes, Ryan was three over par and tied for sixtieth. As she walked around the end of the ninth green to reach number ten, Katherine caught up with her.

"How do you feel?" Katherine asked.

"Actually, not too bad, considering my score. Maggie is about to have a cow, but I'm just having a little trouble with the greens. They're so different from the ones back home, and I had no time to practice here." Ryan stopped a minute to talk to her. There was less of a crowd now, so they could actually get to each other pretty easily over the rope. At the beginning of the round, her old reputation had drawn a decent crowd, but her disappointing play had caused the fickle group to find more successful players to follow.

"You're doing great. Your swing looks amazing and…" Katherine used encouraging words.

"Katherine, it's okay. I'm out here, and you're right. It feels good." She squeezed Katherine's hand. "I gotta go. I might not make the cut, but I gotta try."

Katherine nodded and let her leave.

Maggie was a few steps behind and called out to her as she approached the tee box. "Listen, you can pick up those three strokes if you just settle down."

She stopped in front of the tee box and spun around, stopping Maggie. "Really? Settle down. That's your advice? You're one of the most sought-after swing coaches in the LPGA, and the way I make up three strokes is to settle down?"

"Your putting sucks. I've never seen you three-putt so many times in one round, especially in only nine holes."

"Yeah. Perhaps not being familiar with the greens might be the real problem. Not playing a professional tournament in over two years might have something to do with it too. Did you really expect me to walk out here for the first time in two years and win?" She reached for her driver.

"I guess I did," Maggie admitted. "I'm sorry, Ryan. I just realized what a shitty thing I did." Maggie tugged at her arm to get her to look at her.

"Well, Mags, we're in it now." She tried to turn away, but Maggie held on to her.

"No. You can drop out. You don't have to do this."

"Are you too embarrassed to finish with me?"

"Of course not." Maggie shook her head.

"Then come on and tell me where to put this ball. I'm having too much fun to quit." She led Maggie up on the tee, where her playing partners were waiting for her.

Chapter Twenty-eight

"Do you want to watch the rest of the tournament tomorrow?" Katherine asked as she reached across the heavily starched linen tablecloth to hold Ryan's hand. She had made plans for this dinner even before Maggie had convinced her that Ryan should play in the Open.

"Actually, I'd rather spend the rest of the weekend with you," Ryan said. She hadn't made the cut after Friday's play, and they now had the whole weekend to spend together. Even though she'd adjusted to the greens and was playing much better on Friday, she'd fallen too far behind on Thursday to catch up.

"Hmm. I'm glad to hear that," Katherine said. "You were so close Friday."

"Yeah, well, one below or fifty below—it's all below the cut. That's okay. I truly did have fun, and I'll never tell Maggie, but I'm glad the two of you made me play."

"I'm so relieved. So back on the tour?" Katherine smiled and held up her wineglass to toast. "It's where you belong. The way you were out there this week—it was like you'd never left."

Ryan raised her glass and clinked it with Katherine's. "Yeah. I hope you're right. I have to tell Rebecca and Eddie, and the board is going to kill me. Also, I'm going to need some sponsors. I don't know. I hope I'm not making a mistake."

"You're not. So what's the plan?"

"Well, as soon as we finish dinner, I plan to lock you in that hotel room for at least the next twenty-four hours," she said and winked.

"Hmm. That sounds nice, but I was thinking a little more long-term."

"Maggie is probably on the phone right now trying to get me a sponsor, but even if she doesn't, we're going to prep for Newtown Square, Pennsylvania in two weeks. That will give me time to put something in place for Los Alamos and prepare a little better than I did for this tournament. Will you come back with me? You could help me get ready, and you'd have plenty of quiet time to write."

"I'd love to, but I've been wanting to tell you something. I wanted to wait until the Open was over so you could focus."

"Oh." Ryan hesitated. "What is it?"

"It's not bad, but I can't go back to New Mexico with you. I sold my second book."

Ryan jumped up and pulled Katherine out of her seat into a big hug. "That's awesome. I'm so happy for you. I haven't even read the first one yet." Several patrons turned to stare, so Katherine quickly guided her back to her chair.

"Ah…well, yes, you have."

"What? I'd remember if I read a Katherine Reese book." Ryan released her, and they both sat down.

"Yeah, but I saw a K.T. Rivers book on your chair the first time I went to your house." Katherine held out some business cards she'd already had made at a local printer—K.T. Rivers, Author, HarperCollins Publishing.

"You're K.T. Rivers? I loved that book. And HarperCollins. Katherine, that's amazing." It was hard to contain her excitement.

"Yeah, so I have to go sign a contract and start book three. They're expecting three more from me. They want the next one in a year. It's going to take a lot of focused work."

"I'm so happy for you. This is where you should be." She took both of Katherine's hands in hers and squeezed.

"Yeah, but we're probably going to be separated a lot. I won't be able to follow you on tour, at least not all the time."

"Oh." Ryan nodded. "I guess I should've known that, but you know I don't have to play every tournament. We could work out some kind of more reasonable schedule so we can see each other."

"Well, we can talk about that later, but you need to play—now, while you're at the top of your game." Their waitress brought two Caesar salads and set a shrimp cocktail between them.

"Yeah. Let's talk about it later," Ryan said.

❖

Time flew after Ryan got back to New Mexico. Katherine had been keeping Rebecca and Eddie informed, so there were no surprises. They were extremely encouraging when Ryan arrived back in Los Alamos. She was surprised that the golf-club board of directors was excited for her as well. They'd always used Ryan as part of their marketing, whether she was there or not. Her being back on tour was a good thing for the club. The board agreed that Eddie could run the course until they could find a new pro.

Ryan was relieved that she hadn't made anyone angry with her crazy antics, but she was also a little disappointed to find that she was so easy to replace. After a bit of logistics to arrange for her house to be cared for and bills to be paid automatically, she was ready to go in only a few days.

"So when do you leave?" Rebecca asked while pouring them each a cup of coffee.

"I fly out to San Diego to spend the weekend with Katherine on Friday, and I'll be off to PA on Monday." She took a quick sip of coffee. "Can you believe I'll be back on the tour in less than a week?"

"I'm so happy for you." Rebecca sat next to her, and they watched the driving range from Ryan's favorite table as regulars hit balls before going out to play a round.

"I'm going to miss this." She nodded toward the range. "And you, Bec. What will I do without you? And I won't get to see you get all big and pregnant."

"Oh, Ry. I'm going to miss you so much too. It's been so good having you back home with us, but you belong on the tour." She rubbed her belly. "I'll send you pictures, and maybe you can take a week off when he or she is born."

"Of course I will."

CHAPTER TWENTY-NINE

Ryan's American Airlines' flight touched down at San Diego's International Airport almost ten minutes early. Phones all around her started binging almost as soon as the flight attendant gave the passengers permission to turn on their electronic devices. It took her old phone a little longer to connect to service than her neighbors', but as soon as it did, she saw the text she was hoping for.

I'm in the cell-phone waiting lot. Text me when you land, and I'll pull up at arrivals. I can't wait to see you.

She smiled. She couldn't stop herself. For some reason, she was as nervous to see Katherine today as she had been when she arrived in North Carolina only three weeks ago. She'd planned for a week of cheering and watching Katherine win. Wow. Had it turned out differently than what she'd expected.

In three weeks she'd gone from I'm-never-playing-on-tour-again to playing in the most important major in the LPGA tour. If someone had bet her everything she owned, she'd be homeless right now. She'd said no way would she ever go back on tour, but here she was getting ready to play in a regular season tournament in just a few days. First, though, she planned to spend time with Katherine. Their feelings were clear, but they still didn't know about each other and had so much to share.

She kept looking at her watch. Like the last few days at home, when she was getting Eddie ready to take over and didn't have anything to do because he'd spent the last two years teaching her, time wouldn't move. And neither would the passenger in the aisle seat next to her.

"I'm sorry. You don't mind waiting, do you?" The woman she'd sat next to quietly the entire flight pointed at her ankle wrapped in a black medical boot. "I'm so slow going down the aisle. I don't want to make anyone angry."

"No. I don't mind. We all get out eventually, right?" She turned on her winning smile, even though she wanted to say, "Oh, yes, I mind. The most beautiful girl in the world is waiting for me, and I'm trapped here behind you."

"You're right. I can never understand why everyone wants to push and shove to get out so quickly," the lady said while turning half around to see the passengers standing in the aisle.

"Mmm." Ryan grunted as she finished her text.

Stuck in the plane a bit longer. Give me another ten minutes.

The line was finally moving, but when she looked back behind her, she saw several more people still waiting.

Involuntarily, her leg started bouncing. The lady next to her must've felt the movement because she looked over at her. "It won't be long now. I'm sorry. Are you waiting to see someone special?"

Ryan put her hand on her knee and stopped the motion. "Yes, but I can wait. We have the whole weekend together."

"As soon as these folks get by, I'll let you go so you won't have to wait on me," the woman said. "What's your name? I can't believe we sat next to each other the whole way, and I didn't even get it. You seemed pretty interested in all those papers. I figured you were working and didn't want to be disturbed. I'm Sally."

"Oh. I'm sorry. I guess I was a bit preoccupied. My name is Ryan." She watched the last person go by.

"Well, Ryan, looks like you can get out now." Sally pulled herself out of the seat and moved back so Ryan could get out. "Enjoy your visit, Ryan."

"Thank you. You too." She jumped up and took long strides toward the front of the plane, but before she reached first-class, she stopped and turned back toward Sally. She watched for a split second as she tried to get her bag down from the overhead storage compartment, but her short legs and restricted movement were making it difficult. Ryan jogged back and lifted the case out with ease. "I forgot my manners for a second." She sat the bag on its wheels.

"Oh, thank you. You didn't have to do that."

Ryan stepped to the side, holding both her bag and Sally's. "You go ahead."

Sally nodded and moved through the aisle as quickly as she could. Ryan started tugging the bags slowly behind her. As soon as they reached the jetway, Sally tried to take her bag. "Thank you."

"Is someone meeting you in the terminal?" Ryan held onto the bag.

"Yes. My son and his new baby girl." Sally's face lit up.

"Then I'll take it."

She had to meet Sally's new granddaughter, and it took far more than the ten minutes she'd promised Katherine, but she felt better for having helped.

As she jogged through the exit doors, she realized she had no idea what Katherine drove. She grabbed her phone to send a text as she scanned the long line of vehicles outside the terminal.

"Ryan," Katherine called. "Ryan! Over here."

She turned at the sound of her name to see Katherine standing in front of what appeared to be a brand-new BMW convertible. Ryan trotted quickly over to the car. "Nice ride." She pretended to give it special attention, sliding her hand along the aerodynamic lines.

"Hey. Run those hands along these curves instead." Katherine stood up straight and pushed her chest out. The V-neck tee shirt she wore exposed an ample amount of cleavage, and Ryan forgot the car.

"Hmm. Well, if you put it like that." She pulled Katherine into a hug. "You look amazing, and you feel even better." She tightened her grip slightly to feel Katherine against her. As she ran her hands down Katherine's back to her tight, round ass, Katherine took her face in her hands and kissed her. It was exactly the greeting she was hoping for. Katherine's tongue pushed gently between her teeth, and she met it with her own. That familiar rush when she was close to Katherine filled her, but before Ryan could move her hand to the bottom of Katherine's shirt to slide it up her side to feel her soft flesh, someone abruptly interrupted them.

"Ladies, is this your Beemer?" The airport security guard was standing uncomfortably close to them.

They both jumped and backed away from each other. Then Katherine responded. "Yes."

"This is a pickup area, not a parking lot. You'll need to move the car." According to the name tag on his shirt, his name was Miller.

"I was greeting the person I was picking up," Katherine said and smiled at the guard. He nodded but stood firm in his place. "Okay, we're leaving." Katherine directed Ryan to the passenger door.

Katherine pulled out and headed toward the exit. "Oh, dang it. I was going to let you drive," Katherine said as she hit the interstate and began moving quickly through the gears.

"I'm enjoying watching." She stared at Katherine's tanned legs, exposed high on the thigh in her short shorts. "You're hot when you drive a fast car."

After about thirty minutes of driving up I-5 with the sun and breeze on their faces, Katherine turned into the tiny one-car garage under her condo.

"Woo, it's a tight fit." Ryan carefully opened the door to avoid hitting the concrete walls.

"Yeah, sorry. Did I give you enough room? It's the only thing I don't like about this place," Katherine said as she reached across the open car to grab one of Ryan's bags. As she did, Ryan had an amazing view as her shirt gaped open. She stood there without moving while Katherine strained to stretch across the car. "A little help here."

"Mmm-hmm." Ryan still didn't move.

Katherine finally looked up. "What…Oh, I see." She stood back up.

Ryan lifted out her bags. "Can you blame me?" She smiled and waited for Katherine to lead the way into her home.

"No. I guess not. I've been told they're nice to look at." Katherine walked to the door, unlocked it, and held it for Ryan to walk in. "If you're lucky, you'll get to do more than look."

Ryan dropped the suitcase and computer bag on the floor of the big open kitchen she'd just walked into and spun to catch Katherine. "How about now?" She was aware of the curves she'd just admired pressed against her, causing her to heat from head to toe. She pulled Katherine into a tender kiss until it wasn't. Their lips parted, then met again. She tilted her head to gain better access, and then she could no longer hold back. She ran her tongue over Katherine's lips and heard a small sound as she moved her hand under her blouse to caress the soft skin there. They both moaned as Ryan slipped her tongue through Katherine's lips and slowly explored Katherine's mouth as their tongues intertwined. Pleasure rushed through her as Katherine offered her more, opening her lips, so Ryan deepened the kiss.

❖

While they were still kissing, Katherine started slowly pushing Ryan toward the living room to the stairs leading to the bedroom. Finally, she broke away from the kiss and led Ryan up the stairs, walking backward so they could be face-to-face. She watched Ryan's long, muscular, bronzed legs as she slowly followed. Ryan was slim and athletic, but her hips had just enough roundness to emphasize her femininity, and Katherine nearly stumbled as she admired the woman inches from her. Also, she couldn't help but notice that Ryan remained focused on the cleavage that was even more exposed after Ryan had stretched her shirt for greater access.

When they reached the top of the stairs, she turned forward and led Ryan to the master bedroom. It took up most of the second floor, with only one small guest room across the hall. Huge and bright, it had windows facing the ocean and a sliding-glass door leading to a large deck. She had spent the morning setting up candles she'd intended to light and spreading rose petals in a path leading to the bed. She'd even set out wineglasses and an ice bucket for wine. As soon as they entered, Ryan turned to take it all in. "Oh my God, Katherine. This is amazing, and this room is bigger than my whole house. It's—"

She spun around and stopped Ryan's words with a rough, demanding kiss. The candles would not be lit, and the wine would remain in the refrigerator. Katherine didn't want to wait another minute for Ryan. They'd have time for the fantasy later—this couldn't wait. Their kiss continued to underscore a seemingly endless need. Ryan returned it with the same passion Katherine had initiated. As she tasted Ryan's sweet mouth, Ryan's hand slipped under her blouse—this time with success. She felt a rumble in Ryan's kiss. Ryan leaned back long enough for her to see her hunger reflected. Three weeks was too long to be apart. As she reached for the button on Ryan's jeans, Ryan pulled Katherine's tank top over her head. Freed of her blouse, she quickly unbuttoned Ryan's shirt while blazing a trail of kisses down her neck and across her shoulder as she removed her shirt. She threaded her fingers through Ryan's short hair, her breath growing more ragged and the kisses greedier.

When they finally ended the kiss to come up for air, Katherine licked her lips to replenish some of the moisture. Before she could move toward the bed, Ryan had reached around her and unclasped her bra. She stood there, allowing Ryan to stare. She had always thought her breasts were too big, but Ryan's appreciation was obvious, and she was pleased to allow Ryan time to cherish them.

After only a few seconds, she couldn't stand it anymore. She moved forward and reached behind Ryan, working the clasp of Ryan's bra. Ryan's breasts were smaller than hers but full and firm, with nipples hardened by desire. She placed her hand over Ryan's heart and slowly moved it lower and covered her breast. As she gently caressed the ivory skin, then lightly circled the nipple with her fingertip, Ryan sucked in a deep breath.

CHAPTER THIRTY

After spending most of the morning at the San Diego Zoo and the afternoon and early evening on a harbor cruise, Ryan had convinced Katherine that going to bed early was a good idea. They'd had a wonderful three days that had raced by far too fast.

"I'm not sure what I was expecting for our future, but I hadn't realized we'd be spending so much time apart," Katherine said as she lay in the crook of Ryan's arm on their last night together. She'd been planning to join Ryan in Pennsylvania before the tournament was over but was informed by her agent, before Ryan arrived, that she'd be starting a book tour that weekend—scheduled for thirty-eight cities over the next three months. None of those cities matched up with the LPGA tour.

"Yeah. I'm trying to be excited for you. I realize this is great for your book and your career, but I'm disappointed that you won't be with me. I'm being selfish, I know, but it's going to be hard to get back in the groove." Ryan caressed Katherine's arm as she spoke.

Katherine grunted, "Mmm-hmm." But Ryan would have no problem getting back into the groove of tournament play. She'd just participated in the USGA Women's Open without the slightest hesitation. Ryan was a natural, and while she was so happy to see her excited, she was also concerned about their nascent relationship. "Have you and Maggie discussed a schedule yet?" She turned on her side so she could see Ryan better.

"Schedule?" Ryan didn't move. "We're going to follow the tour."

"Oh. I thought you planned to schedule a week off now and then." She tried to hide her own disappointment. If Ryan wasn't going to miss any tournaments, it might be months before they could see each other again.

"It's just…I've missed so much of this season already and the past two years. I'm so far behind my peers."

She lay back down so Ryan couldn't see her face. "Yeah, of course. Maybe I'll have a break, and I can meet you somewhere."

"Next week is the PGA Championship in Minnesota. I'd love to have you there." More to herself than to Katherine, she said, "I hope I have a caddie by then. Mags is going to make me crazy."

They didn't make love that night. She couldn't have pretended not to be disappointed that she wouldn't see Ryan for several weeks. But, worst, Ryan was so preoccupied she didn't seem to notice that she simply rolled over and fell asleep.

❖

Katherine was up and out of the bed before Ryan woke up. When she reached over to snuggle next to her, she found the bed empty and cold. She rolled out of bed and went downstairs in Katherine's beautifully decorated seaside townhouse and found her sitting on the deck off the kitchen holding a cup of coffee.

"Hey, beautiful. I missed you." She walked up behind Katherine and put her arms around her. "Couldn't sleep?"

"Yeah. A lot on my mind." Katherine started to get up. "Do you want me to make you some breakfast?" She picked up her phone from the side table next to her chair. "It's only eight. We have a few hours before we're due at the airport."

"Hmm. I can think of something better than breakfast to occupy those few hours." She pulled Katherine to her and into a kiss, but Katherine didn't return it with her usual passion. "Are you okay?"

"Yeah. I'm sorry." Katherine backed away, walked into the kitchen, and jerked a pan out of her cabinet. "Omelet?"

"Ahh…okay?" She grabbed a cup and poured herself some coffee from the nearly full pot. "Maybe we should talk first." She put her hand in the center of Katherine's back and guided her to the breakfast nook.

After they were both seated, Katherine spoke without being prompted. "I'm ruining our last day together. I need to get over it and enjoy the time we do have." She started to get up.

"Katherine, wait." She caught her arm and held her in place. "In my experience, we don't *just* get over things. Talk to me."

"I'm being stupid." She tried to pull away.

"Please." Ryan stood up next to her. "Just tell me what's on your mind."

Katherine finally sat back on the bench across from her. "Okay, but I know I'm being silly, and I'll work through this."

Ryan sat too. "Go on."

"It was such a relief to finally allow myself to stop chasing a ghost and not be tied to the tour. I guess I had this vision of us spending time together—lots of time. I was hoping for a future for us. Ryan, I…" Katherine hesitated.

"What is it?" she asked.

"I'm in love with you, but I pushed you back into the tour. I know it's right for you, but I can't help but be jealous of it now."

She grabbed Katherine's hands. "Oh my God. I love you too. And please never stop thinking of our future together. I can't wait until we can make plans. We'll figure this out. We can both do what we love and be with each other." She stood up and slid into the booth next to Katherine, then gently kissed each of her cheeks, tasting the salt of the tears that slowly trailed down her face.

"Can we figure one thing out now?" Katherine asked tentatively.

"Yes. Let's come up with some plans. That'll make us feel better." She jumped up. "Let me get my phone. I downloaded the schedule into my calendar."

When she returned, Katherine had her phone and day planner in front of her.

"Where are you the week after the PGA championship?" She flipped through her phone.

"I'm actually going to be back here most of that week. I have something to do then, and it would mean so much to me if you'd join me."

"Done! I'll order tickets after we finish. How about we plan to spend the week before the Evian Championship in New Mexico?"

"That actually works. I'm supposed to be in Austin that weekend and could drive over at the beginning of the week. It will be nice to see Rebecca and Eddie." Katherine made a note on her calendar.

"That feels a little better, doesn't it?" she asked.

"Yeah. It does. I'm sorry I'm being so needy. I…I guess I just want to know that we're strong enough to build a relationship when we're apart so often."

CHAPTER THIRTY-ONE

Ryan stood at the first tee of The Golf Course at Glen Mills outside of Philadelphia. She'd never played the course before, and she couldn't stop moving around at the side of the tee box. Oddly, she was even more nervous than when she played in the Open two weeks earlier, probably because she didn't have time to think about it—she just played. Over the past couple of weeks, she'd spent hours studying the Pennsylvania course where she now stood. She'd planned and replanned strategies for each hole, walking the fairways in her mind.

"What's wrong with you? Stop fidgeting, or you're going to piss everyone off." Maggie stood next to her new touring bag with no sponsor's logo. As hard as she'd tried to get a big supporter, all Maggie could solicit was a small token from Callaway, who had sponsored Ryan generously in the past. She was wearing their shoes, hat, and shirt, but their contributions barely covered the cost of entering the tournament. They didn't begin to pay for the week's expenses—airfare, hotel, rental car. That cost was coming straight out of her savings. To find some backing, she'd have to prove herself again. Her quick departure and lengthy absence had caused the big-money sponsors to shy away.

She grabbed the towel Maggie held and wiped the sweat rolling down the side of her face. "What is it here, like a hundred degrees?" She tossed the towel back to Maggie.

"Calm down, Ry. It's the humidity. You'll get used to it. Think about Katherine or something. You're freaking out a bit." Maggie reached out to pat her shoulder.

She moved away from Maggie as if she were infected with typhoid. "Telling me to chill out does not help," she snapped back.

Then the announcer called her to the tee. Maggie handed Ryan her driver, but she shook her head and reached for her 3-iron. "What are you doing? You have a clear shot."

"I'm not feeling it." She walked away and placed her ball on a tee. She moved from her perfect stance to a position behind the ball and then back again at least three times before she finally swung. The ball took a bit of a turn to the right that she didn't like, but it was okay. It landed short of her competitors by several yards on the right side of the fairway. Not a great position, and she had a long shot to the green, but she was safe and well in play. She let out a heavy sigh and handed the club back to Maggie.

Maggie shrugged and took it.

The rest of the day went much like that first shot. She struggled with every hole, making the game more like work than it had ever been for her. But somehow, she managed to stay in the top twenty and could still make the cut if she played better in the next round, though winning was a distant goal.

As they walked off eighteen, barely making par, Maggie, who'd kept her mouth shut most of the day, obviously couldn't hold back now that the round was over. "What the hell was that?"

"Give me a break," Ryan snapped and continued walking toward the clubhouse.

"No," Maggie said, and Ryan stopped and turned to look at her. "Seriously, if your mom was—"

"She isn't. She isn't here!" Ryan yelled, drawing attention from the players on the practice putting green and the few spectators milling around hoping for autographs. When she realized she was being stared at, she turned and walked away. Maggie followed without a word.

When they finally reached the locker room, Ryan plopped down on the bench and put her face in her hands. "I can't do this. That's why I quit. I knew it, but I…at the Open it seemed…well, possible. And with Katherine there…"

"Ry, look. I'm sorry. I shouldn't have said that." Maggie sat next to her.

"It's not your fault. You're right. I played like an amateur." She finally raised her head and looked at Maggie.

"Well, I wouldn't go that far. You're tied for twelfth in a professional tournament." Maggie put her arm around her and squeezed her.

"The memories are haunting me."

"I'm sorry. I…" Maggie paused. "Listen. I knew your mother. She'd hate that playing is causing you so much pain. Maybe you were right to stop the tour."

"She'd be disappointed in me. That's for sure." She took off her golf shoes and started to change her clothes. "Thanks for listening, Mags. I might have to work this out on my own, but I can't quit, not now."

"Okay. I'm here for you." Maggie gave her another quick hug. "Are you going back to the hotel?"

"Yeah. I think I'll see if I can get ahold of Katherine early today."

"That might help. Want me to go back with you?"

"No. I know you're dying to watch the rest of your girls play. I'll see you in the morning—8:10 tee time, right?" Maggie coached several other LPGA players and liked to watch how they were doing so she could help them make adjustments after each round.

"If you're sure."

She nodded. "See you at six?"

"Okay. Call if you need me." They headed out in different directions.

❖

Ryan made it back to the hotel in only a few minutes with the limited midday traffic. As much as she wanted to forget the round she'd just played, she couldn't help running it through her head. Even in the shower as she tried to rinse it all down the drain, she kept thinking of her poor play and all the things she should've done differently.

As soon as she dressed, she found her phone and punched up Katherine's number. If she had any hope of getting it off her mind, Katherine was it. She was supposed to wait until six for their daily call, but based on her calculations, Katherine would've had time to land at JFK, make it across the city, and reach her hotel by now, so she couldn't wait.

"Hello, beautiful." Katherine answered, and all Ryan's anxiety fell away.

"I miss you so much."

"I miss you too. Is your round over already?"

"Yeah. I played so badly. I'm embarrassed. I can understand why no one wanted to sponsor me." She chuckled.

"Oh, Ry. I'm sorry. When you say badly, what do you mean?"

"Well, I'm four over in the first round. The leaders are five under. I'm tied for twelfth, with eighteen players ahead of me." She was trying hard not to be whiny, but in her own ears, she sounded like a spoiled kid not getting what she wanted.

"Ryan, that's great!" Katherine's voice went up an octave or two with her excitement. "What did you expect in your second tournament in two years?"

"I expected to at least play par golf."

"Well, perhaps you should give yourself a break. I might've heard words like that from my coach this spring," Katherine said and laughed. "You kept telling me to stop having expectations and just enjoy the game. You should give it a try."

"Or I could finish this tournament and join you on your book signing and go back home." She wasn't sure if she was joking or not.

"Oh, Ry. You know I'd love us to be together, but I'm also not sure you'd be happy. You need to at least finish this season and then decide. We'll work it out for this book tour, and then I can travel with you. I'm used to writing on the road, so it might even help me be productive."

"Really? You'd want to follow me?" She was truly surprised. She'd imagined she'd be on her own again.

"Of course. I want to see you play. I love watching you—not just your swing." Katherine laughed.

"Stop it. I wish you were here now."

"Me too. What time do you tee off tomorrow?"

"Ten after eight."

"I don't go to the book signing until ten thirty, so I'll be watching."

"Thanks, Katherine. You're my golfing muse."

"You're going to do great. I love you, but I have to go to a social tonight, and I need to get ready. Can we talk after?"

"Oh, I'm sorry. Of course. I love you too." She ended the call, grabbed the course-yardage book, and carefully replayed every hole. As she wrote down each club she'd used next to where her ball landed in tiny script, she began to realize what she'd done. She'd let fear dictate her decisions. She'd played it safe and wasn't likely to miss the cut, but she sure as hell wouldn't win if she continued to play that way. She had to find that winner's arrogance that she was sometimes criticized for. This was her game.

❖

Ryan's drive landed over a hundred yards from the center-cut pin location on the third hole of the second round. It was a three-hundred-and-seventy-five-yard par four, and she was set up to birdie for the third hole in a row.

"What the hell did you do last night? You're playing like the old Ryan." Maggie handed Ryan her 9-iron. Ryan could land that club wherever she wanted.

"The old Ryan is back. I'm a professional golfer, and I intend to play like one." She took the club from Maggie and walked in front of her to her ball.

"Hey, Ryan Gibbs. I watched you play two years ago in San Antonio. You're awesome!" Ryan heard the yell from the crowd on the right side of the green and turned toward them and waved. She did feel like her old self, and she was having a blast, with no concern about the next fifteen holes.

As she predicted, she played nearly flawlessly. She finished the round at four under par, putting her one over for the tournament. She was now seventh on the leaderboard, with no worries about missing the cut and a real possibility of winning. Because she was doing so well, she was moved to a later tee time for the Saturday round, so she and Maggie decided to have a mini celebration.

"How about Mexican food? A margarita sounds good," Maggie asked as she drove them out of the hotel parking lot.

"Are you kidding me? Did you forget where I'm from and the amazing New Mexican food you had when you visited? How about Italian? I could use the carb load, and wine sounds safer than margaritas," she said.

"Oh, you're no fun, but you're right about the great food in New Mexico. Okay. I heard Vetri Cucina is great, and it's only a few blocks away."

It was a quick drive to the restaurant, and since they were so early, they were seated immediately. They both ordered wine before the host walked away.

"I'm starving," Maggie said. "I guess carting golf clubs around a course kicks my ass. I've gotten lazy. I haven't done that in years."

"Yeah. I know. Thank you, and I'm looking for a caddie. Any ideas?" she asked as the waiter approached the table. He introduced himself and poured the wine and started to walk away.

"Ah, excuse me." Maggie stopped him. "We need menus."

"Oh. I'm sorry. I thought you knew it was a *quattro piatti* menu, and since you selected your wine, I thought you had made your food choices." The waiter returned to the table and handed them two small cards, explaining that each night the chef prepared only a few items in each course of a four-course meal, and most customers chose their wine based on their main course.

"Well, since we are clearly not cultured enough to eat here, could you select the courses that would go well with this wonderful wine?" Maggie held up her glass. "We might be a little backward. Besides, we're so hungry we're guaranteed to enjoy whatever you bring us."

The poor confused waiter nodded and returned to the kitchen.

"Are you sure you're going to like what he brings? What if this wine pairs perfectly with snails?" Ryan asked, and they both laughed.

"I don't think I've ever had snails, but I bet I could eat them now." Maggie took a sip of wine. "Back to the caddies."

"Oh, yes. Ideas?"

"As a matter of fact." Maggie slid a piece of paper with names and numbers on it across the table. "After your shooting today, I was nearly attacked."

Ryan wasn't surprised. Caddies could be as fickle as the sport sponsors, and they made a percentage of their players' winnings. Ryan had played like a winner today, and she didn't plan to change that approach, so her caddie was likely in for a big paycheck. "I know you like to have a woman caddie, but Jason Mathers is on that list, and I think you'd work well with him."

"Mathers? What happened with him and Rose? He's been her caddie for years. I don't want drama. There's enough of it on the tour without stealing someone's caddie."

"Seems it was a mutual decision. Rose has been having some trouble, and Jace said he'd stay with her, but she let him go, telling him she'd decided to do a complete makeover to work on her game."

"Hmm. Well, okay. Let's call him when we get back."

"Good, because I don't want to carry that bag even one more loop."

"Oh, come on. It wasn't that bad, was it?" she said as a tall man with a chef's hat came out with several plates, their shy waiter was behind him carrying several more.

"I'm Chef Vetri, and Joe told me two beautiful women out here were wanting him to choose their meal. Well, Joe has trouble with decisions, so I've brought you all of tonight's selections." He started arranging plates on the table.

"Oh my gosh, Ry. What have we done?"

❖

Ryan finished the tournament in the money with Jason Mathers on her bag. It wasn't a huge payout, but it was encouraging to be at the top of the leaderboard on Sunday. She and Jason had made it through the last two rounds with no issues, and by Sunday they were joking and enjoying the teamwork they'd established before they made the turn at number nine. Ryan was lucky to get him. Jace was a great caddie. He knew most of the LPGA courses like his own backyard, and when he didn't, he studied and walked one until he did. He also knew when to advise and when to "shut the fuck up," his words. And he knew exactly when and how much to push.

Ryan had originally planned to surprise Katherine with a quick visit since she was going to be in Cincinnati next week. It was a relatively short drive from PA. She could've spent Monday and Tuesday there and still had Wednesday at the championship course at Hazeltine National in Minnesota. But after talking with Jace, he'd convinced her that she could win, and if they got there Monday morning, they'd have three days to strategize and play the course. She desperately wanted to see Katherine, but the pull of the game and the possibility of a win was too strong. She'd rationalized that, since they hadn't planned on it and after the championship she was going to go spend a week with her, Jace was right. They should spend as much time as possible on the course.

So after she collected her money, gave Jace his percentage, and paid all her expenses, she was only slightly above where she'd started, but she felt good. She finished packing and headed for the lobby. She had arranged for her and Jace to fly out Sunday evening and had even managed to get two rooms and a rental car despite the eleventh hour. Maggie was waiting for her in the lobby.

"You're back! Your game is back." Maggie said with a huge smile.

"I'm back." Ryan nodded and walked over to Maggie. "I owe it to you and Katherine. Thank you."

"I'd like to take credit, but she's the reason you're here. She's a terrific woman. Don't lose her."

"I know. I won't. Trust me." She moved closer to give Maggie a hug. "In case you're waiting in the wings to have her for yourself."

"Oh, Ryan." Maggie punched her arm. "It'd be you I'd wait for, but I know where we stand." Maggie quickly changed the subject. "I have someone expecting me upstairs, so I'll let you get on the road."

"Who?" Ryan asked and then shook her head. "I don't want to know."

"Right. Now don't forget what we talked about with your long irons, and I'll see you Wednesday."

CHAPTER THIRTY-TWO

It was late when they got in, and both Ryan and Jace were exhausted from the early morning on Sunday, followed by a long day of golf and their late flight, so they agreed to go directly to their rooms and get some rest. They planned to meet at nine for breakfast and get to the course in time for the ten o'clock tee time Jace had managed to secure for her. He knew a guy, apparently. She didn't care how he did it; she was just glad to get on the course with such short notice.

After two full rounds of walking every inch of the par seventy-two course, countless hours on the driving range, and even more on the putting greens, she was as ready as she' d ever be. Despite her efforts to not care, she couldn't help but dream of winning this tournament. If she could, it would be the first of what she hoped would be many majors. Winning a major was a big deal for all golfers, but for her it was so significant because her mother loved them. Janet watched one in its entirety, regardless of what needed to be done at work; she always said it could wait. Then she'd talk about it for weeks afterward. Even though Ryan was too young to remember the game, she knew every stroke of Nancy Lopez's tie-breaking round in the 1997 US Women's Open Championship, because she'd heard Janet talk about it over and over. Winning a major would be the highlight of her career.

She sat at her desk in the hotel room, reviewing the notes she and Jace had made in the yardage book, when her phone finally rang. She'd been waiting for Katherine's call since they left the course around eight that evening. Though she knew Katherine was still at an evening event, she'd tried to phone when she got out of the shower. She desperately wanted to talk to her and then get some good rest for her early tee time. Even though she'd done well last week, she was a long way from the top of the money list. Until she could remedy that situation, she'd have to settle for early morning tee times. Only the best players got the midday ones.

It was nearly eleven when the phone rang. "Hello! Finally. I was beginning to think you weren't going to call." She tried to keep the irritation out of her voice.

"I'm so sorry. I know it's late and you need your rest for tomorrow. Did I wake you?" Katherine asked.

Hearing Katherine's voice softened her immediately. "No. I couldn't sleep until I heard from you. How was your event? Did they serve cordon bleu?" She and Katherine had joked about how often it was the main course served at large event dinners.

Katherine laughed. "No. Actually it was roast beef, the second most popular food served at event dinners. My day was good. I'm actually excited. Can I keep you up for a couple more minutes?"

"Of course." She had the phone on speaker and was crawling between the sheets. "I'd stay up all night for you."

"I'm being considered for a book award. I never dreamed anyone would ever even want to read my books, let alone want to award me for one."

"Oh my gosh. That's amazing and well deserved. Your writing is incredible. I could read your prose for hours." She was excited, her voice elevated. "Congratulations."

"Thank you. It's only a small independent award, and I might not get it, but it's an honor to be considered."

"In the words of my wise girlfriend, how about not expecting anything and just enjoying it," she said, and they both laughed.

"Yeah. Everything's working out for me. And it's all because of you."

"Well, I don't think I can take all the credit, but you and I together…well, we're great together."

"We are, aren't we?"

"I know you need to get to bed, but I can't wait to see you next week. I'll head back to Cali as soon as I finish here on Sunday. I'll see you at my place on Monday?"

"Yes. I can't wait. I love you. Talk to you tomorrow." She said her good-byes, set her phone on the nightstand, and waited for sleep. It was slow in coming, but eventually she relaxed and slept all night.

❖

As soon as Katherine hung up, she changed out of her evening gown and into pajamas, then prepared to call her mom. She hadn't talked to her much since starting the book tour, but her mother had been so encouraging when she told her she wasn't going to play competitive golf anymore. She'd always supported Katherine's writing and was her best critic—good and bad. Her father, she could tell, was a bit disappointed, but he didn't say a word. He was also supportive of her writing, but he loved golf so much. He'd been proud of telling his law buddies that his daughter was on the LPGA tour. Even so, he'd be proud to tell them she won a book award too, if she won.

The phone rang several times, and she was about to hang up when Clarice Jackson-Reese answered with what remained of her once-thick Southern accent. Even after over thirty years in California, her faded Alabama accent was unmistakable. Clarice, everyone called her Claire except her Alabama family, had been born and raised in Huntsville and then attended Auburn University, like her father and grandfather before her. If it hadn't been for a law conference held at Auburn during Claire's senior year, she'd probably still be in Huntsville living the genteel life she'd been reared to enjoy. But even the Jackson Southern roots weren't deep enough when it came to Darrell Reese's charms. They had married the year after Claire graduated, and together they got Darrell through law school at UCLA. To hear him tell it, he wouldn't be practicing law if it weren't for Claire. What everyone thought was an unlikely match had turned out to be the perfect partnership. They had Marie two years later, and Katherine two years after that. Claire and Doc, the nickname everyone called Darrell for no good reason, had rarely been apart since the day they were wed.

"Hello, darling," Claire said.

"Hi, Mom. Sorry it's so late." She looked at her watch. It was midnight in Cincinnati, making it ten o'clock in California. Her mother was a night owl, so Katherine knew she'd be awake, but she rarely answered the phone after nine because she didn't think it was civilized for someone to call after that time.

"I'm glad you called. How are things going?" Claire asked.

"Great, actually. I was nominated for an award tonight."

"Oh, Katherine, that's wonderful. I knew that book was special. It's my favorite so far. Congratulations, darling." Claire's accent thickened a bit in her excitement, and *darling* came out in a slow drawl.

"Thanks, Mom. I'm excited." She leaned back on the pillows. "Well, I actually called to find out if you plan to go with me next week."

"Oh, honey." She could hear the disappointment in her mother's voice. "I thought we decided last year not to do it anymore."

"You decided." She tried not to sound angry. "I'd like you to come with me. Ryan will be there, and I'd like for you to meet her. Perhaps it could be good."

"It's…well, it's hard." Claire seemed to stop short, but she understood what she was trying to say.

"I understand, Mom, but would you think about it?" She wasn't mad now and felt bad for pushing, but she wanted her mother there.

"I'll think about it, but wouldn't it be nice to bring Ryan here? Your father would like to meet her, and we could plan something special at the house. Maybe we could all go play a round of golf."

"Well. Maybe we could do both."

"Maybe."

"I should get to bed, Mom. I'll talk to you again before I fly back. Good night. I love you."

"I love you too, darling," Claire said, and the phone went dead.

CHAPTER THIRTY-THREE

Beautiful. Beautiful shot, Ry," Jace said and took Ryan's 5-iron, wiped it clean, and put it back in her touring bag that now had a small Bette and Court logo on the side. Ryan wasn't a big fan of their clothing line—a bit too girly for her tastes—but she did like having another sponsor.

As she headed toward the green, she moved closer to the rope along the fairway to talk to some of the ladies and a couple of dudes who'd been following her for three days in a row. She'd played so well the first day she'd drawn quite a group of fans, and because her play had remained consistent, their numbers had grown. She was six under and alone in third place with three ladies ahead of her—two were in second. She had a real shot at winning and was making every effort to stay focused and calm. They'd just made the turn, and she was set to birdie number ten, her ball sitting pin-high, only inches from the hole. If she could play the last eight holes the way she'd done the rest of the week, she'd end the tournament at eight under, but she could do better.

Everything had fallen into place. She felt like she'd never left, and only occasionally did she allow thoughts of her mother to make her feel guilty. She'd mostly figured out a way to use her memory to push her to do better. The occasional phone call to Rebecca helped. Knowing her best friend was so excited for her boosted her confidence, and Rebecca always knew what to say to push her past any sadness or guilt when it cropped up.

Ryan was paired with one of the players tied for second, Martha Daniels. Ryan knew of her from her time on the tour, but she'd never played with her. She was extremely intense and competitive, and because of that attitude she was annoyingly quiet. For Ryan, golf had always been a social event, so having such a silent playing partner made her a bit uncomfortable. To energize herself, she took advantage of the crowd and her caddie.

Jace handed Ryan her putter on the green at number eleven, where she was set to make yet another birdie. When the ball clinked into the bottom of the cup, putting Ryan in second by herself and one ahead of her playing partner, Martha finally spoke. She'd been completely silent since she greeted Ryan when they first teed off. "Damn, Ryan. You're like a freaking birdie-making machine. Are you going to birdie every hole this side?" And she actually smiled.

"I'm certainly going to try," Ryan said, and stepped back to allow Martha to finish her putt for par.

Ryan didn't quite birdie every hole, but she did well and ended at nine under. As she watched the last two players come in after her, she knew winning was a long shot. Keri Hall was ten under and set up for an easy par. She'd have to do something incredibly stupid to bogey and set Ryan up for a tiebreaker round.

Jace stood next to her as they watched Keri walk to the green. The crowd in the stands surrounding eighteen was already clapping. "Well, Ry, you played some great golf. Let's shake some hands, get a paycheck, and hit the road. With the roll you're on, you've got Illinois in the bag."

The next tournament was in a course outside of Chicago, and Ryan had played well there in the past. "Jace, I can't play Chicago. I promised Katherine I'd meet her in California."

"Ryan, next week would be a better one to take off. It's a small purse in Virginia, and only a few big names will play there. Chicago is a big tournament with a big purse and lots of key players. You shouldn't miss it. It says something to sponsors when you play in a small tournament and miss a big one." Jace turned, picked up her bag, and started walking to the clubhouse as Keri's ball slid over the lip, putting her in first place alone.

"What? Are you serious?" She caught up to Jace. "I'm not going to let the tour dictate my actions like I did in the past."

"Right. Okay." He shrugged. "Mind if I pick up a player next week if the opportunity presents itself?"

"Seriously?" She'd been frustrated about Jace's sponsor comment, but now she was outright mad at his disloyalty.

"Ry, listen. It's not about you. I want you to play. I want to carry your bag, and I'll be there when you come back, but I need the money, and you should be playing."

She was still angry, but she did understand. It cost a lot to be on tour, and the caddies made money only if their players did. If she wasn't playing, Jace should still get a paycheck. "Really?" she said to his back.

He stopped and put down the bag. "You need to do what's right for you personally, but for your golf game, the best thing is to play. You have back-to-back top-ten finishes, and you're on a roll. This is a big tournament with a lot of people watching. It could make a huge difference and keep you in the groove. You've missed so much of the season. Don't miss this tournament. Can't you wait one more week to see Katherine?" He knew Katherine Reese by reputation alone, but in the last two weeks, he'd heard a lot more about her as Ryan pined over her distant love.

"Let me think about it," she said and walked past Jace to collect their winnings.

Chapter Thirty-four

It was after ten when Katherine landed in San Diego, and the first thing she did, as soon as the flight attendant announced that it was authorized, was to turn on her phone and check for a voice mail from Ryan. She had seen the end of the tournament on ESPN prior to boarding, so she knew how well Ryan had played, but as much as she was excited for Ryan's success, she wanted to know Ryan's arrival time. It had been more than two weeks since she'd seen Ryan, and she couldn't wait to pick her up in the morning. She smiled when the voice-mail notice popped up on her screen. She punched in her number and listened.

"Hey, sexy. I miss you so much. Ah…I need to talk to you about a change of plans. Call me when you get in, no matter how late. I love you. Ahh…I…okay, bye." She had heard Ryan's voice trail off, and it seemed as if someone had wrapped a rope around her chest and squeezed it tight. As much as her fingers itched to hit the call button and ask what the hell, she tried to calm down. It was probably bad, but she didn't actually know what was going on.

After she collected her bag, she punched up the Uber app and was heading to her house within minutes. She had plenty of time to call, but again she waited. She had no idea what was up, but it would most likely be better to have the conversation in private. Besides, her Uber driver wouldn't stop talking long enough for her to even comment, let alone make a phone call. When the driver asked what she did, she had innocently answered that she was an author. It felt good to say that, but the driver turned out to be a twenty-one-year-old French-literature major, and during the forty minutes from the airport to her house, she had to hear about all the great French authors and their works—she recognized only a few of them.

"Here we are, Ms Reese." The driver stopped mid-sentence as she pulled into Katherine's driveway.

"Thank you. Be safe out there." She practically ran to her front door. As soon as she got through the door, she tossed her luggage aside and grabbed her phone.

"Hello. Are you home?" Ryan answered a little too enthusiastically.

"What's going on, Ryan?"

"Oh…well…I…"

"You aren't coming, are you?"

"Katherine, listen, I—"

"Just answer me. Are you coming?" She practically yelled as she spoke each word distinctly.

"No. I'm playing in Chicago, but I'll meet you in Atlanta as soon as I finish, and we can spend two weeks together. I'll go…"

"We had a plan. I…" She stopped to keep from crying.

"I'm sorry. I know we did, and I won't do it again, but I'm so far behind in the season, and I'm on a roll. I need to assure sponsors that I'm back and that I'm playing well."

Silence.

"Katherine?"

"Yeah." She cleared her throat. "Okay. I just wanted you here. It's a special thing and…It's okay. I should never have expected—"

"Of course you should. It's just this one time. I promise I'll make it up to you."

"Hey. It's okay." Her voice was so soft she had to make herself speak up. "I'm tired, and it's late there. I'll talk to you later." She didn't wait for Ryan to speak. She hung up. All the energy she'd had when she landed had been zapped. It was as if she'd been running for hours and had nothing left. With her phone still in her hand, she walked to her balcony and stood in the cool ocean breeze.

Finally, after several minutes, she found her mom on the phone and hit the send button.

Claire answered on the first ring this time, despite the late hour. "Hi, darling. Are you home?"

She nodded and then quickly realized she needed to speak. "Yeah. I got home a few minutes ago."

"Oh, good. So we'll see you tomorrow. I decided to go with you. Do you know what time Ryan will arrive?"

"No, Mom. You're right. We shouldn't do it anymore. It's time to move on. Ryan's not coming. She has to play in Chicago."

"Oh, no. Doesn't she know why you wanted her to be here?"

She heard true concern in her mother's voice and had to fight tears again. "No. I didn't tell her. I…well, I didn't want to put pressure on her. She needs to do this." Tears began to flow down her cheeks. "This might not be right for us."

"Oh, sweetheart. I'll come get you tonight."

"No." She sniffed and wiped her tears. "I'll come in the morning. Let's do something fun. I need to move on. Ryan and I are on two different paths. Being with her just isn't right." She stopped, her voice cracking and unable to fight the tears again.

"Don't give up. I can tell how much you care for her. I'll be there in an hour."

She could tell her mother wanted to make it all better. She wished she could, but she had to decide for herself. "Mom, I love you so much, but no. I'll be there tomorrow. I'm exhausted. I just want to go to bed."

"If you're sure."

"I'm sure. Good night, Mom." She set the phone down after her mom said good night and dropped into the lounge chair on the balcony. A flash of a memory caused tears to flow again. Ryan had sat in that chair every time they watched the sunset when she was visiting.

CHAPTER THIRTY-FIVE

Good morning, Ryan. What the hell are you doing here?" Ryan heard Maggie's familiar voice calling from across the hotel dining room, where they were serving a buffet-style breakfast. As much as she'd wanted to sit in silence this morning, she headed for Maggie's table. She'd barely slept all night. Her thoughts of Katherine kept coming in a mix of sadness and anger. She desperately wanted to see Katherine, but she was frustrated because Katherine didn't seem to understand why she needed to play this week.

"Hey, Mags."

"Sit. Breakfast is amazing. Get yourself some food, and then tell me why you're here." Maggie was too loud for so early in the morning.

"Okay. If you promise to talk a little quieter."

"What? Are you hung over?" Maggie seemed to get louder.

"No. I…I'll be back." She shook her head and went to the buffet.

When she returned in a few minutes with a small pile of runny scrambled eggs and a cup of black coffee, Maggie looked her up and down, then stared at the sparse amount of food. "I was kidding, but are you sure you're not hung over?" She whispered this time.

"I'm fine, Mags. I'm just not hungry, and I didn't get much sleep."

"Oh. What's up?"

"Jace convinced me to play this week, and I had to tell Katherine I couldn't come visit until next week."

"Jace is right. You're doing great, Ry. You were so close to the win last week."

"Thanks. I know I need to. That's why I'm here."

"I'm sure it was a hard decision." Maggie finished the last of her breakfast.

"Well, yeah, but I thought Katherine would be more understanding. I can't believe she's making this so hard. I mean, she was the one who pushed me back on the tour. I was happy where I was." She moved her eggs around on the plate but didn't take a bite.

"But were you, really?" Maggie put her hand over Ryan's, stopping the scraping sound she was making with her fork on the plate.

"Yes, I was, but I'll admit I'm glad to be back. I love being on tour. It suits me, but she should understand. You have to play to win, and you have to win to play. I can't sit out any ol' time I want." She let her fork drop and moved her hand away.

"I imagine she'd be more understanding any other time."

"What do you mean? Why not now?"

"Oh. You don't know." Maggie set her coffee cup down and took Ryan's hand again.

"Know what? What are you talking about?" She tried to pull her hand away again, but Maggie held on.

"Tuesday is the anniversary of Marie's death."

"What? No." She looked at her watch to check the date. She'd heard about it back when the accident happened, but she had no time reference. Katherine had told her all the details, but she was pretty sure they'd never talked about when it occurred. "Oh my God. I'm a fool." She got up and left her breakfast and Maggie.

Chapter Thirty-six

When Katherine drove around the circle drive of her parents' grand house, she could see her mother standing in front of the double doors holding a cup of coffee.

"Hi, Mom." She got out of her car and walked into her mother's hug.

"Hi, darling. I've missed you." Her mother released her and opened the door for her to enter.

"Me too, Mom." She headed directly to her mother's office in the back of the house, which overlooked a beautiful flower garden that consumed nearly an acre of their ten-acre grounds. Claire spent most of her day there, still doing a lot of Doc's legal reviews and editing. Katherine knew he'd told her she didn't have to do it anymore, but he was delighted that she continued.

As soon as she walked in, she plopped down in the leather chair across from Claire's desk. She'd spent many hours in that chair doing everything from drawing and pretending to be working like her mother when she was small to participating in serious and often emotional conversations as a teenager. She even came out to her mother in that chair. Not that she needed to. Claire seemed to know everything about her and Marie and didn't seem surprised at all.

She had walked over to Katherine, wrapped her arms around her, and said, "Let's go tell your father." While his reaction included a bit more surprise, Claire had helped him come around, and she didn't give him much time to figure it out.

Her mom stopped short of sitting behind her desk and sat next to Katherine in the matching leather chair. "How are you feeling this morning?"

"Better. Well, tired but better. I didn't sleep much."

"Oh, darling. I'm so sorry." Her mom grasped her hand. "Well, why don't you go lie down for a bit. We can have a late snack for lunch and then meet your father at the club for dinner. He has an evening meeting, and I suggested we eat at the club so it's not too late when he gets home."

"Okay. That sounds good." She started to get up.

"I have everything arranged for tomorrow. We'll get started early and be there when the sun rises. Helen will prepare us a lunch so we can make a day of it." Helen had been Claire's maid for over twenty years. "She'll probably even cut the crust off for you." Claire laughed.

Katherine sat back down. "Oh, Mom. You're so wonderful, but you're right. We shouldn't do it anymore." For the past three years, on the anniversary of Marie's death, Claire and Katherine had driven down to the site of Marie's tragic car accident. It was about forty miles down the interstate, north of the Tijuana border crossing. They'd spend the day telling stories about Marie and sharing her dreams, but mostly they cried. After the second year, Claire had suggested that perhaps Marie would want them to move on. It was hard on her to support her own emotions and Katherine's too, but Katherine had insisted that they make it an annual event.

"Really?" Claire leaned forward and crinkled her eyebrows. "Are you sure?"

"It hurts a lot, doesn't it?" she asked.

"It does. It hurts you too." Claire nodded.

"Yeah, and you're right. Marie wouldn't want us to keep hurting. I'm beginning to have happy thoughts of Marie when I think of her, not sad ones. Going there would just bring the sad ones to the top again."

"I agree, darling. I'm glad to hear you say that." Claire stood, and Katherine joined her. Claire pulled her close and squeezed. When she finally released her, she started leading her up the stairs. "After your nap, let's plan for a different outing."

"Mom, I'm sorry, but I've decided to meet Ryan in Chicago. My flight is in the morning."

CHAPTER THIRTY-SEVEN

Ryan was on hold with her travel agent, Carol, when she knocked on Jace's door. He must've been ready to leave, because he opened the door immediately.

"Hey, Ry." Jace's giant frame filled the doorway.

She pointed to her phone. "Carol. Oh, thank God it's you. Can you give me one second?"

She heard papers shuffling, and then Carol replied. "Yeah, sure."

Ryan pulled the phone away from her ear. "Jace, I'm going to San Diego."

"Oh." Jace leaned on the door frame.

"It's a long story, but I just found out an important event is happening this week, and I can't miss it. I'm sorry, but I have to go. Please feel free to caddie for someone else, and I'll meet you next week. It doesn't matter that it's a small tournament. I'll be there. I—"

"Ryan, it's okay. You don't have to explain to me. You have to do what's right for you. I'm sorry I pressured you. I'll be there for you next week." He leaned down and gave her a hug.

"Thank you, Jace…for understanding." She backed away and pointed to the phone again. "I gotta get a flight."

"Right. Good luck, and be safe."

She nodded, put her phone back to her ear, and started walking away, but then she turned back to Jace. "Hey. Maggie is in the dining room. She might know if someone needs a caddie."

"Thanks, but I think I'll sit this week out and be ready for you."

She smiled. Even though she didn't want him to miss a week's pay, his loyalty thrilled her. They were becoming a team. "Hey, Carol. Sorry about that. I need a ticket from Chicago to San Diego as soon as possible."

"Oh, I thought the tournament was in Chicago this week," Carol said, and Ryan heard keys clicking in the background. She had never met Carol, but they had become virtual friends due to many conversations booking flights and making other travel arrangements. Often they were stressful conversations when flights were canceled or delayed, but Carol always made things work. Sometimes when Ryan climbed on a crowded flight with every seat filled, she wondered who got bumped for her to get a ride and how Carol had managed it.

"Looks like I can get you out at six in the morning. Want me to reserve a seat?"

"Oh." She'd been standing in the hall outside her room but finally opened the door and slid inside. "There's nothing for today?"

"Hmm. Let's see." After a long delay, Carol came back on the line. "I can try to get you on standby, but it's a long shot. Looks like the standby lists are filling up. You might spend the day in the airport and never get out."

"Put me on every standby option you can find and then reserve that seat for tomorrow morning. What time is the first standby flight?" She started shoving things into her bag.

"Oh, wait. A Delta flight is leaving at ten till eleven from Midway, with a three-hour stop in Atlanta. It would be a long day across the entire country, but it would get you there at 6:40 p.m."

"Book it." Ryan zipped her bag. She'd call Jace and ask him to transport her golf clubs to the next tournament.

"Can you make it to the airport?" Carol asked, and the sound of clicking computer keys sped up.

She looked at her watch—almost nine. "Yes. You do your thing, and I'll get there."

"Good luck, Ryan," Carol said and hung up.

She punched buttons on her phone as she ran down the stairs. She was on the fifth floor, but her experience with the slow elevator in the hotel had caused her to head straight for the stairs.

"Jace."

"Did you get a flight?" Jace's calm baritone was refreshing in her haste.

"I did, but I'm rushing to the airport. Can you check me out of the hotel and get my clubs?"

"Sure. You want me to drive you?"

"Thanks, Jace. No. I'll get there. See you next week." She jumped off the last stair onto the ground floor and burst through the fire doors.

"Shit, Ryan. Are you trying to kill me?" Maggie grumbled as she caught herself after Ryan nearly knocked her to the ground.

"Sorry, Mags. Got to get to Midway." She was looking down at her Uber app.

"You're going to see Katherine?"

"Yes, but I don't have time to talk."

"I'll take you to Midway." Maggie changed directions and followed her to the parking lot.

"Don't you have golfers waiting on you?"

"Only one. I'll call from the car and tell her I'll be late. She still has plenty of time before the tournament starts for me to mess up her swing." She chuckled and pulled car keys out of her pocket.

"Thanks, Mags."

❖

It was actually a blessing that Maggie agreed to drive her to Midway. She'd grown up outside of Chicago and knew the best route to avoid traffic—most of it. Ryan would've likely missed the flight without Maggie's knowledge of the area and fearlessness in the Chicago traffic.

With Maggie's help she arrived, got her tickets, and rushed through security as the last passengers were loading.

"Ma'am, would you like something to drink? And I'm sorry, but you'll need to turn off your phone. They just closed the cabin door."

She looked up from her SMS app that she'd been staring at since she got on the plane. She'd been trying to decide if she should send Katherine a text or surprise her. Her type-A personality caused her to want to send a quick message, but the romantic side of her wanted to just show up on her doorstep. The flight attendant had solved her dilemma.

"Oh, yeah. I'm sorry." She turned off her phone. "I'll take a diet Coke."

She settled in and tried to calm her anxiety. Now that she was on her way, she hoped she was doing the right thing. Would Katherine be so upset with her that she wouldn't even want to see her? Despite all the activity in her brain, or because of it, the flight to Hartsfield-Jackson International Airport seemed to take much longer than the two hours indicated on the flight map. And it was a bit frustrating to know she was going the wrong direction, but at least she was on her way.

Since she was near the back of the plane, she had more waiting to do even after they arrived at the gate. She remained in her seat, making only a small effort to keep her legs from bouncing while she watched the other passengers slowly disembark.

Finally, she reached the terminal. The space and the fresh air made her feel like she'd just been connected to pure oxygen. She walked to the departure screens she'd spotted as soon as she cleared the jetway door. Even though she had a three-hour layover, she scanned the screen for her next flight. When she saw the gate was in the same terminal, she relaxed a bit and suddenly realized she hadn't eaten anything since yesterday's dinner. That little granola bar was long gone.

With plenty of time and her seat secure, she started looking for a place to sit down and relax. The scent of a greasy burger drew her to TGI Friday's. She found a seat at the bar, and even though it was before noon in Atlanta, it was afternoon in Chicago, so she ordered a Blue Moon and a burger. She turned on her phone and started scanning the news, no longer feeling the need to message Katherine. She'd be there soon enough.

Somehow the extremely long three hours passed, and she was finally boarding the flight that would take her to Katherine. She'd managed to kill most of an hour with the bartender at TGI Friday's. If it hadn't been for the lunch crowd that caused him to be so busy, she probably could've spent her whole layover there. He was a big fan of golf and knew who she was. But, best of all, he was from Williamsburg, Virginia.

She and Jace had originally thought it would be a good one for her to skip, but since she was missing this week's, she wanted to play even if the purse was relatively small. She'd found the course layout on her Chromebook and started studying it while she waited for her lunch. The bartender identified it at once. Before she left when he got too busy to talk, she felt like she'd actually played each hole.

She managed to endure the rest of her layover with a book she'd found at the Hudson Booksellers across from the bar. She'd read several pages and was struggling to stay awake with her stomach full and pure exhaustion from no sleep. When they finally announced the flight, she was relieved at the possibility of falling asleep on the plane.

She waited and waited. It seemed like the entire flight had boarded before they called her group, but finally she got on and settled in. It was her lucky day. She was next to the window, with no one in the center seat. She folded her jean jacket into a pillow and was asleep before the wheels were up.

❖

Ryan woke with a start at the sound of the pilot on the intercom. “Ladies and gentlemen, you have nothing to worry about, but we are being diverted to Dallas/Fort Worth.”

She’d fallen so deeply asleep, she wasn’t sure she knew what she’d heard. She turned to the young lady in the aisle seat in her row. “Did he say diverted?”

“Yeah. Dallas,” she answered and, like the rest of passengers, began looking out the windows.

“Did something happen?” Ryan asked.

“Yeah. I can’t believe it didn’t wake you.”

“Oh, really? I was out. What was it?”

“A few minutes before the announcement there was a loud popping sound. Most of the passengers squealed, including me.” She was looking around, obviously trying to listen to the nearby conversations.

“Oh. That can’t be—”

“Ladies and gentlemen, please remain calm. It appears one of our engines isn’t restarting, so for safety they’ve asked us to land, but you have nothing to worry about. We have three operational engines and will be on the ground in Dallas in a few minutes.”

CHAPTER THIRTY-EIGHT

"Hey, honey." Katherine's dad wrapped her into a hug as soon as she approached his table at the club. "You look amazing."

"Thanks, Dad. You too." She sat in the seat her father held out for her and then watched him kiss her mother and hold the chair for her as well. When she was a teenager, she'd been embarrassed by his chivalry and always tried to get in front of him so he couldn't open doors and hold chairs for her, but now she loved him for it. It made her feel special.

"Your mom tells me you're leaving in the morning. I was hoping you'd hang around for a little while and play a round with me." Darrell Reese took off his Brioni suit jacket, but before he could drape it over the back of the chair, the host was taking it out of his hands.

"I'll hang this up for you, Mr. Reese."

Doc nodded and released the coat, returning his attention to her as he sat down. "Is she worth it?" he asked.

"Mom, what did you tell him?" She glanced toward her mother, who shrugged. "Yes, Dad. She is." She reached for her phone and glanced at it. It was nearly seven and would be nine in Chicago soon. She expected Ryan to call within the next hour.

"Well, she's one hell of a golfer." Doc turned as their waiter approached. "Wine, ladies?" he asked.

"Yes, please," Claire said and confirmed with a quick look at Katherine, who nodded back. "That pinot we had last week. I think Katherine would like it."

Doc turned back to the waiter. "Ask the sommelier if he has any more of the 2018 Swanson's Pinot Grigio."

"Yes sir." The waiter disappeared.

"Katherine, your mother and I just want you to be happy. I know it's been hard for you these past three years."

"I know, Dad. I'm sorry I've been such a downer, but things are much better, and Ryan is the reason. I'm not sure I would've realized how truly unhappy I was until she helped me see that it was okay to let go. She recently lost her mother." She quickly glanced at her phone again and then set it next to her plate.

"Waiting for a call?" Claire asked and frowned. She knew how much her mother disapproved of cell phones at the table.

"Yes, I'm sorry, Mom, but I can't miss it."

She went on to tell her parents how much Ryan meant to her. Doc adored her, and who she loved had never mattered to him.

Dinner was amazing. The three of them ended up laughing and telling stories about Grandpa and the club most of the time. When they finished, Doc walked out with her on one arm and her mother on the other. The valet had his Mercedes and Claire's Lexus waiting at the door when they exited.

"Do you mind if she rides with me?" Her father turned to Claire. "We can visit on the ride back since she's leaving us in the morning."

"Of course not. Drive safely. I'll see you at home in a few minutes." Claire kissed him and climbed into her car.

He opened the passenger door, and Katherine climbed in. She loved her father, and because he was always so busy with work, one-on-one visits with him were rare. He took advantage of the opportunity, and after the forty-minute drive home, he showed her around the development, pointing out the new property he'd recently purchased.

She'd completely lost track of time, and when their grandfather clock struck ten, she quickly said her good night and good-byes for her early departure before she headed up to her room. As soon as she closed her door, she started sifting through her purse for her phone. The minute she dumped the contents of her bag onto the bed in a panic, she realized where it was.

She ran downstairs to find her parents sitting in the living room still talking. "Dad, can you call the club?"

"Sure. Why?"

"I left my phone on the table." She was so disheartened. Ryan had probably tried to call and would be sure she wasn't answering on purpose. "And Mom, can I use yours?"

"Of course, darling. It's on the hall table." Claire started to stand up.

"I'll get it. I'm such an idiot. She probably thinks I'm mad at her, and now I have to wake her to tell her otherwise."

"If she's everything like you said, she'll understand." Doc pulled his phone out of his jacket pocket. "I'll tell the club to send your phone to the house. We'll get it to you. In the meantime, pick one up on the way to the airport."

"Take mine." Claire got up this time and went to the front hallway. "Here. I'll use yours until you get back."

She took it. "Are you sure?" She started punching in Ryan's number, glad she hadn't put it in her phone during most of her stay in New Mexico, or she probably wouldn't have remembered the digits. She'd refused to add Ryan to her contacts during the first two weeks of her stay because she'd been convinced that she didn't want contact with her after she left. She laughed, thinking of how silly she'd been, but her good mood was cut short when Ryan's phone went immediately to voice mail.

CHAPTER THIRTY-NINE

It was after seven when Ryan finally put her feet on solid ground inside the terminal at Dallas. As soon as they touched down and gave the okay, she went for her phone, but because she'd almost literally crashed out the minute she sat down, she'd forgotten to turn it off, and the battery was drained. She was looking at a black screen. The lady in her row offered to let Ryan borrow hers, but all she could remember of Katherine's number was the 858 area code. After they landed, they were delayed on the tarmac in the hot, stuffy plane for over an hour and a half without a parking spot because they'd been diverted at the last minute.

Ryan had been so sure she would be in San Diego before time for her normal phone call with Katherine, she hadn't even thought about what she'd do. Now it was getting late, and not only would she not get there, but she couldn't call either. Once inside the terminal she spotted a charging station and plugged her phone in immediately, but that put her at the end of the Delta customer-service line to get a new flight. Without her phone, she couldn't even call Carol for help. She had to wait, again, frustrated at how dependent she'd become on the storage capacity of her cell phone.

As she stood in line, she watched her phone, but nothing was happening. Occasionally, while she waited, she asked the young man behind her to save her spot while she checked the cord and even moved it to different locations, in case the connection was broken, but it wasn't taking a charge. It was way past time for a new one—hers was probably five years old—and it appeared that today was the day it chose to die.

After waiting almost forty minutes, she finally reached the front of the line. "Hi." Ryan greeted the haggard-looking, middle-aged woman behind the counter and could tell this wasn't going to go well. Her ponytail was falling out all around the woman's face, and her mascara was smeared in a black streak below her left eye. Without pleasantries or eye contact, she asked for Ryan's ticket.

"I'm trying to get to San Diego—tonight if at all possible," Ryan said, and slid her unused boarding pass across the counter.

"Hmm." The lady grunted. Her name tag said Sara, so Ryan tried pouring on the charm.

"Sara, I appreciate you helping me out. It must be frustrating having to deal with a plane-load of unhappy people."

"It happens all the time, and it's my job," Sara said abruptly and again without making eye contact, but she was clicking keys and scanning her computer screens. "Looks like the best I can do is five in the morning."

"There's nothing tonight?"

She finally looked up. "No."

"Nothing with a layover that might get me there late tonight? Or from another airline?"

"No. I can't book with other airlines. Do you want this one, or do you want to try somewhere else?"

Ryan stood there thinking—apparently too long.

"If you want to step back to make a decision, I'll help the next person," Sara said.

"No. I'll take it." She probably would've tried another airline if she'd had access to her phone and Carol, but with no communications, she didn't want to risk losing the morning flight. She collected her new boarding pass and started looking for a place where she could make a call to book a room for the night. She had no idea if the airport still had pay phones, but she followed the signs to an information desk and found a lonely row of four phones there. As she was about to pick up a headset, she realized she had no way to search for a place to stay, and it was nearly ten o'clock now, so she decided to grab a snack and find a place to rest in the airport.

Despite the uncomfortable conditions, she made it through the night. She was able to find a decent chair that allowed her to recline a bit and stretch out her legs, but the worst part was the cold. Before morning, she'd woken several times and pulled out more items of clothing from her carry-on. But by three thirty a.m. she stopped fighting the cold and the discomfort and took her carry-on to the nearest ladies' room, where she brushed her teeth and washed her face. She glanced in the mirror and regretted that she would have no opportunity to shower and make herself more presentable for Katherine, but at least they'd be together.

After strolling through the terminal to her departure gate, while she was relieved to see the gate showed the departure to San Diego, she was saddened that most of the food vendors wouldn't open until after she'd boarded. She found a soda and candy machine and purchased a diet Coke and a cheese Danish—probably not the worst of the options she could've chosen, and at least she wouldn't be starving.

CHAPTER FORTY

Katherine was dressed and ready to go to the airport before six. Her flight wasn't until nine, but it would take almost an hour to get there, so she grabbed her bags and headed for the door. Besides, she was so anxious, she needed to get moving.

"Wait." She heard her mother's voice just before she closed the front door.

"Oh. Good morning." Katherine stopped. "I'm sorry. Did I wake you?"

"No. I'm taking you to the airport." Claire was dressed, her purse in her hand. "Your father put your car in the garage. I'll drop you off."

"You don't have to. I can leave it in long-term parking." She was still holding her bag in one hand and the door handle in the other.

"Come on, darling. I want to."

She shrugged and followed her mother through the kitchen to the garage. "Thanks, Mom."

"Did you finally get in touch with Ryan last night?" Claire asked as she backed out of the drive.

"No. I'm sure she's upset with me, but the sooner I get there, the sooner I can fix this." She watched the road, though it was too early for much traffic.

Her mom was not a morning person, so they exchanged only a few words on the trip, but Katherine was grateful not to have to worry about parking the car and finding transportation over to the terminal.

The drive was uneventful, and within thirty minutes of her mom leaving her at the departure doors, Katherine dropped off her luggage, made it through security, and had a cup of coffee while she waited at her gate. First-class would be boarding in twenty minutes.

❖

While Katherine sat at gate 21 waiting to be called to board, Ryan arrived at gate 36—nearly two hours late due to weather delays in Dallas. If she hadn't wanted to see Katherine so badly, she might've given up around seven in the morning after Delta announced yet another delay. As she walked toward the terminal exit, she began to worry that she might be reversing the numbers in Katherine's house number, but she knew the street name. If she had to, she could walk up and down the street until she saw Katherine's condo.

With no phone, Uber was not an option, so without hesitation, she approached the first cab in a long line. At this point she didn't care if it cost her a million dollars; she was getting to Katherine, and, finally, she was only minutes away. She told the driver the address as she remembered it, and he punched it in his GPS.

"I'm sorry, ma'am. That address doesn't come up."

She couldn't identify his thick accent, but she thought it was Eastern European. On any other day she would've enjoyed asking him questions about his home and culture, but today she just wanted to wrap her arms around Katherine and end the *Twilight Zone* episode she was stuck in.

"Oh, I may've remembered the digits in the wrong order. Will you try them in reverse?" She repeated the numbers.

She watched over the backseat as the man punched in the number. "Okay. that worked. It looks like a residential area. Nice part of town."

"Yes. Yes, that's it. Get me there as soon as you can."

"It might take about an hour in this morning's traffic." The driver aggressively drove into the traffic flowing out of the airport. "But I'll do my best." Within a few minutes they were easing down Interstate 5 with cars for miles on all sides. It was nearly nine when the driver finally pulled up in front of Katherine's condo. Ryan was so relieved to see the familiar home, she paid the man and rushed to the door.

She knocked lightly. She didn't think Katherine would still be asleep, but she didn't want to be obnoxious even though she was nearly crawling out of her skin with nerves and anxiety. After several seconds passed, she pushed the doorbell and heard it ring faintly behind the door, so it was working. Again she waited—longer than she expected it would take even from the farthest location in Katherine's condo. Finally, she pounded on the door with her fist. Her excitement had dropped from sixty to zero, and disappointment took over as she realized she'd literally flown across the entire country, and no one was home.

She plopped down on the small concrete porch and leaned against her bag. She had no idea what to do now. She desperately needed a shower and some rest in a real bed, but getting to a hotel was going to be a challenge with no phone. In desperation, she pulled hers out of her pocket and stared at it as if she could will it to work, despite the fact that it had failed the other dozen or more times she'd tried it.

❖

It was already hot in Chicago when Katherine got to the Uber line, but the app said her car was only fifteen seconds away. She breathed a sigh of relief when she climbed in the air-conditioned Honda Civic. After she gave the driver the address to the golf course, they rode in silence for the fifty-minute trip. She saw familiar faces as soon as she got out of the car at the clubhouse.

"Hey, Kat! I thought you were on a book tour. Speaking of, I read it, by the way. It's amazing." Jennifer Collins, one of Maggie's other clients, spoke as Katherine entered the building.

"Hi, Jen. Thanks. I'm on a break. I came to watch Ryan play this week." She wasn't sure who knew about her and Ryan, but it was safe to assume that it was pretty common knowledge by now, since news on the tour traveled fast, especially romances. "Have you seen her?"

"Ah. No. I haven't seen her… Actually, I haven't seen her since we left PA."

"Hmm. What about Mags or Jace?"

"Yeah. Maggie's on the practice green with Taryn, but I haven't seen Jace either." The women's tour was small enough that everyone knew each other. In spite of some disadvantages, mostly it was fun.

"Right. Thanks." Katherine wasn't familiar with this course but knew the putting green would likely be right behind the clubhouse. She passed through to the back like she knew where she was going, and sure enough, she not only spotted the putting green but saw Maggie immediately.

She walked slowly over to where Maggie was talking to Taryn Ramsey, a young golfer, new to the tour this year. She wanted to find out as soon as possible where Ryan was, but she also didn't want to be rude. As she was about to interrupt, Maggie spotted her.

"Katherine! What are you doing here?"

"Looking for Ryan."

"Ahh. Well." Maggie hesitated, then turned to Taryn. "Excuse me for a few minutes. Keep working on that, and I'll be right back." She walked off the green, gently took Katherine by the arm, and moved her to the club patio.

"What are you doing? Just tell me where she is." She backed away.

Maggie looked at her watch. "Well, she was supposed to have arrived in San Diego last night, but since you're standing—"

"What?" Katherine pinched her eyebrows together and processed what Maggie had just said.

"I told her about the anniversary of Marie's death, and she got a flight out of here yesterday morning. I took her to the airport about ten, and she was supposed to have arrived around like sixish, maybe seven, Pacific time."

"Oh my gosh. I was at my parents' house. Why didn't she call?" As she finished her sentence, Maggie reached for her silenced phone in her pocket.

"I don't know the number. I better take it. Hold on." Maggie tapped the phone. "Hello."

"Mags, I'm here, but I can't find her. She must've gone somewhere and I—"

"Ryan, she's standing in front of me."

"It's Ryan?" She reached for the phone.

"Hold on." Maggie handed over her cell.

"Ryan, where are you?" she yelled into the phone.

"Oh my gosh. It is so good to hear your voice." Ryan let out a big sigh and continued. "I'm at a Hampton Inn. I think it's called Mission Valley. What are you doing in Chicago?"

"I came to be with you. I miss you so much. Why didn't you call me, and whose phone number is this?" She glanced at the number and recognized the San Diego area code.

"It's a long story, but I'm using the hotel landline. I'm about to go buy a new phone because mine finally died. I didn't have your number. Don't say I told you so." Ryan spoke so quickly she was stumbling over her words.

"Slow down. We'll figure this out."

"I'm so glad you aren't mad at me, and that I can finally hear your voice."

"I'm not mad. I was disappointed, but after I had time to think about it, I understood. Now we have to figure out how to get together. You should come back here. There's still time before the tournament starts, and you could play."

"No!" Ryan snapped, then paused. "I just want us to spend some time together—just you and I. No book, no golf—only you wrapped around me without reality."

"Mmm. That sounds nice," She walked a few steps away from where Maggie was standing.

"Just bring me my phone." Maggie took the hint and headed back to her golf client.

"You want to meet somewhere?" she asked. "Maybe Denver? Oh, or we could go back to New Mexico."

"No. Come back here," Ryan said.

"Okay. Are you sure?"

"Yeah. Give me your phone number so I can put it in my new phone. I'll call you when I have it, and you can tell me your itinerary."

"Okay. I'll get a return flight as soon as possible." She quickly explained why she had her mom's phone and gave Ryan the number. "In the meantime, please call my mom. She has my phone." Again she rattled off a phone number. "She'll come get you. It'll be more comfortable than waiting at the hotel."

"Oh, I couldn't do that," Ryan said quickly. "I can't wait to meet them, but I think an introduction would be much better than me just showing up on their doorstep. Besides, I'm exhausted. I'll rest here until you get back, and then you can take me to meet them."

"Okay. If you're sure. I love you."

They said their good-byes, and Katherine returned Maggie's phone. "So can you take me to the airport?"

"You two!" Maggie shook her head. "Yes, of course. Do you have a flight yet?"

"No. Give me a minute, and I'll see what I can find." She was flipping through her mom's contacts for her father's travel office. Unlike Ryan, she was able to get a direct flight that would get her back to California before six p.m.

CHAPTER FORTY-ONE

As soon as Ryan got off the phone, she showered, then ate and found a cell-phone store. It all took less than three hours, but by the time she had a new phone and called Katherine back, it went straight to an unfamiliar voice mail. While disappointed not to get to talk to her, she guessed she was already on her way back—and that was a good thing.

After all that had happened in the last twenty-four hours, she was sure she wouldn't be able to sleep, but as soon as she stripped down and climbed under the sheets, she was out.

❖

Katherine saw a missed call and a voice mail as soon as she touched down in San Diego. By the time she got into the Uber, it had been less than fourteen hours since she'd taken off that morning. She stopped herself from calling Ryan and told the driver to take her to the hotel. When she arrived, she realized they wouldn't tell her what room Ryan was in.

She scrolled through her missed calls and hit send. The phone rang and rang and finally went to voice mail. The message indicated the user had not set up the voice mail and clicked off.

"Are you kidding me?" She walked toward the front desk, mentally rehearsing all the options she could try to convince the young man to tell her Ryan's room number. But before she could start her fast-talk, her phone rang.

"Are you in San Diego?" Ryan's voice echoed through it.

"Yes. What's the number of your room?"

"You're here in the hotel?" Katherine could hear shuffling and thumping.

"Yes. Tell me what room you're in."

"Fifth floor. Room 524."

"Okay." She clicked off and rushed to the elevator, only to have to wait for one of the two cars to make it to the ground floor.

She rushed toward the room Ryan had told her about, having to force herself to walk, not run, to the door. When she was nearly there, a door opened, and Ryan popped into the hallway. Her hair had that just-slept-in look, and she was wearing pajama pants low on her hips. She looked amazing. It had been two weeks since they'd been together, and she'd missed Ryan so much. She walked into Ryan's arms and kept moving into the room so they could close the door. Before either of them could say a word, she kissed Ryan long and hard, instantly tingling all over as Ryan's tongue entangled with her own and the passion built. Ryan kissed her neck and began to fumble with the buttons of her blouse, while stringing kisses down her neck and across her collarbone. She'd missed Ryan's touch so much.

"Oh…I'm so glad to finally be with you," she said in breathy gasps. "You feel so good." Then she began to tug at the bottom of Ryan's tee shirt. They briefly stepped away from each other as Ryan reached the last button. Katherine shrugged out of her blouse and jerked Ryan's shirt off. She had on Ryan's favorite pale-blue lacy bra. It provided practically no support, but the look in Ryan's eyes as she lightly ran her fingers across the lace at the top was worth it. She shivered as Ryan touched her. Ryan was wearing Katherine's favorite too—nothing at all. Her small breasts didn't require much support, and Katherine loved the perfect curves. She cupped her hands under each, and Ryan sighed. She pushed them together and began to kiss the cleavage she'd created. At the same time, Ryan was working on the button of her jeans.

"You're so beautiful, Katherine Reese. How did I get so lucky to find someone like you?"

She moaned and pinched one of Ryan's perky nipples between her lips.

Ryan pushed at her waistband, and she backed away to remove her own pants. She watched Ryan as she revealed the matching thong.

"Oh my God, woman." Ryan grabbed her waist and spun her before pushing her onto the rumpled bed. She lay there, purposely spreading her legs, teasing Ryan as she pushed her pajama pants down, along with her underwear.

She smiled at the beautiful athletic woman who was about to climb onto her.

"What?" Ryan asked as she lay on top of her, placing one muscular thigh between her welcoming legs.

"I've been dreaming of this since the last time we were together," she said and pulled Ryan to her lips. She tasted the peppermint from Ryan's Crest toothpaste, and then Ryan rolled her to her side and reached for her bra clasp. She relaxed and let Ryan do her thing, and with one hand and a quick flip, the little support the bra provided gave way. Ryan rolled them back over and took her bra off. She liked what she saw in Ryan's eyes as she looked down at her breasts, but she liked better the feel of Ryan's tongue on her nipple. At that warm gentle touch, a tingle traveled down to her core, and a wetness began building.

"Oh, Ryan, that feels so good." She squirmed under Ryan to move her thigh closer to her swollen clit. Ryan obliged with a pressure that made her gasp with pleasure.

"You like that." Ryan raised up briefly before refocusing on her other breast.

"I do—so much. I could come." She pushed up to meet the pressure and rocked gently. She tried to hold back, but little moans escaped as her climax began to rise.

"Hmm. Like this." Ryan raised up and put her hand under her thigh, pressing harder as she found Katherine's rhythm. "Oh, beautiful, you are so wet. Your underwear's soaked."

"Don't stop, Ryan," she called out in breathy syllables as the intensity increased, and then she called out as she reached her climax. "Oh, my…that felt so…" She stopped to inhale deeply.

"I think I know what it felt like." Ryan leaned down and gently kissed her lips. "I love you so much." Ryan rolled to the side and pulled her toward her so she could put her head on Ryan's shoulder. "I'm sorry."

She raised up to look at Ryan's face. "Why are you sorry? You just made me very happy." She smiled and laid her head back down, snuggling into Ryan's warmth.

"I'm sorry I did it again. And I won't ever let it happen again."

Katherine raised up and this time turned onto her side. "I sure hope we're not talking about what you just did, because I don't think I could stand it if you never did it again."

"I'm not going back on tour."

"What? You're doing amazing. You're going to be winning every tournament and back at the top of the leaderboard before the end of the season. Ryan!"

"It consumes me, and then I miss out on the things that are most important to me." Tears fell from her eyes.

"Oh, Ryan." She wrapped her in a fierce hug. Ryan's tears were warm on her bare breasts. "We'll figure it out."

"I keep making the same mistake I made with my mom. I shouldn't have cancelled on you." Ryan sniffed and wiped her face with the top of the sheet she'd pulled over them.

"You didn't know. We just need to communicate better."

Ryan raised up, tension in her face. "You did communicate. You told me it was something special, but I shut down. I got sucked in."

"Listen, I appreciate that you recognize what happened, but maybe I shouldn't have asked you to leave while you were climbing. Jace gave you good advice. You should be there tomorrow." It had gotten dark since she arrived, but she wasn't sure what time it was. "We could probably get a redeye and be in Chicago in time to tee off." She turned to reach for her purse she'd dropped with her carry-on as soon as she entered the room.

"No! Stop!" Ryan yelled. "No. I'm not going anywhere." She softened her voice and pulled Katherine back to her.

❖

Katherine pulled away from Ryan's embrace and sat up on the bed facing her. Her perfect breasts were a bit of a distraction, but she forced herself to focus on Katherine's eyes.

"Ryan, we love each other, right?" Katherine said in a flat, serious tone.

"Yes. That's not the problem."

"No. It's not. It's the solution. We're going to help each other do the things we love." Katherine took her hand in both of hers. "And we're going to keep loving each other too."

"But what if I screw it all up 'cause I…'cause I can't see clearly when I start competing."

"You've helped me so much, Ryan. Now, I get to help you." Katherine paused.

She rolled her eyes. She wanted to believe what Katherine was saying, but the fear of losing this wonderful woman was too real. She'd spent the last nearly forty-eight hours terrified that she'd ruined the best thing she'd ever had.

"It's frightening, and we're going to make some mistakes—both of us—but I don't want you to ask me to stop writing, so I could never expect you to stop playing golf."

"I could still golf. I—"

"Ryan, you're a professional golfer with world records in you. I want to be the one by your side when you set those records, and I want you to be by my side when I write an award-winning novel."

"I just don't know. How can I be sure I don't lose you because I lost focus on what's most important?"

"I'll help you. You have to believe in us."

"I do. But I don't believe in myself."

"Well, I do." Katherine squeezed her hand. "In just a few weeks I'll finish my book tour, and I'll be able to travel with you. We'll make decisions together for each of us."

"Are you sure you want to travel from city to city with me?"

"Absolutely." Katherine kissed her. "I love to write in hotels. It's where I've written most of my best stuff, and I can be there for you on the tour. Also, we can take time off when it's right and maybe find a place of our own."

"Really?" Hearing Katherine's positive tone made her feel like such a life might be possible. "Where would you want to get a place?"

"We don't need to worry about that now. I have to finish something here first." Katherine pushed her back down on her back and began to trail kisses down her naked body.

Epilogue

Ryan drove the rental car up in front of the Albuquerque Sunport arrival gates. Katherine would've already collected their luggage and had probably been waiting a while, since it had taken so long to get the car. She saw Katherine standing with a stack of luggage near the end of the long line of cars. She drove up behind the last car and stared at her beautiful girlfriend. Katherine was looking at *The Alibi*, a local weekly newspaper featuring entertainment and activities around the greater Albuquerque area. Ryan loved that paper and wasn't surprised that Katherine had found it.

Four months had passed since they left San Diego, and she was living in a dream. Everything had worked out much like Katherine had promised her. After the book tour ended, Katherine joined her on the LPGA tour and watched her play the weekend rounds. The rest of the week, while she was practicing, learning a new course, or playing the first two rounds of a new tournament, Katherine spent her days in coffee shops or libraries outlining, writing, and editing her new story. She would even occasionally play a round of golf with her.

It was perfect. Ryan had won two tournaments and consistently placed in the top ten. All her sponsors were back and even more fans. She'd missed only one tournament since Katherine joined her. They'd spent an extra week in the Napa Valley after a tournament in Nevada. Katherine's parents flew over to join them, and Ryan finally met them.

And now here she was, watching this beautiful woman, who loved her, read a newspaper. Her hair was down and blowing slightly in the warm Albuquerque fall breeze. As she was trying to figure out a way to discreetly take a picture, Katherine looked up and waved. She tucked her phone away and crept up in the slow-moving line to meet her.

"You look so beautiful," she said as she jumped out and gave Katherine a quick kiss before she grabbed two of their bags and tossed them into the trunk.

Katherine pulled the remainder to the back of the car and threw them on the others. "Don't be silly. You just left fifteen minutes ago. I look the same."

"The same beautiful." She opened the passenger door and then ran around to get back in the car.

"You're crazy," Katherine said as she climbed into the plain white Toyota Camry. "Subaru wouldn't spring for a car." Ryan had recently signed a deal with Subaru.

"Maybe next time." She smiled and exited the airport toward Interstate 25.

"I'm so glad to be back here." Katherine looked out the window as they made their way out of the city limits. "My life changed here."

She took Katherine's hand. "I'm glad you like it. I might not always live here, but it'll always be home."

As they hit the first reservation lands outside of Albuquerque, her phone rang. "Would you answer it? I didn't set up the Bluetooth."

"Mmm-hmm." Katherine picked up Ryan's phone. "It's Eddie. Hello, Eddie. It's Katherine. Ryan's driving." She pushed the speaker button so Ryan could hear.

"You're in Albuquerque?" Eddie's voice went up an octave or two.

"We're not far from the Bernalillo exit." Ryan spoke up. "How are your baby girl and your amazing wife? She still doesn't know, does she?" Rebecca had given birth to a daughter about twenty-four hours ago and insisted Eddie not call Ryan until her tournament was over. But he couldn't wait. She had dropped out of the tournament in the middle of the fourth hole the moment Katherine told her Eddie had called, and Katherine got them the earliest flight available.

"No! She doesn't know," Eddie said. "She'd kill me if she knew I called you. And they're doing great, by the way. She's gorgeous, just like her mother. She's a little doll."

Katherine and Ryan looked at each other and laughed. They could hear his excitement, and it was so cute. "The doctor is going to let me take them home this afternoon. That's why I'm calling. I thought maybe you all could pick up some food and be at the house to surprise her when I bring them home."

Katherine piped up. "No. We'll cook."

Ryan looked over at her with wide eyes.

"I'm a good cook," Katherine said.

"Okay, if you want." She shrugged. "How much time do we have, Eddie?"

"Oh, I don't imagine we'll get home until after six—by the time we do all the paperwork and stuff."

"We'll get there in about an hour, right?" Katherine asked Ryan.

"Yeah, about."

Katherine turned back to the phone. "We have plenty of time, Eddie. We'll make something nice and have it ready when you arrive."

"Thank you. I can't wait to see you both." Eddie hung up.

"What are we going to fix?" she asked.

"Hmm. I don't know." Katherine shrugged and stared out the window.

❖

By the time they arrived in Santa Fe, Katherine had a plan, and she picked up all the items to make chicken piccata with angel-hair pasta and a salad. They even had time to drop off their bags at Ryan's place before preparing the meal at Rebecca and Eddie's. By six p.m. the table was set, and Ryan was pacing from one end of their ranch-style home to the other.

"You're going to wear a hole in the rug." Katherine stopped her and held her in a hug.

"I'm so excited. I can't wait to see the baby, and I've missed Bec so much."

As Ryan was about to relax a bit in Katherine's embrace, she heard a car door slam and ran to the front door. "Don't go out. We're supposed to surprise her," Katherine said, but Ryan was already outside.

"Ryan." Rebecca squealed from her seated position next to the baby seat in the backseat.

"Bec." Ryan yelled back and rushed to the car.

They tried an awkward hug over the baby seat, but finally Rebecca stopped her. "Let me get out."

Ryan started to back away to give Rebecca room but was captured by the tiny person in the car seat. "Oh, Bec. She's so little, and oh my gosh, Eddie was right. She looks so much like you." She lightly stroked the small cheek with the back of her index finger. "Can I hold her?"

"Yes. Of course she wants Aunt Ryan to hold her, but you need to get out of the way so we can get out." Rebecca was calmly unbuckling the baby seat.

"Back up for a minute, Ryan." Eddie approached and nudged her out of the way while handing her the baby bag.

"Oh, sorry," she said.

Katherine joined them at the car and took her by the arm. "You suck at surprises."

"I surprised her. Didn't I, Bec?"

Rebecca was out of the car now and pulled her into a hug. "You did. Why are you here?" She was scolding her but continued to hold on.

After a long exchange of hugs, Eddie was finally able to herd them all into the house. The baby slept through all the calamity and didn't wake up until their meal was nearly over.

"I need to feed her." Rebecca eased herself from the chair to get the baby.

"We'll clean up while you feed her." Katherine started collecting plates at the table.

"No. You ladies cooked. I'll clean up. Go sit with Rebecca," Eddie said.

"If you insist, Eddie," Ryan said as she followed Rebecca into the living room. "Can I rock her after you feed her?" She and Katherine had struggled to keep their hands off her from the minute Rebecca set her next to the table while they ate.

"Of course. And Katherine, would you like to hold her?" Rebecca had already settled in her recliner and was opening her shirt to nurse her.

"May I?" Katherine's eyes lit up like a child getting a scoop of ice cream.

"I didn't know you liked babies." Ryan sat next to Katherine on the sofa.

After nearly an hour of taking turns rocking the baby, they both agreed that, as much as they'd love to stay there all night, they should let Rebecca get some rest.

"Yeah," Eddie said. "You gotta leave, or baby Janet will think she needs to be held all the time."

The mention of her mother's name stopped Ryan. She turned back to Rebecca, tears streaming down her face. "She'd love you so much for that."

Rebecca met Ryan in the middle of the room and held her close. "Don't be sad, Ry. It's in her honor. I hope you don't mind?"

"Oh, no. I don't mind one bit." She sniffed hard and wiped her eyes. "It's perfect. I just wish she could see her. You know she wouldn't leave, and she wouldn't have let anyone else hold her either." They both laughed.

"You're right. I wish she was here too."

"She knows." She backed away. "Okay, tomorrow? I'll give you a call."

"Love you, sis," Rebecca said, and Ryan and Katherine finally made it out the door.

❖

In the car, Ryan turned to Katherine. "Would you like to have kids?"

"I would. What about you?"

"Yes," Ryan said, backing out of the drive and heading in the opposite direction of her house.

"Where are you going?" Katherine tried to identify where she was, but her short visit in the spring hadn't been long enough for her to remember the landmarks. "To the cemetery?"

"No." Ryan paused for a long moment. Finally, she spoke again. "I'm taking you to one of her favorite spots though. You've been there before."

"I don't think you told me."

"No. Probably not." Ryan pulled into the parking lot of the golf course.

"Oh, of course."

"No. Follow me." Ryan got out and met her at the front of the car, then took her hand and led her across greens and tee boxes.

"Ryan, I can't see." She slowed the pace to watch her step more closely.

"Don't worry. I know every dip and bump out here." Despite the darkness, Ryan walked on without hesitation.

Finally, they reached the bench next to the tee box on number fifteen. "Sit," Ryan told her.

She sat down and looked in the direction Ryan was facing, across the course at the moon hovering inches above the Pajarito Mountains. "Oh, Ryan, that's amazing."

"It is, isn't it? I never appreciated it as a kid when she'd drag me out here in the middle of the night." Ryan backed up and sat next to her.

"I know this is soon. We haven't even known each other for a year, but I'm so in love with you, I can't wait." Ryan got down on her knee in front of Katherine.

"Ryan." She smiled big enough to light up the space.

"Katherine Reese, will you marry me?" Ryan held her mother's engagement ring in her hand. "It's small. I can get something bigger."

"Ryan, I love it. And I love you. Yes. I'll marry you."

Ryan slipped the ring on her finger.

About the Author

Jan Gayle was raised in a small farming community in central Illinois. Upon graduating from college with a B.S. in social studies education, Jan joined the U.S. Air Force. She later accepted a commission and served for twenty years as an Air Force officer. As a new lieutenant, she deployed to Desert Storm. She returned to the Middle East for another deployment to Operation Iraqi Freedom fourteen years later. While on active duty, Jan visited over forty countries and was assigned to locations all over the United States. She continues to work for the Air Force as a civil servant, but her true passion is her small woodworking business where she builds custom wood furniture.

Jan lives with her wife Jules and their two boys. She started writing on a dare and was immediately hooked.

Jan can be contacted at jggourley@gmail.com
Froggy Builder Woodworking: http://www.froggybuilder.com/
Jan Gayle's Author Website: http://JanGayleAuthor.com

Books Available from Bold Strokes Books

Business of the Heart by Claire Forsythe. When a hopeless romantic meets a tough-as-nails cynic, they'll need to overcome the wounds of the past to discover that their hearts are the most important business of all. (978-1-63679-167-8)

Dying for You by Jenny Frame. Can Victorija Dred keep an age-old vow and fight the need to take blood from Daisy Macdougall? (978-1-63679-073-2)

Exclusive by Melissa Brayden. Skylar Ruiz lands the TV reporting job of a lifetime, but is she willing to sacrifice it all for the love of her longtime crush, anchorwoman Carolyn McNamara? (978-1-63679-112-8)

Her Duchess to Desire by Jane Walsh. An up-and-coming interior designer seeks to create a happily ever after with an intriguing duchess, proving that love never goes out of fashion. (978-1-63679-065-7)

Murder on Monte Vista by David S. Pederson. Private Detective Mason Adler's angst at turning fifty is forgotten when his "birthday present," the handsome, young Henry Bowtrickle, turns up dead, and it's up to Mason to figure out who did it, and why. (978-1-63679-124-1)

Take Her Down by Lauren Emily Whalen. Stakes are cutthroat, scheming is creative, and loyalty is ever-changing in this queer, female-driven YA retelling of Shakespeare's Julius Caesar. (978-1-63679-089-3)

The Game by Jan Gayle. Ryan Gibbs is a talented golfer, but her guilt means she may never leave her small town, even if Katherine Reese tempts her with competition and passion. (978-1-63679-126-5)

Whereabouts Unknown by Meredith Doench. While homicide detective Theodora Madsen recovers from a potentially career-ending injury, she scrambles to solve the cases of two missing sixteen-year-old girls from Ohio. (978-1-63555-647-6)

Boy at the Window by Lauren Melissa Ellzey. Daniel Kim struggles to hold onto reality while haunted by both his very-present past and his never-present parents. Jiwon Yoon may be the only one who can break Daniel free. (978-1-63679-092-3)

Deadly Secrets by VK Powell. Corporate criminals want whistleblower Jana Elliott permanently silenced, but Rafe Silva will risk everything to keep the woman she loves safe. (978-1-63679-087-9)

Enchanted Autumn by Ursula Klein. When Elizabeth comes to Salem, Massachusetts, to study the witch trials, she never expects to find love—or an actual witch…and Hazel might just turn out to be both. (978-1-63679-104-3)

Escorted by Renee Roman. When fantasy meets reality, will escort Ryan Lewis be able to walk away from a chance at forever with her new client Dani? (978-1-63679-039-8)

Her Heart's Desire by Anne Shade. Two women. One choice. Will Eve and Lynette be able to overcome their doubts and fears to embrace their deepest desire? (978-1-63679-102-9)

My Secret Valentine by Julie Cannon, Erin Dutton, & Anne Shade. Winning the heart of your secret Valentine? These award-winning authors agree, there is no better way to fall in love. (978-1-63679-071-8)

Perilous Obsession by Carsen Taite. When reporter Macy Moran becomes consumed with solving a cold case, will her quest for the truth bring her closer to Detective Beck Ramsey or will her obsession with finding a murderer rob her of a chance at true love? (978-1-63679-009-1)

Reading Her by Amanda Radley. Lauren and Allegra learn love and happiness are right where they least expect it. There's just one problem: Lauren has a secret she cannot tell anyone, and Allegra knows she's hiding something. (978-1-63679-075-6)

The Willing by Lyn Hemphill. Kitty Wilson doesn't know how, but she can bring people back from the dead as long as someone is willing to take their place and keep the universe in balance. (978-1-63679-083-1)

Three Left Turns to Nowhere by Nathan Burgoine, J. Marshall Freeman, & Jeffrey Ricker. Three strangers heading to a convention in Toronto are stranded in rural Ontario, where a small town with a subtle kind of magic leads each to discover what he's been searching for. (978-1-63679-050-3)

Watching Over Her by Ronica Black. As they face the snowstorm of the century, and the looming threat of a stalker, Riley and Zoey just might find love in the most unexpected of places. (978-1-63679-100-5)

#shedeservedit by Greg Herren. When his gay best friend, and high school football star, is murdered, Alex Wheeler is a suspect and must find the truth to clear himself. (978-1-63555-996-5)

Always by Kris Bryant. When a pushy American private investigator shows up demanding to meet the woman in Camila's artwork, instead of introducing her to her great-grandmother, Camila decides to lead her on a wild goose chase all over Italy. (978-1-63679-027-5)

Exes and O's by Joy Argento. Ali and Madison really only have one thing in common. The girl who broke their heart may be the only one who can put it back together. (978-1-63679-017-6)

One Verse Multi by Sander Santiago. Life was good: promotion, friends, falling in love, discovering that the multi-verse is on a fast track to collision—wait, what? Good thing Martin King works for a company that can fix the problem, right…um…right? (978-1-63679-069-5)

Paris Rules by Jaime Maddox. Carly Becker has been searching for the perfect woman all her life, but no one ever seems to be just right until Paige Waterford checks all her boxes, except the most important one—she's married. (978-1-63679-077-0)

Shadow Dancers by Suzie Clarke. In this third and final book in the Moon Shadow series, Rachel must find a way to become the hunter and not the hunted, and this time she will meet Ehsee Yumiko head-on. (978-1-63555-829-6)

The Kiss by C.A. Popovich. When her wife refuses their divorce and begins to stalk her, threatening her life, Kate realizes to protect her new love, Leslie, she has to let her go, even if it breaks her heart. (978-1-63679-079-4)

The Wedding Setup by Charlotte Greene. When Ryann, a big-time New York executive, goes to Colorado to help out with her best friend's wedding, she never expects to fall for the maid of honor. (978-1-63679-033-6)

Velocity by Gun Brooke. Holly and Claire work toward an uncertain future preparing for an alien space mission, and only one thing is for certain, they will have to risk their lives, and their hearts, to discover the truth. (978-1-63555-983-5)

Wildflower Words by Sam Ledel. Lida Jones treks West with her father in search of a better life on the rapidly developing American frontier, but finds home when she meets Hazel Thompson. (978-1-63679-055-8)

A Fairer Tomorrow by Kathleen Knowles. For Maddie Weeks and Gerry Stern, the Second World War brought them together, but the end of the war might rip them apart. (978-1-63555-874-6)

Holiday Hearts by Diana Day-Admire and Lyn Cole. Opposites attract during Christmastime chaos in Kansas City. (978-1-63679-128-9)

Changing Majors by Ana Hartnett Reichardt. Beyond a love, beyond a coming-out, Bailey Sullivan discovers what lies beyond the shame and self-doubt imposed on her by traditional Southern ideals. (978-1-63679-081-7)

Fresh Grave in Grand Canyon by Lee Patton. The age-old Grand Canyon becomes more and more ominous as a group of volunteers fight to survive alone in nature and uncover a murderer among them. (978-1-63679-047-3)

Highland Whirl by Anna Larner. Opposites attract in the Scottish Highlands, when feisty Alice Campbell falls for city-girl-about-town Roxanne Barns. (978-1-63555-892-0)

Humbug by Amanda Radley. With the corporate Christmas party in jeopardy, CEO Rosalind Caldwell hires Christmas Girl Ellie Pearce as her personal assistant. The only problem is, Ellie isn't a

PA, has never planned a party, and develops a ridiculous crush on her totally intimidating new boss. (978-1-63555-965-1)

On the Rocks by Georgia Beers. Schoolteacher Vanessa Martini makes no apologies for her dating checklist, and newly single mom Grace Chapman ticks all Vanessa's Do Not Date boxes. Of course, they're never going to fall in love. (978-1-63555-989-7)

Song of Serenity by Brey Willows. Arguing with the Muse of music and justice is complicated, falling in love with her even more so. (978-1-63679-015-2)

The Christmas Proposal by Lisa Moreau. Stranded together in a Christmas village on a snowy mountain, Grace and Bridget face their past and question their dreams for the future. (978-1-63555-648-3)

The Infinite Summer by Morgan Lee Miller. While spending the summer with her dad in a small beach town, Remi Brenner falls for Harper Hebert and accidentally finds herself tangled up in an intense restaurant rivalry between her famous stepmom and her first love. (978-1-63555-969-9)

Wisdom by Jesse J. Thoma. When Sophia and Reggie are chosen for the governor's new community design team and tasked with tackling substance abuse and mental health issues, battle lines are drawn even as sparks fly. (978-1-63555-886-9)

A Convenient Arrangement by Aurora Rey and Jaime Clevenger. Cuffing season has come for lesbians, and for Jess Archer and Cody Dawson, their convenient arrangement becomes anything but. (978-1-63555-818-0)

An Alaskan Wedding by Nance Sparks. The last thing either Andrea or Riley expects is to bump into the one who broke her heart fifteen years ago, but when they meet at the welcome party, their feelings come rushing back. (978-1-63679-053-4)

Beulah Lodge by Cathy Dunnell. It's 1874, and newly engaged Ruth Mallowes is set on marriage and life as a missionary… until she falls in love with the housemaid at Beulah Lodge. (978-1-63679-007-7)

Gia's Gems by Toni Logan. When Lindsey Speyer discovers that popular travel columnist Gia Williams is a complete fake and threatens to expose her, blackmail has never been so sexy. (978-1-63555-917-0)

Holiday Wishes & Mistletoe Kisses by M. Ullrich. Four holidays, four couples, four chances to make their wishes come true. (978-1-63555-760-2)

Love By Proxy by Dena Blake. Tess has a secret crush on her best friend, Sophie, so the last thing she wants is to help Sophie fall in love with someone else, but how can she stand in the way of her happiness? (978-1-63555-973-6)

Loyalty, Love, & Vermouth by Eric Peterson. A comic valentine to a gay man's family of choice, including the ones with cold noses and four paws. (978-1-63555-997-2)

Marry Me by Melissa Brayden. Allison Hale attempts to plan the wedding of the century to a man who could save her family's business, if only she wasn't falling for her wedding planner, Megan Kinkaid. (978-1-63555-932-3)

Pathway to Love by Radclyffe. Courtney Valentine is looking for a woman exactly like Ben—smart, sexy, and not in the market for anything serious. All she has to do is convince Ben that sex-without-strings is the perfect pathway to pleasure. (978-1-63679-110-4)

Sweet Surprise by Jenny Frame. Flora and Mac never thought they'd ever see each other again, but when Mac opens up her barber shop right next to Flora's sweet shop, their connection comes roaring back. (978-1-63679-001-5)

The Edge of Yesterday by CJ Birch. Easton Gray is sent from the future to save humanity from technological disaster. When she's forced to target the woman she's falling in love with, can Easton do what's needed to save humanity? (978-1-63679-025-1)

The Scout and the Scoundrel by Barbara Ann Wright. With unexpected danger surrounding them, Zara and Roni are stuck between duty and survival, with little room for exploring their feelings, especially love. (978-1-63555-978-1)